WARD'S SIREN

STEPHANIE HUDSON

Ward's Siren
Lost Siren Series #1
Copyright © 2022 Stephanie Hudson
Published by Hudson Indie Ink
www.hudsonindieink.com

Ward's Siren/Stephanie Hudson – 1st ed.
ISBN-13 - 978-1-913904-87-6

I would like to dedicate this book to Claire L Monaghan,
Author of the Midnight Gunn series.
A lady, who's strength utterly astounds me and who selfless acts
towards others reminds you every day the true nature of
kindness and humanity. Claire went through breast cancer and
after experiencing all that Cancer can do to a person's life and
family, she came out the other side wanting only to help others.
She founded the Steel Petals name and published the book,
***Steel Petals Voices: Poems that speak a thousand words**.*
All proceeds raised under the Steel Petals name go to different
Cancer charities and the book features poems by others that
have been affected by the disease.
I consider myself privileged to know Claire and am honoured to
have the gift of her words in my book...

Journey is a dirty word

A journey full of pain and fear
Is not a journey I revere.
This journey, isolated and alone
Is not a journey I condone.

Journey is a dirty word
In suffering company, rest assured.

Forced upon a road less travelled
Struggling, choices momentarily shackled.

Oh, unwanted companion
Journey is a dirty word.

-C. L. Monaghan
Author ©2021

CHAPTER I

WHEN LIFE GIVES YOU STEAM TO CHOKE ON
EDEN

Evergreen Falls.

That's what the sign said, one I might have missed had the sun already set, due to one broken headlight. Hence why I pushed this tin can on wheels to near breaking point, and myself driving it to the point of exhaustion.

I just had to make it.

This was my last hope.

"Edie, this is just one big mistake… and there you go, talking to yourself, yet again," I said after glancing at myself in the cracked rear-view mirror. Now, how anyone gets a cracked rear-view mirror was beyond me, yet here I was, talking to myself with a crack in my face. Of course, that crack hadn't helped me at all when trying to get the price of this heap of shit knocked down. But that's what happens when you are desperate, you end up putting your life in danger every time you get in your car. One that you prayed didn't get you pulled over by the cops, because your taillight was busted and your bumper was held on with duct tape.

Yep, my life had officially hit the shitter.

What was I thinking, my life had hit the shitter six months ago!

Just thinking about it had me looking at myself in the mirror, trying to force down the tears that threatened to fall from my light olive-green eyes. Eyes that hadn't seen a lick of makeup since I could last afford the luxury. At least I had long dark lashes that didn't need mascara, only a bit of curling as they mainly grew straight. Dark brows framed a pair of sad eyes that once upon a time had the sparkle of life in them, a light that had died out what now felt like an age ago.

At least I had managed to keep my bangs trimmed, though they always naturally split in the middle as I was always pushing my hair back out of habit, which made me often wonder what the point of having a fringe in the first place was. My bangs merged into the shorter parts that always came loose from the ponytail I had my hair up in now, a style I had usually kept cut at my shoulders. But then haircuts had been another luxury I couldn't afford, meaning it was now slightly past my shoulder blades and would only get longer, as I wasn't about to take up trying to cut what I couldn't see. My bangs barely looked straight as it was, which meant for the first time, I was thankful for my natural wave as it masked my mess ups quite well.

As for the rest of my face, I had been blessed with my mom's high cheekbones that matched my slightly pointed chin and slim nose, all of which made my eyes appear larger. However, I had no doubt inherited my lips from my dad, whoever the guy had been, as my mom had never spoken about him. But whoever he was, then I would have bet on his lips being full and a natural darker shade of pink like mine were. My mom had also been pale, so my easy blushing complexion I could also thank him for, I guessed, that and the slight speckling of freckles under my eyes. However, the scar under my chin and an inch along my jawline had been all me… the result of hitting a trash can with my bike as a kid. My meagre eight years of life had flashed before my eyes as I flew over the handlebars and landed into some rubbish that had overflowed from the trash can, part of which was a half-broken bottle.

I had just been thankful that it had only meant stitches in my face and the palm of my hand, and not a pierced jugular that would have meant no more years after those eight. As for the rest of me, I was short like my mom, at only five foot tall, had small feet that meant buying my sneakers in the kids' section, and because of this I looked more top heavy than I was as my waist was narrow. It also meant that a pair of jeans was rather tight on my thighs or baggy on my waist, so there were the joys of that, I thought with a roll of my eyes.

Like now, driving this car with my belt buckle undone so it wasn't sticking in my belly as I drove, but at the ready to do up the moment I had to leave the car so they wouldn't fall down. Something they tended to do a lot more now I had lost weight due to only being able to afford to eat once a day. It was also the reason I hid most of myself away under a big navy knitted sweater that always fell off one shoulder. Three more layers lay under this, being a grey tank top, a long-sleeved red thermal, and a navy-blue T-shirt that had gold feathers falling to the hem floating down. But this was because I always seemed to be cold, something that became considerably more so since I was forced to live in my car.

Yep, a twenty-seven year old from the small town of Edenton, North Carolina, with a population of just over five thousand. A town I was named after, as my mom wasn't exactly religious and hadn't decided to name me after the biblical paradise, like some may think. No, instead she had named me after what she considered her own paradise, this being her hometown. Man, she had loved that town, loved it so much she

3

had named her only kid after it. Well, despite everyone who knew me only ever calling me Edie, myself included. But then, when my mom had passed away, I could no longer bear being there, as it was just too painful. Every shop, street, corner and house seemed to hold a memory of us together, and I wasn't on my own in feeling like this as my stepdad had moved us the day after the funeral.

That had been the last day I had seen Edenton.

It was also the reason that after losing my mom at the young and tender age of ten to cancer, I had clung onto the only family I had left. My stepdad and stepbrother, Jimmy. And Jimmy, well, he was the reason I was in this mess to begin with, that and my sentimental need to feel as though I had some shred of a family left.

Of course, had I been okay without it, then I would have been in this very moment blissfully unaware of any underworld drug cartel that involved him, and would be continuing to live my safe, mundane life. But, thanks to Jimmy, well he seemed to be a chip off the old block in regard to his father, who is currently serving life in prison for grand theft auto.

But I'm getting way ahead of myself and the reason I was currently driving to some gothic nightclub in the middle of nowhere, one mysteriously named Afterlife. It all started six months ago, and I knew the moment I opened the door to Jimmy to find him with a black eye, my life was only going to get worse from then on out. Just how much worse I never could have imagined.

It turned out that Jimmy had turned into the real-life version of 'Gone in 60 Seconds' promising some mob boss, drug lord person named Felix Gomez that he could deliver to them what they wanted, which I assumed was a car full of drugs. Even though Jimmy had been hazy on the details, from what I could gather the drop off went wrong, and the promise he made was

4

broken the moment the DEA got involved, making Jimmy run for it. Well, now Gomez wanted what Jimmy had promised or else he would be swimming with the fishes... yep, Gomez liked to keep it old-school gangster, *clearly*.

I also knew that those weren't the only bruises he had the moment he came inside and winced as soon as he'd sat on the couch. That was the day he told me he needed money and if he didn't get it, they were going to kill him. That was also the day that I said goodbye to my comfortable safe life.

Because I was a sentimental sucker who was desperate for a family, I could be a part of.

So, I let Jimmy guilt me into believing all I needed to do was get out a loan for him and he would pay me back. Needless to say, Jimmy never paid me back. which meant I had to sell everything, just to keep afloat and soon it became one loan to pay off another and another loan to pay off the other two and so forth and so forth. It also meant that with one glance in that cracked mirror I could see everything I possessed that was left of my life, which included a rolled up sleeping bag because I had been evicted and had been sleeping in my car for the past week. As for Jimmy, he was in the wind and up until two weeks ago, I was unaware that he hadn't paid these people off. Oh no, in fact he had taken the money I had given him and done a runner. As for me, well, unfortunately the people that he had owed this money to weren't big on letting shit like this happen and thanks to Jimmy, he had led them straight to me. Meaning that it didn't take long before coming for what they considered the next best thing...

Me.

So you see, I was out of options, thanks to Jimmy, my shitty little stepbrother. Of course, I tried to make all the excuses under the sun for him, but those excuses got pretty thin the moment two big heavies turned up at my office and threatened me in front of my boss. Someone who I was pretty sure had shit his pants as he ran to the toilets not long after. Then, the moment he had finished cleaning up whatever mess he had made, I was swiftly asked to leave the premises and now found myself without a job. Which meant I was running from my own debt, Jimmy's debt, and the icing on the tasteless cake was the thugs who had threatened to keep breaking bones until I paid up. Needless to say, I liked my bones the way they were.

I mean, I was a data analyst for Christ's sake, I baked cookies on the weekends for my neighbour, and bought cat food for a cat I didn't own and was pretty sure was getting fed by every other person on my block. This was not the way life was supposed to go. I paid my bills, I paid my taxes, I saved up for the nicer things I wanted to buy yet made sure I didn't overindulge. I'd had a nest egg for those dream moments, that one day I may need it for a wedding or a deposit on a house. Or if I still hadn't found a boyfriend by then who wanted to take the next step, then maybe I would take that trip around Europe I'd always dreamed about. And well, I doubted any guy would be interested now, as I felt like my name had been stained with the dirt and grime of the underbelly of crime.

No, this was my last hope because I needed to try and find Jimmy so that he could sort out this mess himself, and after he did, I might then be the one to castrate him myself! That was if I could actually get to this Afterlife, because wouldn't you know it my car was overheating yet again, and smoke was coming from under the hood.

"No, no, no… not again, damn it!" I complained as it had continued to do this for the last hour of my journey. And like before, I pulled over to the side of the road so I could add more water to the radiator and let the crappy thing cool down, praying it would start up again.

As soon as I turned off the engine, I stared down at the

steering wheel not knowing whether to punch it, scream at it, or start laughing hysterically. All I knew was that in those few minutes of staring numbly at it, they were enough to get me to calmly tighten my belt buckle and get out of the car. Then, once on the side of the road, I opened up the hood and I wanted to cry as even more steam bellowed out.

I opened up the side door for the bottle of water I knew should be there and again I felt like crying the moment I found it empty. I had forgotten to pick some up at the last truck stop.

"Damn it! Damn it, fuck, fuckity fuck, fuck!" I had to say it felt good swearing, but not as good as being sat in my car driving along the road and on my not so merry way. I looked along the road just as I saw one truck drive past me, and I realised I was going to have to try and flag someone down and beg for water, because it wasn't as if I had roadside service to call. Hell, I didn't even have a phone anymore.

So, I grabbed my dark green parka jacket that had a cream faux fur hood, from the back seat. One that had been a life saver on those cold nights. Then I went to stand by the side of my car and waved as the first two people drove straight past, and when it was coming up to the third, well I very much doubted they would stop either. This was because the car looked expensive enough to have paid for a new house, paying off all my debts and giving these people whatever money Jimmy owed. I had to say that if I had owned a gun in that moment, I would have been quite tempted to try and steal it. Hell, it felt as though I was already a criminal so why not go the full hog.

It was a brand-new Mercedes-Maybach that looked like a cross between a limousine and some sleek black panther ready to pounce.

"Yeah, like you're going to stop… what… no way…" I muttered as the chauffeur driven car actually stopped, and my mouth hung open at the sight. And this was not just at the sight of the beautiful vehicle but also at the fact that whoever was sat inside it cared enough to help a woman on the side of the road… or should I say, the driver had.

"Are you having problems?" the guy said as soon as the window came down, a lot smoother than mine did, considering I had to crank it down like you had to do in the nineties. It also jammed halfway down, so there was that little joy.

As for the guy, he looked to be a lot more than just a driver as he was a powerhouse of muscle, and I knew then that he also must have been a bodyguard. Yet, despite how intimidating his size would be for most, it had to be said that for such a big guy, he had kind eyes. The kind that crinkled at the sides when he smiled, which transformed his face and instantly put me at ease. It also made me relax enough to talk, and I wondered if this had been a practiced grin of his considering how menacing a man of his size could be, especially to a single woman stranded on the side of the road. Though it did make me question which body he was supposed to be guarding as I couldn't see into the back.

"Hi, yes… sorry… erm thank you so much for stopping. I'm afraid my antique over there has failed me yet again. I don't suppose you have any water, do you?" I asked in my mumbled way, seeing that the privacy screen between driver and passenger was still up. Thankfully, the driver gave me a smile, and one that didn't creep me out like one of the two heavies that had come to the office and threatened me had. No, Rocco and Benny had been nothing like this guy, someone who looked kind and only too willing to help, they were the kind who tried to take advantage… Rocco had made his thoughts of how I could start paying off the debt perfectly clear as he was trying to feel me up. I shuddered at the thought and how much it repulsed me.

Nope, don't think of that, Edie.

But as for this guy, he nodded once and looked as if someone was speaking in his ear before he replied,

"Sure thing, let me just get one from the back." His knowing grin went with his easy tone, making me question what that had been about? Had he been wearing a com unit?

The big guy got out of the car and my eyes grew wider as I knew he was big, but I didn't know he was colossal. Jesus, but I felt like a child stood next to him. Of course, the buzz cut of dark blonde hair screamed military and didn't necessarily go with the standard black suit that tried to scream he was all business. Mr. Colossus then walked to the passenger door and I walked closer to follow him. But then as soon as he was close enough, the window rolled down and my lungs failed me.

For sat there in the back was a being that could only be described as two things.

The first would be a living God, as he was the most handsome and most beautiful man I had ever seen in my life! Christ almighty, I didn't even know that men could be manly and beautiful at the same time!

Oh, and as for the second, he could have been the Devil himself, as he was hotter than Hell and, in that moment, I just knew in my heart, this man had the power to…

Burn me whole.

CHAPTER 2
OWNED HEARTBEATS

Oh God, what was happening to me?

I swear it felt as though I was drowning in adrenaline as my heart pounded in my chest. Christ, but just trying to catch my breath at the sight of the man was proving difficult, and I couldn't understand why. It was like momentarily trying to breathe under water, knowing the second I did I was a goner!

Just who was this man?

A man who had ignited such a response in me, a response that didn't even seem rational despite how breathtakingly handsome he was. Because sat inside that car was the most gorgeous man I had ever seen in all my life, and yet my response to him seemed to be caused by so much more. He was like a real life, living fantasy and was destined for someone who was most likely just as beautiful as he was. For anyone who must have been lucky enough to be blessed by God himself, just spending one night with this man and I just knew in my gut, it would have been like spending a night in sexual heaven.

He was stunning.

He had such a raw masculinity that made me squeeze my thighs together. I swear if my lady parts could have spoken in that moment they would have sighed. But I knew, as well as every inch of me did, that a girl like me would never have a chance with a man like that. He was the King, and I was the pauper.

The living God sat in the back must have been in his mid-thirties, with dark brown hair that was cut short at the sides and back, the top styled longer… begging to have a woman's hands raking through it. Now, as for that flawless face of his, then it started with a square jaw dusted with dark stubble I wanted to kiss along, giving him a slightly rough look that I adored. But these peppered kisses I wanted to bestow would then have ended up on his perfectly shaped lips, where the bottom one was slightly bigger than the top and begging to be sucked. A pair of dark brows and long black lashes framed the lightest brown eyes I'd ever seen, they had an unusual darker ring on the outside and an amber ring around the pupil. They made him look exotic and also dangerous, as I swear the amber turned to a gold that looked to be glowing for merely a second as he took in the sight of me.

As for his clothes, unlike his driver, he wasn't wearing a suit but instead, a leather biker style jacket with a dark T-shirt underneath. Something tight enough to show the impressive amount of muscle I knew was concealed underneath.

His eyes flashed to me and I found myself squirming under his heated gaze, not knowing where to look and failing the silent challenge he gave me. I also wondered why he would need a bodyguard as he was just as colossal in size as his driver. I could see that from the thickness of his neck and the size of his shoulders, which no doubt strained the leather every time he moved.

Just the sight of him gave me chills and as I braved another look, I shivered even more so when he frowned at me. A frown and a look that soon turned into one of questioning as he handed his driver a bottle of water. I swallowed hard knowing I needed to step closer to retrieve it, and it was suddenly like being faced by a dangerous situation you needed to get closer to in order to survive it. So, I held out my hand to take it, but then when it wasn't passed to me, I was the one left frowning in question.

"Deke, go and see what you can do about that piece of shit car… as for the lady, she will stay here," he ordered in one of the deepest voices I'd ever heard, and one that had a natural authoritative bite to it, as if he was used to giving people orders and having them obeyed. I swallowed nervously at the idea of 'the lady's staying here' and was almost afraid to find out exactly what that would mean, because I sure hoped it didn't mean me talking to this guy as I was going to end up sounding like a mumbling idiot, I just knew it. Heck, but just trying to get my words out without swallowing my own tongue at this point would no doubt be classed as a bonus!

I was also slightly insulted about him calling my car a piece of shit, even though it was and even though I myself had called it far worse. However, I didn't think it was the most polite thing in the world to call someone else's car a piece of shit, especially not when you were riding around in the back of something that cost half a million! Something I only knew thanks to an old work colleague of mine who felt like she had won the lottery when meeting some rich guy online and getting picked up in one on a date once. Although, it had to be said that having a guy telling me the cost of his fancy car within the first five minutes of a date was a bit of a turn off for me. But for Stacey, well I think she was ready to quit her job because of it and could already see the imaginary ring on her finger. I had even asked her if he was handsome, making polite conversation and all. I didn't take it as a good sign when she screwed her nose up and muttered that he was old but what did she care, he had a black credit card, whatever that meant.

As for this guy, well, I still thought that pointing out our obvious differences in wealth, as in me having none and him having lots, was a little insensitive. Although, he might have made up for it slightly by calling me a lady, as I had to admit, that part had been nice.

"What is your name, my little Carino?" he asked, and I swear a lady quiver was added to the lady parts' sigh, as Christ almighty did voices on men like this really exist?! I mean with that voice, how the bejesus was a girl to have a chance? Although now, I wanted to know what Carino meant but was too embarrassed to ask.

In fact, I was too embarrassed to say anything, and he must have noticed.

"I know you can speak, little doe, as I heard it when you spoke to my driver," he said, giving me yet another nickname, and just hearing that I meant enough for him to do so made me want to sigh right along with my lady bits.

"I... I can," I answered after swallowing down a lump called lust.

"Then would you prefer I call Deke back over here?" he asked with a smirk, and I shook my head a little in confusion before mumbling,

"Erm I... why would...?"

"Why, so you can tell him your name first and then he can relay it back to me, seeing as you converse with him far easier than you do with me," he pointed out, making me blush. Jesus, but this guy didn't let up, as he could have made a hobby out of twisting me up inside so that my nervousness could amuse him.

"I... erm..." Yep, this was my lame answer, and once again he seemed to be enjoying himself as he barely fought a grin.

"Or will you grant me your name in good faith, considering I told my driver to stop and come to your aid?" he asked in what I knew was a teasing tone, as this time he allowed himself the grin and man, it was a freaking knock out at that! No way this guy was playing fair!

This was when I decided I needed to show him that I wasn't just a pathetic nervous wreck and could actually form more words than I had so far.

"Thank you for, erm… doing that, the water that is, and stripping… No! I mean stopping! I mean stopping as it is going to be, I mean is much appreciated," I said in reply, and I wanted to hit myself on how stupid it sounded. Especially after he chuckled when I got my words mixed up and said what I wished in my head, which was of course to see him strip.

Damn it, Edie!

I looked down at my feet as I needed to get away from that amused gaze of his that felt as if it had the power to hold me captive. I also hated that I was in a cheap pair of worn shoes that were the only ones not worth anything on eBay, and by looking down I was also alerting him to the same fact. For that matter, all of my outfit looked shabby and suddenly it made me want to run and hide from the shame.

But then something in him must have shifted as he was no longer sounding amused but more like… *Concerned.*

"Hey, eyes on me, beautiful," he said, making me near choke on my own saliva, had there been any because it felt as though he had sucked it all out of me. Unfortunately, that was only figuratively speaking, as right now I would have loved for him to have sucked it all out of me in a mind-blowing kiss. But wait, what did he called me? My gaze snapped to his as if this softly spoken order was one I had no choice but be compelled to obey, then I started out,

"I'm not… I mean that's nice, but I… I mean…" He cut me

15

off with what I swore sounded a bit like a growl before telling me in an impatient tone,

"Unfortunately, I don't know what you mean, as you are yet to say, along with granting me your name for that matter." At this, I closed my eyes for a moment to try and gain some semblance of normality, and then said,

"What I'm trying to say, is thank you for the help and for stopping. As for my name, I don't know you well enough to give it yet... no, not yet, I don't mean yet, because I won't see you after this point of course, so then there won't be another chance for a yet..." At this point he looked thoroughly amused by my nervous ramblings and even more so than before, so I powered on and said,

"And thank you for the compliment, although I know I'm not beautiful, but that was very charming of you to say. Can I at least pay you for the water?" I said, and suddenly he burst out laughing as if I was the funniest person he'd ever come across, and I would have been insulted had the sound not had me utterly enraptured. Just the way his corded neck tensed and that deep baritone sound of hilarity bursting from him, had been worth making a fool of myself just for that moment alone and who knows, perhaps it would help keep me warm on those cold nights shivering in my car.

"Upon my word, I have never known another like you and no, beautiful, you can't pay me for the fucking water," he added with a bite to the swear word he used, and I had to say it made my toes want to curl, that, and knowing he had purposely chosen to call me 'beautiful' again, as if trying to prove a point... oh yeah, that was nice and definitely going to keep me warm.

After this it was clear my little shit bag on four wheels was fixed as the hood was banged shut, making me jump and I winced at the strength used to do it, wondering if that was something new to bite me in the ass later. Yeah, like when the whole crappy thing came flying off my car, cracking my windscreen.

"I think it's time to trade in, my little Carino," he said, nodding to the current bane of my existence. I laughed nervously and rubbed a hand to the back of my neck before telling him,

"Yes, that would be nice." The quiet way I said this didn't go unnoticed as he frowned for a moment, as if trying to read the hidden meaning in the oh so many things I didn't say.

"Anyway, thank you again, and thank you, Deke," I said after his driver had finished with my car. But then, as soon as I had said it, something flashed in my mystery man's eyes. It was as if he was annoyed at hearing me calling his driver by his name. I wondered why that was and suddenly I felt guilty that I hadn't given him my name after all. But then again, he hadn't offered his name either, so maybe it was better that way. Although, it would have been nice to be able to put a name to the fantasy that would no doubt last me for the rest of my life.

But as for reality, then really what was the point of swapping names, as it wasn't as though I was ever going to see him again, other than this brief exchange, one that had certainly brightened my year. And for a man like him, well, I knew he was so far out of my league and that was even before my life had been ruined and sullied.

I mean sure, I wasn't butt ugly by any stretch of the imagination, but I certainly wasn't going to kid myself on my chances with a man like him. He was an Olympian God and as for me, I would have been one of those servants holding a golden bowl full of grapes out for him to enjoy. A thought that would no doubt end up twisted into one of my sexual fantasies tonight, as master and the servant girl was such a classic!

Speaking of the clear master of this situation, he released a sigh as if he was being forced to make a decision he wished he didn't have to make. Something that was odd considering what he said next.

"Very well, then I will bid you on your way, my little Carino, and hope for a safer journey on your part."

"Thank you... Erm, good day to you too... well, I mean good night now, as it will soon be dark," I said in an unsure tone, not missing the classical hint to his words, making me wonder who these days actually said that 'I bid you' anything. It was especially a bit old fashioned for someone who looked to be in their thirties. But then I had to say, it was quite nice, and no doubt would be yet another thing to add to the fantasy. Maybe tonight I would make him a Duke or some nobleman from the era of Jane Austen.

At least my dreams were free, but these days it was all the happiness I got. The moment I could close my eyes, I was then free to pretend that my real life was actually the nightmare, and my dreams were the ones that I could wake up to.

He smirked at my reply as if I amused him again and said,

"Yes, and around these parts, it's the night time that can be the most dangerous, especially for a beautiful woman out here stranded alone." His words made me blush and I looked down at my feet, telling the ground,

"That's... erm... nice of you, but I will be okay." At this, he made a 'huff' sound as if he didn't believe it but had no other option than to leave it at that.

"And if I offered you a ride somewhere, what would you say?" he asked, making me pull at the cuff of my jacket just for something to do with my hands out of nervousness. Then I looked back at my car and knew that if I did that, then the fear was being unable to get back to what was essentially the place I lived at the moment, which was beyond depressing to admit, even to myself. So, despite how much I would have loved to have been able to throw caution to the wind and go for it, I knew I couldn't. Even if I was giving up my last chance at spending a little more time in his presence, something that I knew given half the chance I would have easily become addicted to. Because he was the stuff of dreams and unfortunately for me, I knew that was all he was ever going to be.

The hero in my dreams.

"I would say thank you for the offer and how I wished I could accept it but…" I said, and despite letting my sentence trail off he got the hint.

"But… you are a beautiful girl stranded on the side of the road, and I am but a stranger who doesn't even know your name. Very well, then I will say goodbye for what I hope isn't the last time, for you never know… *fate might bring us back together again,"* he said. This made me grin, and I swear I felt that same wish down to my toes. But then he seemed to mutter a hissed, *'fuck me'* to himself and my head snapped up at the sound. What I saw must have been a trick of light as his eyes seemed to be glowing again like liquid gold, but then a blink later and it was gone.

"Word of warning, my little Carino, if the Fates are good to me and that next time ever happens, then I will be classed as a stranger no more and that name of yours… *it will be mine!"* he said, growling the words at the end, which made me shiver as it sounded as if he meant so much more than my name belonging to him.

It sounded like a sexual claiming.

After this, he nodded to his driver, and I hadn't even noticed that Deke had got back in the car, I had been so focused on my mystery man. Someone who winked at me before the window rolled back up and darkness cut him from my view forever. Then, as he pulled away, I sighed and said,

"In that case, I hope the Fates are good to both of us... now back to reality, Cinderella," I muttered as I walked back to my piece of shit car with not a glass slipper in sight...

One I would have sold on eBay in a heartbeat.

A beat from a heart that felt as though it had...

Just been claimed.

CHAPTER 3
TOO FUCKING CUTE
WARD

My little Carino.

Fuck me, but the moment I heard that Siren's song when she had spoken to Deke, I thought I would crawl out of my fucking skin! Gods, but she had no clue, not one single clue how hard it had been for me not to open the car door and drag her inside, stealing her away and forcing her on a very different journey.

But she was forbidden.

Because she was human and I, well… *I was not.*

However, I had to wonder that if this was the case, if she were just human, then how had she managed to call to my soul the way she had? Of course, she seemingly had no idea that she had done so, making me question if she was indeed one of the lost Sirens.

The story and mythology behind Sirens was somewhat twisted in the world of humans, and only speaks of half-truths. As what really happened, was far more nefarious that any textbook would speak of. It was said that Zeus and his older sister Demeter produced a daughter together, Kore, or better known to most as Persephone. She was in the charge of eleven Angels known as Sirens, who were created for Zeus' amusement. They were known mainly for two things, their immense beauty, and their enchanting song. A voice so alluring they could capture the hearts of any and bring powerful beings to their knees by a mere whisper if they wished. Yet, despite these abilities, they were said to each possess a pure soul without malice or cruelty, although their loyalty was with their maker and his will on them was not one to be denied.

This meant that when Zeus had made a deal with his brother, Hades, he was only too quick to involve them. The deal had been for his daughter in exchange for Hades' loyalty, something he needed as the ruler of the Underworld's power started to grow with time. This meant Zeus was paranoid that his brother would one day try to overthrow his rule as King of the Gods of Mount Olympus, as he most certainly had the power to do so.

However, there was one thing that Hades wanted far more than power... *his queen*. But as for Demeter, Persephone's mother, well, she was not as easily swayed for this union to happen and utterly forbade it. Hence where the Angelic Sirens came into it, for Zeus commanded they each play their role in luring Persephone beyond the protected barrier of Mount Olympus and to a secret garden. One where Hades would be waiting for her. This was when she was kidnapped and taken back to the Underworld with him, which was just another realm in Hell ruled by a very different Devil.

But as for the Sirens, Demeter blamed them, and had Zeus cast them out, after foolishly believing in his innocence. This was because he had thrown all blame their way to save himself from his sister's wrath. He was a bastard like that and was not known as a tyrant God and King for nothing. As for Demeter, she too placed a curse upon them as they fell to the human realm. A curse that was whispered as they fell to the Earth after having their wings taken from them,

'Be gone and search for my daughter the world over'.

Eleven Sirens became human that day and have ever since carried the latent gene over into any female offspring they may have had. But it was also rumoured that their generations of daughters each had one chance at getting back their wings and reclaiming who they once were, and that was only after discovering their fated one.

Then, on a single day of the year, during the Greek Summer Solstice, it was when their true nature would be at its strongest and they could then be claimed by their fated mate through a ritual, named the Klidonas. This Greek word translated into the meaning 'sign' or 'oracle', as the Fates deemed this day to be the only one within the Sirens' power to discover the truth.

But as for finding their fated mates, I had heard that this could be possible during anytime of the year, for they would unknowingly call out to them whenever they felt them nearby. Say, to one of the highest-ranking Angels currently situated on Earth and cast here to do the Gods' dark will, who just happened to stop his car and play hero. I released a sigh wondering if this was what had happened? Had she been one of the lost Sirens calling out to me subconsciously and claiming me as her fated mate?

Gods, but could it all be true!?

Was she a dormient and had no idea of her otherworldly powers? I was as old as they came and yet I had never been affected so deeply by a human before, so it would make sense. However, until the Summer Solstice then I could not be certain. Yet, it was unmissable how I felt and for me, I now knew that it was most certainly enough!

"Fuck!" I hissed, making Deke look in the rear-view mirror.

"Problem, boss?" I shook my head and answered honestly,

"I should never have left her at the side of the road." I knew this now, as the further away I travelled from her, the more it pained me to do so. And now I was in two minds whether to go back for her or not. But then, I knew where I was headed and being waved under the nose of the King of Kings was hardly the time to break the law if that was what I was willing to do. For I could not be completely sure of my theory until the Summer Solstice, and that, according to the Greeks was in May, and we were currently in fucking September.

Which meant taking a risk as currently she was human and that, well, that was utterly forbidden in our world. A fact the King of Kings would not approve of, I was sure.

Speaking of whom, we pulled up to one of the many homes the King owned, however this one was mainly used as his place of business…

Afterlife.

Its front to the mortal world was a Gothic Nightclub that allowed humans to indulge in their darker curiosities for an evening. Although, doing so whilst completely unaware of the horrors of the Supernatural world that were seated above them in the higher level of the VIP. On the outside it looked more like a stately home you would have found in Europe due to its age, for the United States was still considered a young country to beings as old as most on the King's council of rulers. As we were known as the enforcers and each of us were classed as a head of state, charged will ruling over different sectors of the world, for the King of Kings was only one being and could only do so much.

As for myself, I had been charged with the ruling of the largest single sector, being that I was the most powerful of his enforcers. Which meant that I had been given Europe to rule over and held my own counsel, who each in turn aided me in overseeing the laws of our people in the different countries within my sector. Now, as for Afterlife, it was our duty to come here once a year to meet with our King of Kings to discuss any matters that had arisen during that time.

I was also one of the oldest members to have been charged with such a position due to my connection with the King's brother, Vincent the King of Angels. As for myself, well I was a rare breed, and both Kings knew this. Hence my position, as most larger countries such as the United States had been split up into four ruling bodies.

But for the Demons and Angels that had been granted the freedom to walk Earth's Realm, then they did so under the strict laws made and enforced by our King of Kings, who ruled over all the entire world. And he was one hard ass, broody bastard named,

Dominic Draven.

The only one that I, like the others on his council of rulers, were bound to, for he was our King. He was the one the Gods themselves had deemed the most powerful among Supernaturals with only few of the other Kings to come close... One in particular...

Lucius Septimus, the Vampire King.

His immortal enemy.

Dominic Draven might have been considered the King of Kings, but just beneath that pyramid of power were the Kings of different species, like his brother was the King of Angels being the most powerful of his kind. Then there was Jared Cerberus, who was the King of the Hellbeasts, and Sigurd Snake Eye, who had yet to claim his title of King of the Ouroboros and ruler of the Shadowlands. But this was only to name a few as, like Sigurd, there were more yet to claim their titles.

25

My understanding was that Dominic Draven's goal was to one day bring together these Kings as a united strength, at a table of Kings meeting. This was where they were to join forces against the impending prophecy that claimed to be the end of the world. However, such a united front had still yet to come onto fruition and needless to say, there was much distrust between the Kings of my world. It was also said that all that was needed was one being strong enough to bridge the gap…

A single, mortal girl.

A human girl prophesized to be the King of King's own Chosen One. A girl that had not yet been found but one that was fated to be the only weakness for the bad tempered, broody, hard ass King. I didn't know whether to feel sorry for the girl or to pray that it happened sooner rather than later, because as the more years that went by between this prophesied girl and the King finding her, the more the King grew restless, and his famous anger and fury seemed to be growing with each passing year.

It was also said that once he found her and claimed her as his Queen, that this would spark the beginning of the other Kings in finding their own fated mortals, and it would mark a new era of our kind and for its rulers. As for beings like myself, despite being a ruler in my own right, it was still forbidden for me to claim a human as my own, hence why I forced myself to leave that beautiful, captivating creature on the side of the road. But by the Gods, I'd never seen anything more fucking cute in all of my years, hence why I had gifted her the nickname, my little Carino, meaning 'cute' in Italian.

However, now that I had more time to think about her possible heritage, it was why I decided that I couldn't just leave her there. Not if it was possible that she was my destined Siren, and I was lucky enough to have been fated with a life mate after all. I couldn't chance losing her now as that would have been like throwing away life's greatest gift sent by the Gods themselves!

"What do you wish me to do?" Deke asked, knowing that I was struggling with this decision, one I knew could risk angering my King and destroy everything I had built within my sector. But then, finding my fated one was more important than anything and came above all else... *every King knew that.*

"Drop me off here and go back to search for the girl. Take her to the hotel and stay there with her. I will find my own way back." He didn't look surprised but did make a point by asking,

"And if she is has already gone?"

"Then we will track her plates to that piece of shit she drives and find her that way." As soon as I said this, I noticed Deke's demeanor change, making me grit my teeth.

"You have something to add?" I said with my tone telling him this wasn't a request. Deke released a sigh telling me this was going to be something I wouldn't want to hear.

"I am not sure tracking her plates would lead you to an address she lives in any longer," he said, giving me a bad feeling about this.

"And what would make you say this?" I asked hoping he was about to tell me he found her car filled with suitcases and moving boxes, telling me she was merely relocating.

"Because it looked as though she was fucking living in that piece of shit, that's why," Deke gritted out, obviously feeling the same as I would about this, something that made me growl at the thought.

"Fuck," I hissed knowing this was fucking unacceptable! Of course, I had known she obviously had very little in the way of money, as that rusted death trap on wheels said as much. But it was also by what she wore, with clothes that were well worn and most likely second hand as they didn't exactly fit her well. She also seemed self-conscious being seen in them, no doubt

feeling intimidated when we showed up in such expense and luxury.

Well, that shit ended now, as there was no way I would allow my woman to continue to live that way! Gods, but I was furious at just the thought of it, and even more angry at myself for being foolish enough to drive away! I should have gone with my gut in the first place and simply taken her by force if she had been unwilling to comply. Kidnapped her if need be, anything to get her safely within my care and keep her there until I figured out my next move.

I was a fucking idiot!

Hence why I got out of the car and slammed the door with enough force, it cracked the window. Then I stormed over to Deke as his side window lowered.

"Go find me the girl. Get her to the hotel as I will be there shortly, for I'm not anticipating this will take long," I said to my right hand general, who had been with me for more years than I can remember.

"And if she is not willing?" he asked, making me tense before needing to grit out yet again,

"Then take her by force, for I will not be so foolish in allowing her to slip through my fingers again."

"You believe her to be your fated?" he asked, because Deke didn't just work for me, he was also my closest friend, and this meant that he knew he could get away with giving me shit as his grin suggested he was doing now.

"That depends, did you hear her Siren calling out to you too?" At this his eyes widened as he too had heard of the legends and knew what this meant.

"Oh, shit man, then you're fucked, Ward," he said, nodding to Afterlife and the belly of the beast I must go in. I looked behind my shoulder and ground out a growled,

"*Indeed.*"

"Don't worry about the girl, I will go now and try to find her, but in the meantime, you go deal with the King, and seeing as I doubt you've got time to jack one off in the car before the meeting, try not thinking about her unless you want them to think you're concealing a fucking weapon in your pants," Deke said, alerting me to the fact that yes, since meeting her I was as hard as fucking granite! Something that most certainly wouldn't help my situation.

"Duly noted, and will not go unforgotten ready for the next time I get to kick your ass in the ring, now go find my girl, dickhead," I snapped, making him laugh and say,

"Right you are, asshole… oh, and try not to let Aurora fuck with your head this time." I growled at this, remembering a particular blonde beauty that tried everything in her power to use me as a way to make the King jealous. Of course, she had tried with many others and just as she did with me, she usually failed, for I was not interested in that black heart of hers despite her being an Angel.

But then that was the most popular misconception made by humans, for not all Angels were good and not all Demons were bad. In fact, our world was a whole spectrum of grey areas just as the human world was. And as for Aurora, well she might have been as blindingly beautiful as the sunrise she was named after, but beneath the vessel and shell of a human form, she was nothing more than that of a rotten soul down to its core.

And trust me, for I could spot them a mile away.

Just as I could spot those who had a pure heart in their blindingly pure soul, just like my little Siren on the side of the road had. Just the thought of her driving in that death trap had my nerves on edge and I gritted my teeth again, just as I had done when she had addressed Deke in such a warm way.

She had said his name, but I had yet the opportunity to give her my own, despite trying to force the issue of knowing hers.

Something I was now determined to know… and fucking soon at that!

My curvy little Siren.

Soon, it wouldn't just be her name I owned,

But her heart as well.

CHAPTER 4
THE KING OF KINGS

I entered through the elaborate doors of Afterlife's grand entrance that I knew would lead straight into the heart of the club. I nodded my silent thanks to the doormen, who instantly knew I was part of their boss's elite as they had held open a pair of wooden doors that could have belonged on any Castle. As for the building itself, it's weathered sandstone was being half overtaken by a blanket of green ivy, meaning the outside remained unassuming and a total contrast to that of the inside. This was because the moment you walked through the doors of Afterlife, it was as if you were walking into a cathedral converted into a Gothic nightclub. This, with its tall arched ceilings where huge wrought iron chandeliers hung, added to the ambient lighting of hundreds of flickering bulbs made to look like candles.

Everything about the large open space screamed Gothic opulence, with its crimson reds and deep purple fabrics to the metal artwork that gave it a raw and dangerous edge. Dominating the club, were the two large staircases that led up to the VIP area that framed either side of a stage in the middle. One that already had a band playing a heavy rock song, which meant the dance floor was crammed full of bodies. As for the bar, this was situated off to the right of the main entrance and ran the full length of the wall, which was a good job as it was currently packed with customers.

I quickly crossed the space, and not wanting to add any attention to myself, I decided on a more subtle way of reaching the VIP. It was through a door situated at the back of the club which led to a back staircase that was guarded. One that remained that way at all times, for no humans were ever allowed in the VIP area, although I had to admit, I never really understood this, as how the King was ever supposed to meet his Chosen One was beyond me.

I nodded to the guards and took the steps in a rush knowing I wanted to get this over with. Then, once in the VIP area, I wasn't surprised to say that I was one of the first Enforcers to arrive, as I had planned it this way. This was because there was a matter I wanted to discuss with the King without others listening. So, I approached the King's table, one that was situated dead centre and at the front of the VIP, so that he may survey the humans beneath him. Vincent was the first to notice me.

"Ward Za'afiel, my old friend, how the Devil are you?" Vincent Draven greeted in that easy manner of his, clasping my hand as he always did. I smirked at him and answered how I usually did.

"The Devil has nothing to fear from me for another year, so I am well." He laughed at this as I knew he would.

"Then our father will be pleased," he replied, knowing that the father they spoke of was a good friend of Lucifer's... their parentage was a complicated one.

It was then I noticed their Demonic sister smiling at me from the table. The beautiful Sophia reminded me of a dark-haired china doll, with skin that was both pale and flawless. Her dark features were closer to her ruling brother than those of Vincent, who was most definitely the light to their darkness. He had a head of tight blonde curls and sapphire blue eyes, combined with kind features that certainly fit the persona of being an Angel. Although, such a look should never be underestimated, for I knew from experience he was one of the most brutal warriors on the battlefield... just like his siblings, as Sophia's beauty was also not one to be underestimated.

Vincent nodded for me to take a seat, telling me,

"We have not long arrived ourselves."

"Ward!" The stern and unyielding voice of my King acknowledged my presence with my name and nodded for me to take a seat at his table. One that was surprisingly sparse, telling me this was for my benefit, knowing that I wished to speak to him without being overheard.

"My Lord," I said with respect and a bow of my head, as he might not have been the warmest of beings like his brother, but he earned my respect all the same. After all, he was a just and fair King, and one who did right by his people. But Dominic Draven, like most other rulers, had one of those naturally intimidating presences that dominated any space he occupied. When standing, he was a few inches taller than I was at six foot four and his build was that of a warrior King, whose bulking muscle was currently hidden by a dark suit that matched his dark features. Eyes so dark they looked almost black and tanned skin that would have suggested a life by the Mediterranean Sea. Yet his vessel was of Persian descent, back when Persia still held its name, and the proud history was one he could claim, for he ruled there as its King of Kings.

Though that was a long time ago, the man had not lost signs of those days. Black hair brushed the tops of his large shoulders and was currently styled back from his stern face, one the female population would consider handsome, no doubt.

Now, I was not a small man by any means and was used to the same reactions I had received earlier from my little Siren whenever I walked into a room. However, despite years of growing accustomed to such, none had ever pleased me as much as when affecting her, my little cute human, who was still dominating my thoughts. But seeing as the sheer raw power from the Gods that created me hummed beneath my veins, then this was of little surprise, as most of my kind would be granted the knowledge that I was considered unbeatable by most beings. However, that same power also recognised one of the few that was more powerful than I, sat around the table.

Hence the reason I had been given all of Europe to rule.

"I will get straight to the point."

"And that right there is why I like you, Ward, you cut out all the bullshit," Dominic replied, making me slowly bow a head at the compliment.

"Well, it also helps he is not bad to look at," Sophia replied with a cheeky wink, that would have made a certain Albino growl with annoyance had he been sat next to her like usual. I nodded my thanks out of respect, when really I wanted to get this shit done, for I wasn't here for an ego trip. Now, had that compliment come from the lips of a certain human... then I would have felt it down to my fucking bones.

Gods, what was wrong with me!

Fuck, but I was hard enough to hammer nails into concrete at just the thought of that cute little unsure look she had given me. It also had to be said that for a Siren, she was most certainly a timid little thing. One I wanted to fuck into screaming my name and loosening up that tongue-tied mouth of hers.

Fuck, but get it together, Ward, I warned myself, as I was here to do a job and get it fucking done so I could get back to my own shit, starting with the importance of acquiring who I suspected to be my fated one. So that was exactly what I did, by telling my King what he would most want to know.

"Malphas has been seen in Germany. Munich, to be precise and I think we all know why that would be," I told him, leaning back in my seat and shaking my head at the drink that was offered as I didn't want to be here that long.

"Lucius!" Dominic snarled out the name of someone who had been his enemy since the end of the second world war. I nodded before telling him,

"I believe he has been making enquiries also."

"Well, if it's with the blood sucker then it's not hard to guess what it is," Sophia said, knowing of whom I spoke, but it was the look she gave her brother next to her that made me question what it was they knew. But Dominic responded to this look with a slight shake of his head before hissing out the ancient Latin term,

"My Electus."

His Chosen One.

I often wondered if such a human woman would have the power to thaw what seemed like a frozen heart of ice, for she would have to be a special creature indeed to soften up the hardest bastard I knew.

Speaking of softening hearts, a little time later and my phone vibrated in my pocket.

"Excuse me," I said, making the King nod as I retrieved my phone. It was a message from Deke… It wasn't good news and it made me growl before I could stop the reaction.

D: *I'm sorry my friend, your little Siren is in the wind.*

"Problem?" Dominic asked after taking note of my annoyance, and I had to force myself to take a breath before I destroyed my phone by clenching it my fist.

"Nothing I can't handle… and soon will," I answered, at the same time replying to Deke's message.

W: *Understood. Meet you outside in ten.*
D: *And the girl?*

His reply was instant, and I glanced over towards the glass doors I knew led to an outside balcony, showing me the moonlit night beyond. I almost smirked to myself, knowing it was the perfect setting for the next stage of my plan, as I replied,

W: *Tonight, we go hunting for a little human Doe.*

After this, I slid my phone back in my pocket and quickly got to my next bit of business.

"There is something else you need to know."

"Go on," Dominic replied.

"It is about Gastian," I said, referring to who was currently being a bane in my fucking existence and I wished I could just kill him.

"What has that asshole done this time?" Vincent asked, knowing of my complaints, something that had been continuing for years and I wondered why he was still given charge of a sector. But despite how small it was, being that it was only Morocco, it was still only separated from Spain by the Straits of Gibraltar. Meaning that at its narrowest point, the distance between our two sectors was a strip of water that stretched just nine miles. Which also meant that I had been forced to deal with the fucker more than once, because he clearly wanted Spain for himself. Now why he did, was what I was yet to discover, but my best guess was that it had something to do with one of the few access points into Hell.

The Caves of Nerja are a series of caverns close to the town of Nerja in the Province of Málaga, Spain. They also stretched for almost five kilometers, and in them, lay a hidden portal into a realm of Hell that I knew was one he was interested in. But still, at this point, it was unfortunately all speculation as I had no solid proof. I just knew that he had been amassing large amounts of funds for some big project he had planned and had been slipping some pretty big bribes into human pockets, greasing the hands of diplomats and people in high places that had mortal control over that part of the region.

Well, that was until I cut him off and had his account hacked without being traced, meaning the guy was now nearly broke. Not that I was about to disclose this piece of information to the King, but seeing as I had forced Gastian's hand, I knew I had to at least express my concerns at what I feared he would do next to acquire those funds back.

"My sources tell me that he has involved himself in the Lega Nera, but in what capacity I am as of yet, unsure," I told them, knowing of the illegal auction house that held these events once a year and how Dominic had been trying to get them shut down for as long as they had been running. But due to the high secrecy, the vendors were only given a week's notice in which country it was to be held in, and nothing more than a few days until the actual venue's address was released to the supernatural world's rich list. They sold everything from mortal treasures, and priceless antiques to caged Demons. Most of which were lost, stolen or killed for, hence the punishment to those involved. And now Gastian had been associated with them, meaning his days were numbered.

"The Black League... seriously?" Vincent asked as if shocked, translating its Italian name.

"Dumb fucker," Sophia said on a chuckle, as this news had helped quell her boredom for a short time, one brought about no doubt due to the lack of a certain pale Demon usually glued to her side.

"How do you want me to proceed?" I asked the King, hoping he said for me to finally be allowed to kill the guy. But then I had to admit, for once, Dominic looked distracted by something... and it most definitely wasn't on business for once.

"Dom?" Vincent said, alerting his brother to my question.

"Gastian will be summoned here soon enough, and once here then he will be questioned on the matter. But until then, keep digging, for I will not have any of my Enforcers disobey me and think me blind enough not to discover such defiance." I nodded, telling him that I would, and my grin told him I would enjoy it, making him ask,

"Why do I get the impression you want him to fuck up, Ward?" At this, I outright grinned and told him truthfully,

"Because I can't stand the weaselly little fucker, that's why." Dominic scoffed a laugh and said,

"Fair enough. In that case, should the need arise then you can aid me in delivering my punishment." I didn't think my grin could get any bigger, but it did, and I answered once more with truth.

"Then it gives me something to look forward to, as I have no doubt that day is coming and soon."

Sophia chuckled after first seeming distracted and said,

"It seems like someone else was hoping for something to look forward to, as one of the locals is trying to get lucky by sneaking up here again." I then listened for myself, only to find myself shocked to the core. This was thanks to a sultry little voice I would have remembered until the day my vessel had turned to dust. It also looked like a night of hunting her down wasn't needed after all, for my prey had come straight to me, making me question what exactly she was doing in Afterlife

38

and more importantly, what in Hell's damnation was she doing trying to get up into the VIP?

But these were all questions I would soon discover the answers to, along with finally knowing her fucking name, something I thought on a barely concealed growl! Which was why my back straightened and I tried to let that be my only reaction. This was before I gave the royal Draven siblings an excuse, telling my King as I rose to my feet,

"Then in that case, I beg of you to excuse me as I have a few calls to make." Dominic nodded in response, and I purposely ignored the look Vincent gave me before I gave too much away. Fuck, but that Angel was as perceptive as he was dangerous.

And speaking of danger, it was time to play hero once more.

Hero to my Siren's call for help.

CHAPTER 5
TROUBLE
EDEN

"**O**h, come on, Jerry, he's your nephew," I said to my stepfather's brother... someone who worked as a manager at club Afterlife. Thankfully, my car had made it there and, as luck would have it, there hadn't been much further to go. But I had to confess at the shock when finding the place.

Afterlife was nothing short of incredible!

In fact, it was like nothing I had ever seen before and always dreamed of one day seeing. I had always wanted to travel, going to places where history seemed to be seeping out of everywhere. The architecture was something that astounded me, as the craftsmanship could be seen in what you would have considered as the most mundane of things. Of course, I had only ever seen pictures of these places online, but still had a bucket list sitting in my emails that I dreamed of one day seeing. Needless to say, it was an email account I no longer had access to, due to no longer owning any technology. But it was there at the ready for when there was finally light at end of the tunnel and I could hopefully get my life back on track. A dream to one day get the chance to visit every church, cathedral, abbey, manor house and castle that Europe had to offer. In fact, I had been hoping that one day I would find that special someone to travel with, yet it had never happened and at this point, well, it looked like it never would.

I couldn't help but think back to my gorgeous mystery man, who I was now regretting not giving my name to, or being brave enough to ask for his. A man, admittedly, *I couldn't stop thinking of.*

"Yeah, and he's a waste of space just like my brother," Jerry said in reply as he dumped some empty bottles in the trash behind the bar. I cringed at this as my shoulders tensed, because I knew I couldn't blame him and nor could I think badly of him for saying so. He too had been screwed out of money by his own brother, which meant his gaze soon softened when looking back at me now looking deflated.

"Look, you're a nice kid, Eden, and you and your mom were always too good for my brother. Hell, but the only good thing that my brother ever did was look after you after your mom passed. But as I told you on the phone, there's nothing I can do as trust me, if Jimmy's disappeared then he's a ghost, and one I doubt you'll ever see again."

I squeezed my eyes shut a little bit longer than necessary at the mention of my poor mother, someone who had unfortunately died and that meant leaving me with no other choice than to be brought up by a car thief and his son. Admittedly, my mother had fallen in love with a criminal and like Jerry had said, the only good thing my stepdad ever did was make sure that I stayed out of foster care. He fed me, he clothed me, and he made sure I didn't want for anything. This, despite the illegal ways in which he received that money to pay for everything.

But what Jerry didn't know was that it had been more than that, as in truth he had been the only father I had ever known.

One who, granted, hadn't been too big on hugs and flowery 'I love you' before bed. But he had cleaned my scraped knees and fixed my bike when the chain came off. He had dragged real Christmas trees in the house because he knew the smell of them reminded me of my mom, as she always preferred them to the fake ones. He had made me cocoa when I couldn't sleep and chased away a bully once with a baseball bat. And every year without fail he put flowers on my mom's grave on her birthday, shedding a tear he thought I couldn't see as I cried. I knew without a doubt that he had loved my mom, and in a lot of ways I knew he loved me too, even though I think having me around was painful for him as I was a constant reminder of my mom and what he had lost.

Now, as for Jimmy, well there had even been a time when we had been two peas in a pod and enjoyed each other's company, despite us not being siblings by blood. But then I was also fortunate that by the time my stepfather had gone to jail, I was already classed as an adult, and was making my own way in the world, which meant I didn't have to rely on anyone and that had felt good.

Of course, Jimmy had played on this bond I foolishly believed we had, and as a result I had now sacrificed my life for his. Meaning Jerry was right, Jimmy was a piece of shit.

"But your boss, this Mr. Draven, from what I've read of him he's a really powerful man, surely if you asked him… he could help in some way?" I said, making his eyes grow wide before taking me by the top of my arm and pulling me off to the side, before telling me,

"You stay away from Mr. Draven, he is not who you think he is and trust me, if you think you're mixed up with the bad people now, then the last thing you want to be is indebted to a man like Draven." My eyes strayed up to the VIP area where I knew he was sat, and then Jerry hissed,

43

"Don't even look up there, Eden." I frowned back at him and pulled my arm free before snapping,

"Then what am I supposed to do, Jerry? I'm living in my damn car, and one that's a piece of shit that won't even start half the time! I lost my job, I lost my apartment, I owe enough money that would make your head spin and now, thanks to Jimmy and this disappearing act of his, I'm left with some really bad guys after me... guys who terrify me, Jerry." At this, he truly looked pained as if he really wanted to help but wasn't sure which way he could.

"And the cops, what are they doing about it?" I scoffed at this and said,

"They have them on payroll, Jerry, so what do you think?"

"Fuck, Eden!" he gritted out, making me swallow hard before asking,

"Is there at least a job going here?" I asked knowing that my tone sounded desperate.

"I'm sorry, no... Frank, a mate of mine, just asked for a job here for his sister-in-law who recently arrived from England, that was the last position." I released a sigh wishing suddenly that I was that girl, she clearly had family looking out for her.

"Look, let me at least give you enough money for maybe a couple of days at a motel or something. I'd offer for you to stay with me but after my wife left me, I'm stuck in a one bed apartment until the settlement from the house we shared comes through... plus you know, I have Gary to take care of," he admitted, telling me that he had problems of his own, as his twin brother Gary could be somewhat difficult.

I released a sigh before shaking my head, telling me no, because as much as I needed the money, I wasn't about to take it from someone who already needed it. No, all I could hope for was that something changed before the cold season really set in, or one day someone would find an Eden shaped popsicle lying down in my frozen car after prying the doors open.

"Thanks, Jerry. I appreciate it and I know that you would do more if you could. I'll just hang out here for a bit if that's okay?" I replied with a deflated tone.

"Take all the time you need, honey, and when you're ready for it, drinks on me, yeah?" I nodded my thanks and let him get back to his job, considering the bar wasn't exactly quiet and his staff certainly looked like they needed the help. It was in that moment that I looked behind me, up to the VIP area, and after releasing another sigh I knew I had no more choices left. As there was only one thing left to try and in spite what Jerry had said, I knew my situation couldn't get any worse, so really what did I have to lose?

So, I waited until everyone looked occupied with customers, before I made it across the room closest to one of the doors that I believed was a back way of leading to the VIP. It would make sense seeing as there were quite a few people up there and, as yet, I hadn't seen a single person climb one of the double staircases that dominated the space.

I didn't know how long I waited, but it didn't seem more than ten minutes before some sort of fight broke out and the two men who had been guarding the door started to intervene, giving me my chance. This was when I slipped through the door and inside, finding myself faced with a stone staircase that led straight up to what I could see was a small landing. It also looked like there were two doors up there, one of which I gathered lead into the VIP area and as for the other one, well the place was big enough to be a hotel, so maybe that's exactly what it was.

Unfortunately for me, I made it about three steps up before I was roughly grabbed from behind and yanked down the steps before being pushed up against the wall by a scary ass dude.

STEPHANIE HUDSON

It was in that moment, when faced with the angry guards, that I knew I had failed yet again. I also had another irrational thought slip through my mind, and one that led straight to my lips as I whispered...

"Where is my hero now?"

46

CHAPTER 6
NEEDING MORE

"Hey, come on now, there's no reason to get so grabby!" I snapped when the huge guys started manhandling me and let's face it, I was five foot nothing, so what they thought I could do to escape was beyond me. But then, just before I was marched out of the door, there came a dangerous voice of authority from the top of the stairs, one that didn't sound happy.

No, he sounded furious.

"Let her go... now!" he growled out, and I swear the order didn't even sound human. The guards froze in their actions and my heart felt like it did the same thing, as suddenly my fantasy man was right there once more.

My hero was back, as if... well, *as if he had heard me.*

Obviously, this was a ridiculous thought as of course he wouldn't have heard me. This wasn't a fairy tale. Yet, if that were true then why did it feel as if I was suddenly in one?

He descended the steps quickly, and I wasn't surprised considering how tall he was. Holy shit, but those legs looked as if he was a professional athlete or something. Or maybe he just lived in the gym as those abundance of muscles would suggest as much. His shoulders looked more than big enough for him sit me on them or throw me over one of them, I thought with a blush.

Christ almighty, but he was even more gorgeous this close up and talking of him getting closer, that was exactly what happened when suddenly he hooked a palm behind my neck. Then, at the same time, he stepped right into my space, claiming it as his own as he tipped my head back as his own descended. Now if I thought I couldn't breathe before when just talking to the guy, well now it felt like my heart would burst from my chest and belly flop onto the floor like some dying fish!

"Now, what did I tell you, my little Carino, about wandering off without me?" he said louder, before leaning down further so his lips were at my ear where he whispered,

"Relax, beautiful, and play along." Relax... relax! Was the guy serious!? Okay, okay so he said play along, which meant that this was all an act. I could do this... *couldn't I?* I swallowed hard and did something I hadn't done in a long time...

I used what I called my sultry voice.

"I am sorry, babe, but I just needed to use the little girls' room," I said, lowering the tone of my voice to an almost purr. It was something I was able to do since I was a kid, and it sure had helped to keep me out of trouble. Of course, I had been too embarrassed to do it as an adult thinking it seemed silly. My best friend at school used to think it was a hoot, especially when it helped in buying her cigarettes once. Of course, the fact that I had bloomed into my boobs at a young age always helped with the act of appearing older, so I'm not sure it was down to the voice at all.

But as for now, then I wasn't so sure it was just the boobs after all, as the guards both looked mesmerised, and they weren't the only ones. My mystery man and my hero who was making a habit of saving the day, well, he seemed utterly dumbstruck. His eyes even seemed to get lighter as if the amber in them had flashed gold for just a moment, that must have been a trick of light. Of course, with him staring at me like that, he wasn't exactly helping with our little act and I felt like nudging him back into action. Jeez, but maybe I should start using this voice more often.

"This being, she is with you?" one of the guards asked, finally breaking whatever spell it seemed I had put these guys under. My hero shook his head a little as if trying to rid himself of the effect my voice had just had on him. Then he took his time in answering the guard as he first leaned in closer and kissed me on the cheek, asking me on a whisper,

"Parli italiano, bella ragazza?" (Translation: Do you speak Italian, beautiful?) I frowned, not understanding what he'd said, making him smirk and add,

"I will take that as a no, *excellent.*" He finished this by gripping my chin and giving it a little playful shake before turning back to the guards.

"L'umano è mio per la sera, e ho fame dell'essenza di un'anima pura dopo il mio viaggio… Now fuck off and do not interrupt us further." (Translation: The human is mine for the evening, and I am hungry for a pure soul's essence after my journey.)

He said most of this in a different language that, if I had to guess, was Italian. But it was the sound of his growling voice that ended the sentence that had me taking a quick breath, knowing the strength of this man and his power over others.

Now where had that thought just come from?

Then, after this angry bite to his words in the order he gave them, he turned his attention back to me, not allowing me any longer to think about it. No, this was because he suddenly took possession of my neck again and pushed me up against the wall. I gasped in surprise before his lips descended on mine and before I knew what was happening, this God of a man was now…

Kissing me.

Actually, that seems too light a word for it as it was more like consuming me and taking me whole! Jesus, Mary and Josephine, his kiss was like a branding! It was hot, heavy and had the power to burn the memory of it into my soul for all eternity. His fingers gripped into my flesh harder, making me moan, one that was captured in his mouth as he deepened the kiss, something I didn't think was even possible. And stranger still, as his tongue dueled with mine, it was as if he was trying to burn me to his memory also, as not one second of this felt like an act.

Especially not with the way he trapped me against the wall, his one hand cupping my cheek and the other fisted in the baggy woolen sweater I wore at the base of my spine. Christ, but it felt as though he wanted to crush me to him but was trying to hold back and be gentle. Something he wasn't really being, which told me he had so much more raw intensity left to give…

Left for me to experience.

In fact, it was only when I seemed to struggle to breathe did he pull back slightly, only allowing an inch between us as if he was too afraid to allow me the space.

"*Breathe, my Siren,*" he said, now calling me something new and making me wonder where this nickname had come from… had it been because of the voice I had used? But then, weren't Sirens the ones who lured sailors to their watery graves? I would have frowned at the thought, but I was still in the grips of the euphoria his kiss had created.

Of course, I still didn't know what Carino meant either, but at a guess it was Italian for something, as that seemed to be his second language. But then again, I did notice that whatever he called me, it usually came with a claim to belonging to him, which I had to say, made my heart flutter and my toes curl in a good, warm, gooey kind of way.

Holy Hell, how I would have loved for a man like this to call me his and want to keep me forever! There was just something about him that went so far beyond just his handsome face and sexy as sin body.

It felt as if I knew him, and knew him to my core.

Which meant this had my sentimental and hopelessly romantic brain asking if this was what love at first sight felt like? As if every touch was amplified by a hundred, and every word he said my mind hung on to. As if that kiss had the power to drag me back from the darkness my stepbrother's mess had tried to bury me under. But I needed to test it. I needed to know if that kiss had really been for show or not. So, after a quick look to see that the guards had long gone, I made a little motion to the door, and after first needing to clear my throat, I said,

"I think we fooled them." At this he pulled back a little as if I surprised him, then he told me,

"If you think that is the reason I kissed you, then you're mistaken, for I was fooling no one, least of all you. Now give me your name," he said, and I couldn't help but suck in a quick breath at his words. Good Lord, could a man like this really want someone like me?! Of course, that usual growl to his last five words spoken was more of a demand for my name, than a simple request.

Oh yeah, this was a man who was used to getting what he wanted and being obeyed. To be honest, I didn't know how I felt about that, only that half of me wanted to submit to him and the other half wanted to push him and see where it got me. And well, right now I also didn't know how safe it would be to give him my name, which was why I told him,

"I, erm… well, I don't want to get you in to trouble." Naturally, he frowned at what seemed like an odd reply. But it couldn't be helped, as I knew that if anyone came looking for me whilst I was on the run, I didn't want this blowing back on him. Not that I thought those two thugs would have much chance at touching this guy, as he looked as if he had the power to kick the shit out of the both of them with one hand tied behind his back James Bond style. There was just that raw intensity about it that spoke danger, but the type I wanted to stroke, not the type I wanted to run from.

Maybe that made me an idiot, I didn't know. But right then, still locked in his hold, well, in truth… *I simply didn't care*. But my strange comment made him grant me a questioning look. Then he told me,

"We will come back to that reply in a moment but for now, do as I asked, little Siren, and give me your name." I swallowed hard in a way that had me unable to refuse to tell him what he asked for and as I lowered my head, I told him,

"Eden, my name is Eden Teles… oh!" This was how my sentence ended as he suddenly had me pressed against the wall again, growling down at me,

"Fucking Paradise… *I knew it*." Then he crushed his lips to mine and this time, I knew it didn't just feel like a branding… it burned into my soul like one! Then suddenly it wasn't close enough for him, that or the height difference was frustrating him, as he stepped in between my legs. He grabbed my ass and hoisted me effortlessly up the length of him, making me automatically hook my legs around him. I moaned in his mouth as he held me trapped between his body and the wall at my back he had pressed me up against. He rocked his hips into me, keeping me spread wide for him, as I could now feel the very hard and what I knew was a long, thick length of him against me.

Christ almighty, but I was getting almost dizzy from it, as wave after wave of sensations crashed over me. I gripped onto him as if he was my only safety in this storm he'd built up inside me. But even as he kissed me to a near senseless state, there were still three words I wanted to say.

However, as he tore his lips away from mine, he got there first. and he did this by growling those exact three words,

"I need more."

CHAPTER 7
CLAIMED

fter his confession, I swiftly found my feet leaving the floor and I cried out in shock. This was the moment I also found myself gripping on to his shoulders after he hoisted me further up his hard torso. Jesus, was this guy a body builder or something? It was as though I weighed nothing at all, which I most definitely did! Although, I had to confess that living on dried noodles certainly hadn't added to my waistline, so who knew how much weight I had lost since living in my car.

Seriously, that's what you want to think about now, Edie, how desperate you are for a cheeseburger?! I would have shaken my head at myself had that not drawn attention to the erratic action.

In fact, I felt as if what was happening now was some sort of dream or more like some sexual fantasy. One that only my pink rampant rabbit would have known about. If it hadn't been neglected that was, because, well, batteries were classed as an extra and orgasms weren't more important than gas or noodles. Plus, I had my fingers so hey, there was that...

Jesus, Edie!

Stop it now and get it out of your head because you don't know how to deal with this reality. Because I often did this when faced with a situation that was so far from my comfort zone, I needed my head to focus on utterly mundane things. It was why I had never found a sexual release by someone else before. And how sad was that!

But I knew this was down to me, not the two meagre sexual partners I'd had in my life. I was always too busy focusing on what they were doing wrong or where their hand should be. If they could just move their fingers a centimeter to the left or just go slower or faster. Then I would wonder if they had a hobby baking as they would play with my breasts as if they were two balls of dough. Then that would lead me on to wondering if they might like my recipe for currant buns, that went great with real butter.

Hence my problem.

Laughter shook me out of my thoughts, and I braved looking at the most handsome man I had ever seen, one who miraculously still had me in his arms. Then he said cryptically,

"Fuck me, you're cute, Siren… now hold on, so I can get there quicker." I was about to ask what he meant by… well, all of that, when I ended up having no choice but do as he asked. Something I didn't have a problem with, as it meant gripping onto his sexy jacket as he ran up the stairs at a crazy speed I didn't think was possible. Then, when he reached the top, he took the left hand door that at first appeared to be locked when he tried the handle. Then I heard it click and it opened, which soon left my mouth hanging open at the sight. I was utterly dumbstruck as all those random thoughts left me with a whoosh.

"Wow… what… *what is this place?*" I asked on a breathy whisper, as I never expected to see what faced me now. No, I had been expecting a hallway or another room perhaps, but this… it was like stepping inside a fantasy world. It was a long open balcony that I could see was the same on all sides in a massive square where a section of the mansion had been cut out of the middle, like you would expect in a castle or something!

But then, instead of looking straight down over the edge and finding some courtyard or bailey, what I found didn't make any sense as it looked like some kind of temple!

A huge domed roof coated in what looked like polished copper shone under the moonlight above, and had I not currently been in what felt like an unyielding hold, I would have run to the edge just to see it better. Because, as he continued to carry me along the hallway, I could only just make out the gleaming winged sculpture that was mounted at the very top of the dome. One that I would have liked to have seen in more detail, but my hero seemed to be in a rush, and I had to admit, it was nice to know that he was eager to make me his… *if only for a night.*

As for the rest of the incredible space around us, the four hallways that connected at the corners were decorated with an endless line of stone balustrades that rose up in arches. These then connected to the roof above, meaning that, despite the whole area being open to the elements, there was still cover over the walkways.

But as he had veered off down the left-hand side of the long walkway, we continued to pass doors and creepy lanterns that seemed to explode into light, making me frown and suddenly feel uneasy.

"Erm, maybe we shouldn't be here," I admitted, starting to feel afraid, especially considering I didn't know this guy… Hell, I didn't even know the guy's name yet!

"Afraid?" he asked with a dark smirk, and when he watched me swallow hard and nod a little, it made his cocky gaze soften. Then we came to yet another door, and this time, he stopped

57

there. After this he let my legs go, but kept hold of me so I didn't just drop but could be lowered slowly.

"Thanks for… erm well, I have never been carried… and it was…"

"Let me stop you there, beautiful, for if you say 'nice' I will have no choice but to torture another word from those tempting lips of yours." At this, I outright gulped as he backed me into the door we stopped by.

"And by torture you mean… er…like… in a nice way?" I pretty much squeaked out, making him first throw his head back and laugh before shaking his head and muttering to himself,

"Too fucking cute." Then he told me,

"No, beautiful, not in a *nice way*…" He paused, grabbed my ponytail in his fist and used it to pull my neck to one side before he finished his sentence against my neck.

"…*but in a good fucking way, you're going to like.*" This was said as nothing short of a sexual promise, that was backed up when I moaned, thanks to the way he suddenly bit down on my flesh and ignited that small bite of pain I really didn't think I would like. But holy Hell, I didn't just like it, I nearly ignited because of it!

"Yesss." I couldn't help myself utter the word that slipped out as my head fell of its own accord this time, telling him I wanted more. So, he gave me what I wanted and bit down a little harder, before sucking my flesh into his mouth and soothing the pain. He continued to do this, and by the end of it I was a squirming mess just from having the guy biting my neck! Jesus Christ, but what was wrong with me, I had never had a reaction to a man like this before!

Maybe that's because you have never experienced what it's like with a real man, Edie, I told myself. But then my chance at a real man released a deep breath as if suddenly deciding something and the moment he gave me space, I realised he must have been having second thoughts. I had to say the knowledge hit me in the chest like a hammer and I found myself unable to look at him, so found my feet instead... *something he didn't like so much*. I knew this when he took my chin in between his forefinger and thumb, forcing my head back up to look at him.

"I have to know before we enter through this door, have you been tried before, sweetheart?" I frowned at this before telling him,

"Er... you mean like for a crime in a court or something?" At this, he gave me a warm tender smile as if he was trying not to laugh again. But instead, he held my chin in a firmer grip and pulled me closer to his lips before whispering what he meant.

"Are you a virgin, beautiful?"

"Oh," I replied as it finally dawned on me what he was getting at, and he hummed in an amused tone over my lips before kissing his way up my jawline, still keeping a firm hold on me.

"Oh, indeed."

"No, but I've only had..." At this he pulled back and stopped me quickly, growling out a little with what seemed like a jealous bite. One I had to say made me feel good.

"I don't need the number."

"Jeez, its only two, and each were... well... kind of meh," I scoffed, making him grin this time before saying in a cocky tone,

"Only meh, eh?" I laughed a little and tucked the loose sides of my hair behind my ears after pushing back my long bangs from my forehead out of habit. Something he seemed to watch with great interest.

"How old are you, beautiful?" he asked in a gentle voice that I was starting to become addicted to, especially when he called me beautiful, something that I really wanted to be for him. But then looking down at my clothes and knowing I had no makeup on or had even made much effort with my hair, I had to question how he could think so.

My head quickly snapped up when he growled again, and I found myself questioning if I had said something out loud as he told me firmly,

"You're fucking exquisite as you are, and I will not have you thinking any differently... do you understand?" I swallowed hard at his authoritative tone, one that sent chills through me. He sounded so dangerous, yet his touch spoke of anything but as he caressed his thumb across my lips. Then, with his striking eyes softening, he commanded,

"Now focus on my question."

"I am twenty-seven," I told him, and he grinned before telling me,

"Good, for this pleases me, as I was unsure with you looking so young." I blushed at this, knowing that he was right, as I had been told how young I looked many times before, always needing to flash my driving license to get even so much as a bottle of wine. Not that I had tasted wine in a while, no, that usual Friday night tradition had been one of the first to go.

But I wanted to ask why it pleased him because if he thought that by me being older it meant I was more sexually experienced, then he was about to be disappointed. This was because those two 'meh' partners had only equaled up to a total of five times. Not that I was in any rush to admit this, as I was too embarrassed and for a man like this, well, I wanted to be his everything. I wanted to be utter perfection for him and that meant doing everything right, something I wasn't exactly brimming over with confidence at right now. But then it seemed I wasn't the only one who had doubts, as his handsome face turned serious.

"As much as it pains me to do so, it is time for me to give you the one and only warning you will get."

"What do you mean?" I asked, frowning and wondering what he could possibly have to warn me about.

"If you step through that door with me, then there is no turning back from this." I opened my mouth to speak when he shook his head, and placed his thumb at my lips to silence me, and I soon knew why when he confessed,

"I am not a gentle lover, Eden." A second after he said this, my mouth open on a surprised gasp despite the pressure of his thumb. This meant he used this to his advantage and slipped his thumb inside my mouth and stroked my tongue. I swallowed heavily at the erotic gesture, making me close my lips around him and suck back on it. This in turn made his eyes glow again, making me wonder if they were reflecting off the domed roof or something, as I couldn't see how else it was possible. But it wasn't only his sexual actions that had ignited this feeling in me, as it had also been the way he said my name for the first time. He had made it sound exotic, and strangely as if it belonged to him. As if he had claimed it along with the person it came with... *me*.

"Speak your thoughts, my little Carino," he said after sliding his thumb free from my lips, and in truth it was something I barely wanted to let go of.

"I... well, do you... erm, I mean like tying me up and stuff?" I asked, making him grin. A grin that screamed of all the sinful and dirty things he wanted to do to me. Then he got closer to me and took my wrists in his large hands, shackling them in his strong, unyielding hold before lifting them. With my arms pinned firmly above my head to the door, he looked down at me with that heated gaze of his before he told me,

"Oh, sweetheart, you have no fucking idea of all the bad things I want to do to you, and tying you to my bed is only one of them." He watched as I swallowed down the lustful thoughts

61

he'd just evoked, trying in vain to digest them, making him smirk because of it.

"As for now, well, if you grant me the gift of your trust, then I can promise you that I will take care of you... however, in order for me to do that, you will be walking in that room and surrendering all control over to me. I will own you, Eden... now do you understand?" I shivered this time at his words, and closed my eyes, needing just a moment to escape the intensity of it all. Jesus Christ, this guy was intense!

"Will you... *will you hurt me?*" I forced out the question after the first two words got stuck. He tensed his fingers around my wrists and gritted out his next sentence as if the thought of my question was utterly abhorrent to him.

"No, never... for the pain I speak of will only be the type to enhance your pleasure."

"So, I will feel pain?" I asked with my voice reaching a higher pitch. At this his features softened, and he lowered his head to my neck, licking at the mark I could feel he had created, the one that had made me nearly orgasm. Which meant I knew the point he would make before he whispered it against my skin.

"Tell me, my little captive... Did you like me biting you, Eden?" Again, his hands tightened the moment he said the word captive as if emphasising his point.

"I... well I..."

"Yes and no answers only, sweetheart," he ordered, making me want to shiver again, as the way his voice could switch from gentle to stern in a second turned me on to the point I had to close my eyes and bite my lip to stop the moan.

"Yes," I answered, because I felt as if he couldn't be denied or if I lied, he had the power to know about it.

"Good girl," he praised, and again hearing it felt like a soothing balm across my skin.

"And was my bite painful?" he asked as he continued to make his point.

"*Yes,*" I admitted, again not daring to lie to him.

"Now, I could have bitten you harder. I could have pierced this delicate skin of yours, but then in that moment it would have only hurt you and that is not something I am ever willing to do. Not even to gratify my own pleasure, for I will never put my need above your own," he told me and again, hearing it felt so nice I had to hold back a contented sigh.

"This also means I will always know how to read your body, I will always know what you want and how far I need to go to gain it. For every sexual release you experience I will own, as is my right as your master," he told me, making me suck in a harsh breath at the term.

"*Master?*" I questioned fearfully, not knowing if this was something I could do... *something I could ever accept.* It sounded... well, it sounded a bit barbaric. But then he laughed once and then asked,

"And what would you call me, sweetheart, for I will own you, dominate you and master every inch of your body." I swear I could barely breathe, and it was in that moment he could see my panic building. So, he released my wrists instantly and framed my face with both hands, doing so in a tender way.

"Hey, I won't let anything bad happen to you, Eden," he told me gently, now handling me with such care, it was a total contrast to how he had been seconds ago, making me realise that it was possible for this man to be both, dominating and caring. He could own me like he claimed but treasure me all the same.

"So... I er..."

"Ask it of me, Eden," he said, caressing my cheek with the back of his fingers when he could see me struggling. Admittedly, just the sound of my name coming from those perfect lips was enough to have me wanting to curl up against him and beg him to make me his forever. But then I knew I needed to use my logical brain at some point, and now would be one of those times. As he was trying to be honest with me about what was obviously his kink in the bedroom. Now all I needed to know was how far he was going to take that. As I wasn't naive. I had read the stories, and the books with Alpha characters that were known as Doms, who made punishments seem more like orgasmic treats for female characters. But this was no book, and my life was far from a romantic love story, as I knew there was no way this would go beyond one night.

But still, I also knew there was a lot that could happen in just a night, as that had been all it had taken for my life to go spiraling out of control. Which was why I decided to be brave and ask,

"Will that make me… *your slave?*" The hardest part of this sentence came out in a whisper that made him groan, as if he found pleasure from just the way I said it.

"Mmm, now as appealing as that sounds, the answer is no. You won't be my slave, Eden, you will be my woman. One I will use in the most delicious of ways if you let me. Now, will I expect you to kneel to me? Yes, if I want you there and intend to use this sweet, tempting mouth of yours as will be my right, but with that being said, I will never make you do anything you're not ready for. I will know your limits," he told me, and again I swear I almost had a mini orgasm just hearing it all, as let's just say he was a master at painting a very erotic image of what he wanted to do to me.

"How will you know what my limits are?" I asked, intrigued to know.

"Let's just say I am very good at reading people, *especially those I devote all my attention to,*" he said, lowering his voice at the end into almost a sexual purr that would have had me convinced even if I'd noticed his fingers crossed behind his back. But something in my gaze must have told him differently, and maybe it was admittedly the last hint of mistrust I was holding on to. As it just seemed as if there was something else about him, something important that I still didn't know. And well, if I had to guess I would have said it was something to do with the warning he gave me. But my biggest question of all should have been…

Was he dangerous?

"Do you trust me?" he asked, after releasing a sigh and making me look back towards the way we had come and then back to him as I weighed up my options. He allowed this as one of his hands slid down to the side of my neck, now holding me there and strangely the weight of having his hold on me was comforting.

"What would happen if I said no?" I tested, and I saw the slight tick in his jaw as it hardened as if he hated the thought, but then he said,

"As disappointing as that would be, I would understand it for I am not a good man. However, when it comes to you, then I would do the right thing in a heartbeat, which means escorting you out of here and forcing myself to say goodbye," he said and as soon as he did, I felt an ache in my chest at the thought of never seeing him again. I also had to admit how nice that all sounded, although I knew a smart girl would have at least enquired about the 'not a good man' bit. But then again, for the last six months, when had I ever played it smart? Because so far, I had done nothing but call this man my hero. Or should I now change that to anti-hero?

So what, if this handsome stranger wanted to give me a night I would never forget and a memory that would warm my soul on all those cold nights ahead that faced me? Because I knew deep down that was all it could ever be between us. After

STEPHANIE HUDSON

all, I was tainted and he, well he was worth so much more than what I had to offer.

Though, was I really going to say no to one good thing before I faced my unsure and dangerous future? Was I really going to walk away from that?

Was I really going to walk away from him?

My hero.

There was only one answer to that.

No…

I wasn't going to walk away.

66

CHAPTER 8
TRUST IN DARK
REFLECTIONS

"**N**ow which is it to be, my little Carino?" he said, taking a step back and allowing me the space to slip past him and walk away forever. That was when I knew exactly what this was...

My test.

One I wanted to pass so badly for both our sakes as he clearly wanted this. I also had to question his motives, because the guy was huge and could easily have overpowered me if he wanted to. He could have taken all choices from me or, hell, he could have just not said anything about his preferences in the bedroom and simply left me in the dark. Yet, he didn't do either, but instead wanted to warn me for my benefit, not his own. Well, that to me spoke of a man with integrity and honor. So, despite how he claimed to be a bad man, he obviously wasn't bad enough to lead an inexperienced girl in this room with him blindly without first warning her of what she was getting into... *what I was getting into?* Something that I had to confess, was most likely the best night of my life!

As soon as I thought this, he smirked down at me as if he'd

heard my thoughts and stepped back into me, running the back of his fingers down my cheek, telling me,

"Time's up, my Siren, you had your chance."

"No, wait!" I shouted in a frantic way, now being the one to shackle his wrist as it had lowered from granting me his gentle caress. His other hand was positioned on the door handle, and this too froze as he frowned down at me, questioning my actions.

"I'm sorry, I'm just nervous is all… but I promise you, I do want this to happen… I just… well, in truth I've never been with a man like you before and it, well… *it scares me a little.*" At this, his gaze softened and he raised his hand up so he could kiss the back of my palm as my hand was still wrapped around his wrist. Then, without breaking eye contact with me, he told me,

"Two things, beautiful… first, is that no matter how much I scare you, know that I would never harm you in any way… yes?" he asked wanting me to respond.

"*Okay,*" I muttered, and he kissed my hand again in response before lowering it down, and as I unwrapped my fingers I asked,

"And the second?" This was when he quickly grabbed my own wrist and held it firm as he opened the door, telling me,

"I meant… *you had your chance to run.*"

I swallowed hard at this, knowing I had mistaken him before when he told me my time was up. He wasn't intending on walking away, he just wasn't going to let me do it. The thought made me shiver as he led me inside the room and motioned for me to proceed him. Then, with him still behind me, the sound of the door closing and locking made me jump. I added a little moan to this when I was surprised again, this time, by his touch as he took hold of the tops of my arms. I was shocked that his hands were big enough to circle them, making me want to tremble at the obvious strength he possessed.

"Easy, my fearful little doe, locking the door serves me well, for we will not be disturbed and..." he paused as he walked around me, and I watched as he put the key in his pocket.

"And?" I questioned before he looked back at me, and with a dark grin he said,

"I can't have a captive without a lock and key." He then watched as I swallowed down another fearful lump, making him chuckle as he took off his jacket. My mouth went dry at the sight, as Jesus Christ, who was this man, an axe wielding warrior in another life? Hell, the guy looked like a living action figure as his shoulders and biceps looked sculptured from clay, they were that beautiful. But then, it couldn't be denied that as sexy as his body was, it was also intimidating to someone who felt tiny around him, as I did. Of course, I already knew how easily he could pick me up and carry me around, but after his domination confession, I also had that to combine with every single one of those muscles.

Christ, but what his body was capable of I just didn't know... yet, as wasn't that the whole point I was here. Oh God, I could feel my heart pounding and my breaths getting shorter. Something I think he knew when he looked back at me and released a sigh as if he felt guilty. Now, in only in a pair of jeans and a dark t-shirt, one that was tight across his chest, he sat on the edge of the large bed that dominated the room along with him.

In fact, it was the first chance I got to take in the room, as he had flipped a switch when first stepping inside that had lit nothing more than the two old-fashioned glass lamps next to the huge four-poster bed. The room certainly matched the rest of the place as it looked as if it belonged in a castle.

STEPHANIE HUDSON

The dark slate floors were covered in antique Persian rugs, adding to the luxurious fabrics in the room that covered the bed in a deep red and black brocade velvet. A bed that could have fit seven of me and maybe three of my mystery man, which reminded me, I still didn't know his name!

"Come here, my little Carino," he said, reminding me yet again he knew who I was, yet I was still to learn his name, which was why I told him,

"I still don't know your name." At this, he nodded and replied in that dark tone of his.

"Yield to me by giving me what I want in this room, and you may have it." I gripped onto my sleeves and looked behind me, glancing at the door, prompting him to tell me.

"It's too late for that," he warned, and I swear the intimidation should not have been adding to my arousal, yet I knew it was, as I would having been lying to myself by thinking otherwise.

"Yield to you?" I questioned, ignoring his last frightening statement.

"Come here, Eden," he demanded as way of an answer, and I released a shuddered sigh before forcing my feet to move, not wanting to push him and find out what happened when I made him wait. I suddenly wished I had read every erotic BDSM book that had been available, before my subscription had run out that was. However, the few I'd had a taste of had often found the females spanked, making me wonder if I would enjoy something like that myself. At this thought, I heard him choke back a laugh, and I suddenly feared I had said that out loud, my expressive face no doubt saying as much.

"Fuck me, you're cute, now get your ass over here before I do spank it and we discover the answer to that sexual musing of yours." At this, I covered my mouth with my hands, horrified that I must have said it aloud and he chuckled once more.

Which was no doubt why he decided to help me move the rest of the way... He leant forward and, with ease due to his size, he reached out a long muscular arm and snagged my sweater. Then he curled his fingers into a fist and yanked me the rest of the way, making me stop just in time as his hand flattened to my belly so I wouldn't topple into him.

"Now that's better," he declared as he placed his large hands on my hips, but even with him sat down and me standing, this still put him at my head height as the bed was one you stepped up into, it was that high.

"I am aware that this is all new to you, Eden, which is why I will be lenient with you this first time, but that will only go so far if you don't start doing as you are told because you continue to let your nerves get in the way," he told me, expressing his thoughts, and his hands tensed at my hips to prove his point. I couldn't help but linger on the way he said 'first time' as though he knew there would be more, and I allowed myself the small moment to believe there could be.

"Now, are you willing to do all I ask of you?" His question shook me from this dream, and I nodded.

"Rule one, when I ask a question, I expect a reply... *in words, sweetheart.*" He whispered this last part in a playful tone that contradicted the rules he was giving me, but helped in relaxing me all the same, so I was thankful for it.

"Yes... erm... master?" I replied in a questioning tone, wondering if this was what he expected as I knew in some books this had been what the doms had wanted to be called. His grin told me I had done well, at least I think so as he squeezed my sides and praised,

"That's sweet of you, little doe, but not necessary."

"Then, er... what do I call you?" I asked nervously, making him smile again and I swear it was that blindingly handsome, I sighed.

71

"How about, for now, you just call me sir and we will go from there," he said gently, making me nod a little, feeling that inner shiver from my lady parts in anticipation.

"Good, now strip for me, Eden," he said, and at this my mouth dropped open a little before I could stop it, not even bothering to ask myself how silly it looked. Well, I didn't need to as his smirk told me. But then he just tapped on my chin and said,

"Leave it open, sweetheart, and I will be tempted to put something in it." At this, it snapped shut, making him chuckle before tapping my lips and telling me,

"Consider this one of those lenient times where I allow you to make me wait for your compliance... *one of few, Eden,*" he added, leaning closer and warning on a whisper. Then he nodded down at my body, telling me I could start, and I fisted my hands by my sides silently panicking and asking myself if I really could do this. Okay, so how hard could it be? It wasn't as though he wanted me to give him a sexy little striptease or anything, it was just taking off my clothes.

I could do this.

I wanted to do this.

So, with this in mind, I closed my eyes and took off my jacket, before stopping when he growled,

"*Eyes on me, girl.*" His hard demand made my eyes snap open as if he was the one controlling them. Then, one of his hands left my hip and he held it out to me, meaning he wanted me to hand him my jacket. I did as I was told, and he tossed it over to a wooden chair in the corner that was carved with tall spindles. It was also on top of his own jacket, and I thought the sight looked symbolic, making me smile a little.

He took note of the sight himself before he nodded to my big baggy sweater that looked way too big for me, one that was also frayed a little and definitely well-worn. So, I slipped it off, granting him for the first time more of what my figure was beneath the thickest layer of clothing. Again, he held out his hand for me to place it there, and I couldn't help but noticed the way his gaze heated up as his eyes took in the new sight, scanning every inch of my torso.

"You're doing so well, little one, indeed you please me greatly," he praised, making me blush and lower my head until he forced it back up with a hold on my chin, telling me on a whisper,

"*Now, keep going.*" I nodded slowly, and knowing I had three more layers to go, I grabbed two in one to get it done quicker, as my long sleeved top and t-shirt came off together, leaving a tight tank top beneath. One that was low cut and showed off my cleavage that he seemed fascinated with. In fact, he held out his hand without taking his eyes from me, which admittedly made me feel so good about myself I could almost be fooled enough to believe he wouldn't be disappointed at the very last layer.

My plain, boring white underwear.

"I care little for the wrapping, my little Carino, only for the gift beneath it that is still concealed from me," he told me, as if hearing my thoughts yet again, making me wonder if this was some kind of gift of his? Christ, I hoped not, as just how many times had I called him my hero and fantasied about him. His smirk made me hope this wasn't confirmation that my fears were true.

"Now, bare yourself to me," he said, his voice a little thicker now, and definitely not as cocky, as lust was taking over. So, I did as I was told and grabbed the hem, only to peel it away from my skin, slower this time due to how tight it was. However, the second it was in his hand he lifted it to his nose, before inhaling it deeply, something he hadn't done before. It made me blush, as if he wanted to take in my scent due to some primal need.

Then he released a growling sound like a satisfied rumble, before telling me cryptically,

"I knew you were destined to be mine the moment I first heard you speak and now..." He paused before suddenly grabbing my ass in both hands and twisting his body, taking me with him, so I landed on the bed with a bounce. Then, with him positioned on his knees above me with my legs between his thick thighs, he finished his sentence,

"...*now it's time to hear you scream for me, my Siren.*"

I sucked in a startled breath, that left me on a whoosh a second later as he grabbed the hem of his own t-shirt and lifted it up, revealing the body of a God to me!

"*Wow.*" I shamefully let this comment slip, having no chance at stopping at the sight of him. The man was incredible! Muscles everywhere, and ones I had no clue to the name of. He was solid, every inch of him, and I found myself wanting to explore him with my hands and lips in a way I'd never been interested before in another. It was why I couldn't stop myself from reaching out with a shaky hand, as if ready for his permission or his denying me. But then my questioning eyes went to his and his eyes seem to glow once more before he nodded, telling me silently to go ahead, I could touch him.

So, I did, and the moment my fingertips met his soft skin, he was the one to shiver beneath my touch. He also let his head fall back a little and closed his eyes as if he was savoring it and liked the feel of my fingertips exploring him. So, I got braver still and reached out both hands until they were flat against his pecs, having to lean up a little. Then, I let them caress down, meeting the first line of his abs, the first of eight as his stomach was without an inch of fat. However, the lower they travelled, the more his breath seemed to grow heavier, until I cried out in surprise.

This was because he had shackled my wrists so quickly, I didn't even see him move, making me cry out in fright.

"Go any lower and I won't be held accountable for how hard I take you and I am trying to be as gentle as I can here, but your tender touch is pushing at my limits, Eden," he told me in an almost pained way, making me relax under his tight hold. Because now I wanted to reward him for his confession and knew exactly how to do this, by giving him what he wanted the most. So, I started to lift up my arms, gifting him my submission, and as I leaned back down he had no choice but to travel with me or let me go. Needless to say, *he didn't let me go.*

Then, enjoying the surprise in his gaze, I told him,

"I trust you, sir." At this, he shook his head a little as if astounded with what I'd just given him, and he grinned down at me before pushing my hands harder into the mattress, allowing them to take his weight as he lowered over my body, whispering above me,

"Then I am blessed by the Gods for their gift of you... now to hear you sing for me, Siren." Then he kissed me and by the Gods he'd just thanked, it did more than make me sing, it lit me on fire!

Suddenly it was as if our passion had detonated and we both came alive and desperate to have one another. His hands left mine so he could fist a hand in my hair making me moan at the bite of pain that came with it, one he captured and tasted in his mouth as he continued to consume me with his raw and brutal kiss. The other hand was tearing down one cup of my bra so he could free a breast, soon having my quivering flesh filling his palm. His thumb and finger then pinched my pebbled nipple, adding to the moan of pain that caused my panties to soak. Then his hand left my breast and snaked down the rest of my torso, until he dipped a hand under my waistband and felt for himself how much I wanted him. My back bowed up, forcing his kiss to end as I let out a cry of pleasure at the first swipe of his fingers through the folds of my sex.

"Fuck, yeah, my girl is ready for me… fucking soaked, just like I want to keep you always," he hummed against my cheek before biting me there gently, making me moan again. Then he sat back up, enjoying the needy sound I made at the loss as he grinned down at me. As I tried to sit up to pull him back to me, he suddenly shackled my neck, stilling me instantly. I swallowed down that bolt of fear, making him coo,

"Easy now, little doe." I took in a breath, and it was a shuddered one he felt vibrate against his palm, making his eyes glow again. It was as if he fed from my reactions to him, liking both my submission, trust and fear all wrapped up into one. I tried to question it, but in the heat of the moment I couldn't focus on anything but how he was making me feel. Like when he grabbed my belt buckle with one hand and yanked it free before pulling it from the loops in my jeans, making my body jerk sideways. Then he released my neck and ran the thick leather through his hands, looking down at it as if fighting an internal battle, one he let me in on when he said,

"I will, this once, let you choose, for my choice would be to tie this around that slender throat of yours and tame you with a collar. But if you give me your hands, then I will only use it to bind you." Instantly I knew which one I would .choose so handed him my wrists together quickly, making him chuckle. Then he nodded and turned them inwards and ordered,

"Pray for me, Eden." I swallowed hard at the command and interlocked my fingers together like I was indeed praying. Then he looped the leather around them and tightened it, making me yelp at how tight it was before he released some of the pressure. He was proving that he could read me as he'd said, as he hadn't taken his eyes off me the whole time. Once it was how he wanted it, he snaked a hand under me and wrapped an arm around my waist. He did this so he could hoist my body the rest of the way up the bed until I was closer to the elaborately carved headboard. I was about to question him when he shook his head telling me not to. Because his actions were about to relieve my questioning mind, as he looped the remaining length of the belt through the gaps in the wooden frame. After he was satisfied that I was going nowhere, he then sat back as to admire his handy work and told me,

"Next time, it's my choice and you will wear my collar... but for now..." he finished this by yanking my body down until my arms were stretched above me, making me yelp in surprise.

"...You get to be at my mercy in another way," he growled down at me, giving me no time to think on his words as he was ripping down my jeans, and ridding me of the rest of my clothes. This meant that my panties didn't survive his eager touch as he tore them straight from my body. As for my bra that was next, this thankfully barely survived his rough treatment as the clasp was at the front, this meant that other than having the straps remain at my shoulders, I was completely naked in seconds and spread out before him... *naked and squirming.*

"Gods, but you are worthy of the name, *for you are fucking paradise!*" he said in a hard tone as if it was hissed, and I had to say his words made me feel confident enough to relax a little, no longer worried about what he would think of me.

"It's time to treasure my gift..." He paused to rip open his own jeans and when the hard long length of his sprang free, I gulped, wondering how it was going to be possible to fit all that inside of me. But then he didn't allow me long to wonder as he pushed his jeans down and then spread my legs out wide. After this he took a moment to pause, looking down at his large hands pinning my legs apart, ready for him, and I felt my cheeks burn as he inhaled the feminine scent of me again.

"*Mine,*" he rumbled dangerously, before lowering himself over me and then whispering a dark promise down at me.

"*Time to claim my Siren and make her call out for the one who masters her soul,*" he said cryptically, before he suddenly breached my pussy and impaled me on him making me cry out, screaming in pleasure, and he was right...

I sang for him with my screams.

I tensed around him as the pain of his intrusion made my eyes water. This was when he took a calmer approach, and I knew that despite how dominant he was, what he said was true, he didn't ever want to harm me. The deep concern in his eyes told me that he took no pleasure from the sight of my discomfort.

"Gods, you're so tight for me, sweetheart, try and relax now... ssshh, calm that erratic heart and breathe for me... *let me take care of you, my Eden,*" he whispered tenderly over my lips when he realised I was struggling with his size, making me tell him,

"I'm sorry... it's... it's been years." At this he chuckled slightly, telling me,

"Fuck, my girl, never be sorry to tell me that, as I don't relish the idea of another man claiming what's mine... have no fear for me, Eden, as you're perfection, sweetheart," he told me gently, using his hand to push my hair back from my damp forehead and kiss me there. He continued to give me time to adjust, seeming more than happy to do so and when the pain had dulled, I nodded, telling him he could move. He answered me by kissing me, before taking his time and being something he told me he could be... *gentle.*

I had to say it meant more to me in that moment than anything else ever had, other than when my mom had told me she loved me for the last time. Because since her, no one had ever shown me that tenderness and I knew it was a dangerous thought as I was quickly falling for this man. Petrified at what would happen when I actually fell...

Would he be the one to catch me?

Christ, but I hoped so!

"Trust me, Eden," he said down to me, and I didn't know why. Was my face giving him insight to my vulnerable thoughts again?

Then he told me on a whisper,

"I will always catch you." I sucked in a quick breath, one of astonishment, but before my mind could focus on the impossible, like how he had known what I was thinking, he started moving quicker. He literally fucked the doubts from my mind, and I lost all questioning thoughts to his incredible body and what it was doing to me!

"Fuck... incredible," he said as he started to move even quicker, hammering into me, and I was soon crying out my first orgasm, finding myself tugging at the belt as if desperate to be free. I needed to be closer... I needed to be touching him, wrapped around him. I needed to be a part of him as he felt a part of me.

Our souls joining.

Suddenly my mouth was open, and I swear the sound coming out of me didn't sound like anything human. It sounded like a strange echo of pleasure coming from every corner of the room, and Christ, he was right, it was more like a song!

"YES! Fucking claim me as your Chosen, my Siren!" he roared, making me cry out for the last time when suddenly, the belt snapped, and I looked up to see he had literally torn it free... Christ, just how strong was this guy?!

Again, I didn't get my answer as he suddenly pulled me up, and I didn't need any direction this time as I looped my bound hands over his head, clinging on to him, finally feeling closer to him.

"Yes… yes… oh yes!" I cried out as I felt it starting to build once again, and he suddenly hoisted me up, so he was back on his knees and I was sat impaled deep on his length. Then, with his hands gripping me tight, he controlled my movements, hammering me down over him again and again until I noticed something starting to happen.

I saw shadows around the room begin to swirl and thought I was going crazy when I caught sight of us both in the tall mirror across the room. We were both locked in this tight embrace as he continued to fuck into me, getting lost in his own pleasure and not realising the side of himself he was showing me. I knew that, the moment my vision changed, as no longer was I making love to the sexiest man I had ever seen.

No, now that sight had changed, and he was suddenly a man no more. Because men didn't possess a pair of black wings that spread out past the sides of the bed posts. Nor did the darkness swirl around them like some commanding force summoned by its master. And as for that same darkness, well now it was one that seemed to glow beneath his skin, humming with every thrust of his cock.

But most of all, when I looked back into his face, I knew that he wasn't a normal man at all, because those once glowing caramel eyes started to turn black like that of…

An Angel of Death.

CHAPTER 9
CARING FOR THE CLAIMED

S econds after this frightening moment, he tightened his hold on me before throwing his head back and roaring his release to the ceiling, making his wings shudder in the mirror.

"FUCK! YES... GODS... FUCK, AHHH!" I had no choice but to close my eyes tight, shutting off the image of me being held captive in this dark Angel's hold. And I was unashamed to say that, despite what I had witnessed, my own orgasm couldn't be helped. Because it felt as though he was the one commanding it to be torn from me, making me come to pieces in his bruising hold. Strangely, I then found myself with my head buried in his neck and my teeth sinking in around his flesh where his neck met his shoulder. I hadn't bitten him, but I was now panting heavily against his skin, tasting its saltiness for myself with each drag of air I took.

"*Hey.*" The sound of his gentle voice and his hand cradling the back of my head made me jump in fright, which in turn made him flinch before asking in a serious and cautious tone,

"Did I hurt you?" I swallowed hard, something he felt against the skin I still had my lips against before I shook my head a little, still too afraid to open my eyes. Because I didn't know what would meet me if I did.

"I can feel your fear, Eden, now tell me why?" he asked, and this time his voice came with that hard edge to it. This was when I realised that somehow, it was true, he obviously could read my thoughts. It was unbelievable and crazy but somehow, he could, and now it had me questioning everything I had thought around him.

"Eden!" My name was spoken, and this time it was nothing short of a warning. That was when I knew I had to be very careful, and caution was the key. Now, all I needed to do was open my eyes, something that was easier said than done as like this, holding onto him, and feeling secure in his arms I felt... well, *I felt safe.*

Safe from whatever truth I needed to face.

However, this dark Angel, whoever he truly was, had hit his limit on waiting. I knew this the moment I felt my now loose hair being fisted in a strong hand. A hold he now used on me to pull me back, so I had no other option other than to allow him to peel me from what had strangely been my safety.

"Open your eyes, sweetheart." I knew this was it, I had no other choice, so I opened my eyes, and when I found the man I was falling for back to looking human, I released a deep shuddering breath. Then I pulled from his hold and unless he wanted to hurt me, he had no option other to allow my hair to fall through his fingers.

"Eden?" he questioned before my desperate need cut him off, knowing my mind could be free from all my doubts when kissing him. Of course, as soon as our lips joined he didn't need any other coaxing as he kissed me back, and I felt tears form beneath my closed eyes at the intensity of it. Because I wanted this to last forever. This single moment, I wanted it burned to my memory, every second of it so I could hold on to that feeling until my life was no more.

I knew in that moment that he wasn't just dangerous for my body but mainly...

He was dangerous for my heart.

"Hey, come on now," he said tenderly, after being the first to pull away from the kiss, as if he could feel it was too much for me to bear. As if he knew I was being buried under by all these emotions, emotions I prayed he couldn't hear. Because what I had seen must have been a mistake. Because there was no way that a being that dark could be so tender, so gentle as he was being now. Nothing that evil looking could kiss like that... surely?

Maybe that was finally it then... maybe I was the one going crazy?

"What's wrong, Eden, tell me?" he asked after taking hold of my chin and forcing my gaze to his. I tried to shake my head a little, but he wouldn't allow it and raised a brow at me, as if telling me to stop. So, this was when I told him a half truth.

"I guess I'm just... you know... feeling a little vulnerable... like I said, it's been a long time and..." I struggled out, and finally this was enough to get him to drop it, as he replaced his stern expression with a tender one. He released my chin and instead cupped my cheek, running his thumb under my eyeline to capture a tear that must have slipped free.

"Alright, little one. Here is what is going to happen, I am going to lift you from me and then carry you into the bathroom so I may take care of you. After that I have no other choice but to dress so I can inform my Ki... employer that our meeting will have to wait," he told me, and I wanted to question why he stumbled a little when saying employer and besides, he didn't seem like the type to have a boss of anything.

But then, had I got it all wrong, had that been like a

company car picking him up? Not that any of it mattered, but if he was here for work then why take the chance with me? Oh jeez, but I hope this didn't get him in trouble. At this he chuckled and told me,

"Focus, Eden." I grimaced and then braved to ask,

"Can you read my mind or something?" At this he smirked and said,

"You have an expressive face, sweetheart, and you don't realise when you let words slip out." I frowned at this, making his smirk grow bigger. Instead, I decided to let it go and tell him,

"That's okay, you can go to the bathroom first, I can sort myself out." At this he shook his head and said,

"I know this is all new, but I think you get that I like control and with that comes taking care of your body, it's important to me... do you understand?" he asked, making me blush before nodding.

"What's the first rule, little one?"

"Yes, I understand," I said, giving him my words and feeling my core shiver around him, making him growl in response before burying his head in my neck.

"*Mmm, my girl likes being good for me,*" he murmured against my skin, and again I wished his words didn't so easily ignite that need in me. But then, as if he knew where this would head to, he kissed me over the mark he had made and lifted me off him, making me moan at the loss. And oh boy, his face said it all as he clearly enjoyed my needy reaction. He then shifted his naked body off the bed before turning and grabbing me. This ended with me shrieking out when I was roughly pulled to the edge by my ankle and then tossed over his shoulder. Then he smacked my bare ass making me cry out louder this time. Christ, but I found myself squirming on him as, other than the best sex of my life, it was the second most hottest thing ever done to me.

"I think we just answered your sexual musing on spanking... mmm, this pleases me, my Siren," he rumbled in that deep gravelly voice of his.

"Why do you call me that?" I braved asking, it was easy when I wasn't looking at him, and I currently focused on his amazing behind... in fact, I was impressed I could form words at all! Asses that hot should be illegal!

He laughed, making me jiggle over his shoulder before he answered,

"All in good time, sweetheart."

We walked into a bathroom that felt as though it belonged more in a modern, high class hotel as it was the total contrast to the castle room with its incredible four poster, carved bed. Because where that had been all polished wood and antique furnishings, the bathroom was all black and white tiles, and marble countertops. Oval bowl sinks that had fancy taps that made the water flow out like a fountain. A glass walk-in shower that could have fit a family inside, and a black bathtub that matched the tear shape of the sinks.

He soon brought me out of my curious study of the room when he sat me on counter, and I cried out,

"Ahh, cold!" He chuckled, the bastard, making me glare at him and it was a look he told me his thoughts by, as he playfully shook my chin and told me with that warm glow of his eyes,

"That's adorable you know." I growled at him, and again he laughed, telling me,

"Alright, kitten, you're terrifying... now open your legs for me." At this I dropped the pissed off act and instead went with shocked and started blushing. Especially after he had just soaked a hand towel and was now getting closer.

"Erm, it's okay… I can…" He stopped this by shaking his head at me.

"Now what did I tell you in there about control…? You agreed to yield to me," he said reminding me, and I closed my eyes for a second longer before telling him,

"Yes, but that was about sex." He then ran the back of his wet fingers up my thigh, looking down at my naked body with lust in his eyes as he said,

"That's my seed dripping out of your recently claimed pussy, Eden, what do you think that means to me?" His tone told me this wasn't him playing around this time and I knew with that authoritative edge to it, I should take him seriously, which was why I replied cautiously,

"That you… er… want to care for me?"

"*Precisely*… I told you that I care for what I own, and I claimed you, Eden, I told you this," he replied, making me nearly choke… was he serious?!

"But I thought… thought…"

"I know what you thought, and you're severely wrong if you think that I only want you for a single night. I do not say anything that I do not mean… *ever*. Not even in the height of passion, and that includes the feel of the heaven you create when my cock is buried into that sweet little pussy of yours… *one I claimed*… Now do you understand me?" he said in that no nonsense way of his, and I swear, now I was questioning if he had been a general in the army or something?!

"Yes, you keep saying that, but you can't just claim people's body parts," I argued, making him frown and say with certainty,

"The fuck I can't, especially when those parts are on you."

"And?" I tested gently.

"And now you're mine, so stop stalling and open your legs before I take you back in there and tie them open spread eagle, making more of a mess before cleaning up my girl," he said with that hard edge of promise, and I couldn't help but feel each word as if it had been a stroked finger against my clit.

Holy Hell.

Needless to say, that my legs snapped open instantly, seeing now that he wasn't playing around, and this was far from an idle threat... *this crazy guy was serious!*

"Yep, that's what I thought," he said in a cocky way, as if he'd just won some epic battle with my heart. And I would have responded in some snippy way, had the words not fled me the moment he grabbed the back of my knees and slid me to the edge. Then he spread me wider and at the first swipe of the wet cloth against my tender, abused flesh, I moaned, making him grin again. It was as if he loved the sound, no not just loved it but was... *addicted.*

"You know, you don't play fair," I informed him, and as he continued to clean me, he said without looking at me,

"I never said I would, Eden, and I rarely do when there is something I want." At this I blushed, knowing that it felt good, despite how scary it was because the sincerity in his voice told me he wasn't the bullshitting kind of guy. He just told it how it was and got his way. But then I found myself asking before I could stop myself,

"And you wanted me?" At this he finally looked up at me, and the intensity there again had his eyes looking impossibly brighter.

"Absofuckinglutely... as evidence clearly suggests, sweetheart," he replied, throwing the towel in the sink with a slap and making me flinch. Then, he took hold of my waist and lifted me down, before giving my ass a playful slap.

"Now, get this sweet temptation in there and get dressed, whilst I get myself cleaned up," he ordered, and again I sighed before muttering a playful,

"Bossy, much." Thankfully, he burst out laughing and took it

STEPHANIE HUDSON

in good humor. Because I just hadn't known if I could joke with him or not, as well, he was so intense that I didn't know which way he would have taken my usual smart mouth. One that only came out when I was brave enough to use it.

Back in the bedroom, I picked up all my clothes and started getting dressed, noticing that I would have to go without the panties as they were pretty much useless and beyond saving.

In fact, I was still adding my many layers when he came back out and amazingly, he was dressed, yet his clothes were still scattered around the room. I hadn't seen any spare clothes in there, but then I had been a little preoccupied, and really, given the sight of him, then who could blame me?

Either way, he had obviously had a quick wash as I could see the droplets clinging to his hair when he had been still pulling down a fresh t-shirt as he had emerged. This time it was one that was dark grey and long sleeved that molded to his muscles like a second skin, making me need to lick my dry lips. I swear I had to shake my head to get my senses back as he seemed to have the ability to steal them from me with just a look.

His easy chuckle alerted me to the fact that he found me amusing once more and I soon knew why.

"Not sure we could get any more layers on you, sweetheart," he commented, making me try and hide my own grin as his teasing was funny. Then he retrieved his leather jacket from beneath my own, making me take a step closer to him so he could pass mine to me. But when he didn't, my look questioned why.

"You won't need it yet. Besides, it was like fucking torture waiting for you to take them all off the first time, not going to put myself through that again," he commented, making me raise a brow.

"Well, you're sure of yourself that it will happen again,

88

aren't you?" I told him, again testing the waters, but then he tugged me closer to him after slipping his fingers into the loose waistband of my jeans... *damn, but I was going to miss my belt.*

Then he growled down at me,

"Too fucking right, and I can barely wait, as next time I get to taste your sweet cream..." He paused as he dipped his hand all the way in and dragged two thick fingers through my folds, making me close my eyes and moan at the feel. Then he made my mouth drop open and sing out a cry of shock as he stepped into me, at the same time thrusting his fingers inside me and bringing me up to my toes with the force.

"*Ahh... oooh,*" I called out to him, and to this long, pleasured moan, he responded by granting me a rumbling growl, as he found me soaked for him. But then, just as quickly as he put them there, they were gone, and I opened my eyes to find him putting his now soaked fingers to his mouth and sucking them to taste me. Jesus, but the sight was so erotic, I swear I could have come just from watching him taste me on his fingers. It was too much for me to watch and I was about to take a step back needing the space to breathe, when he made it known he didn't like this. Something I knew when his other hand flashed out like lightening as he collared my throat and captured me, preventing me from going anywhere. Then he released his fingers from his mouth and brought them to my lips, demanding on a growl,

"*Open!*" I shuddered in his possessive hold and did as he commanded of me, feeling it again straight to my core as I now needed to come so badly. Seriously, what was wrong with me, as everything this man did to me seemed to turn me on, making me fucking insane. But then he placed his fingers in my mouth, making me take them and when I tasted myself on his skin, he released a rumbled moan as if I was now the one with the power to turn him on to insane levels.

He pulled his fingers free of my lips and I made a point of sucking the ends, making him grin down at me. Then he tightened his hold on my throat, choking me for no longer than a second as he pulled me closer to his lips. Once I was as close as he could get me, he whispered,

"I'm going to make a fucking meal out of you, my little doe." Then, as my mouth dropped open, he took this opportunity and kissed me, taking the breath right out of me, releasing my neck so he could tenderly take hold of my face, framing my head with his large hands. A possessive kiss that was finished far too soon, but his growl of annoyance told me he wished he had been free to continue, as we both were nearly desperate to.

He placed his forehead to mine and panted through his arousal and I had to say, I had never felt so treasured than in that moment. Christ, but anyone would have thought he was falling in love with me… but that couldn't have been possible… *could it?* Well, if he heard these thoughts he didn't comment, but his eyes heated like they seemed to do often when something affected him.

"I want you to wait here for me. I won't be long." When I merely nodded, he gripped my chin and raised me up until I was almost on tiptoes again, asserting his dominance over me.

"You know the rule, Eden." His stern voice rang out like a warning bell, and a jolt straight to my pussy that was desperate to be filled by him once more.

"I will wait for you," I whispered breathlessly, and he both gentled his hold and his gaze, allowing me to find my feet once more before he praised,

"Good girl." Then he kissed me one more time, making me close my eyes as I let the warmth flow over me. Seconds later I felt him walk to the door, and I was left facing the mirror. But the moment I opened my eyes, my mystery lover was once again…

A man no more.

No, this time he was back to being the Angel of Death I had seen making love to me. The image I had tried to convince myself was all in my head. But then, if that was true, why was the winged figure now nodding his head at me and warning me with a dangerous flick of shadows circling him,

"Remember, Eden, stay here and wait for me." I remained frozen and unable to do anything but squeak out a quick,

"Okay," because I needed him to leave and not reprimand me. I needed him to leave and take the dark image with him, the one that utterly terrified me and had me near shaking. But I couldn't let him see it or he would never leave, as I knew the moment those black eyes frowned that he was looking for the change in me and questioning it, so I swallowed down the fear and tried to make my voice as steady as possible, telling him,

"Until later, my hero." And this was enough, as he smiled. Only this time it was one that was far darker and more dangerous than ever before. It was one that promised me all the delicious and despicable things he wanted to do to me, making me realise I might not survive a next time. Not when it felt as though I had already signed over my soul to him.

Something his words confirmed, when he told me,

"See you soon, *my little captive.*" Then he shut the door, and I finally let a fearful tear fall when I heard the damning sound that made that last sentence a reality,

The sound of the…

The door locking.

CHAPTER 10
SHOT IN THE HEART

As soon as he said this and left, I was thankful I had the time to freak out alone. He clearly didn't realise what I had just seen and thank God he hadn't, or I didn't think he would have ever left. But Christ, what if this was all me and I was really starting to lose it! Maybe it was the cheap noodles I kept eating, as there must have been some unnatural way they achieved that prawn flavor... *right?*

"Oh God, oh God... shit, shit... what... who... shit!" I said to myself before looking around the space and seeing that it was clearly a guest room, making me wonder if this was a hotel after all? Maybe one of those themed ones... Oooh, I wonder if they needed a chambermaid...

"Damn it, Edie, focus! You just saw the guy you had mind blowing sex with turn into some Angel of Death!" I snapped at myself. Although, maybe this was his room, but then where were his bags? Okay, that wasn't important, what was important was counting the last of my lucky stars that I had survived the most erotic experience of my life before discovering who the terrifying guy could actually be!

I could take the most intense orgasm with me as being the

best sexual experience of my life and consider it a gift. One I was half tempted to stay here like he asked me to and wait for him just for the chance that I could experience round two.

"Jesus, Edie, get it together!" I hissed at myself because I knew just what a bad idea that was. And what exactly had he meant, that I was his now? Christ, but I knew he was clearly a dominant lover but seriously, a one-night stand translated into him owning me? Okay, so granted, if I was so repulsed by that idea, why my lady parts were sighing again, I didn't know.

"Of course you know, idiot, it was the best sex of your life!" I mumbled as I searched for my worn sneakers, I didn't even remember him taking them off. Man, but he had been like a wild beast ravishing me, and afterward he admitted that was him trying to be gentle and go slow. I looked back at the snapped leather of my belt still half tied to the headboard and said,

"Yeah, right." Then I picked up the pace, knowing that I couldn't be here when he got back. Not after I had seen what I had. Because it meant I was either crazy, which admittedly, was the one I was kind of hoping for, because the other meant that the guy wasn't...

Human.

Well, he had said that he wasn't a good guy, so maybe that was his version of coming clean and telling me something more? Seriously, you're making excuses for him, Edie. What next, telling him murder was okay but as long as they were just the bad guys he killed...?

"Jesus, please, please, oh please make me be the crazy one," I said whilst I stuffed my feet back into the worn cheap sneakers, a pair that I prayed now, had a hope of helping me when running the hell out of here! Then I went to grab the pair of his jeans he had left on the floor, the ones he had put the keys in when first locking the door, which made me question how he locked it the second time, as I found them instantly. He had obviously forgotten them or maybe he was just hoping I would have. Either way, I grabbed my jacket and stuffed my layered arms through the sleeves in an angry, frustrated way.

But of course, I knew why. Because I was upset and hurt, knowing that I had no choice but to walk away. Damn, he had been so perfect, and the things he had said... oh God, but no man had ever made me feel so safe and protected... *so precious and treasured.*

"Maybe if I just..." I said, pausing before turning the key and leaving the room. But one look back, and I was so close to walking toward the bed and staying there until he got back. Maybe I could have just questioned him about it? But then I shook my head and said,

"He had wings, Edie, what was there to talk about!" Was I to ask how he got them or stick around when he asks just how crazy I was for seeing them? This was the part when I finally left the room, after first sneaking my head out the door as if I was on some kind of mission.

"Yeah, like the one where I escape the handsome Angel of Death before he consumes my soul," I muttered to myself, because high stress situations usually made the whole talking to myself thing so much worse. Although, I had to say that it kind of already felt as if he had consumed my soul, as I could think of nothing else but his touch. Was that part of his power? Had he brainwashed me, or controlled my mind in some way?

"Get a grip, Edie," I whispered, as I slipped through the door and started creeping down the strange open hallway overlooking that incredible temple. One they no doubt did their virginal sacrifices in and other cult stuff... oh God, but what if that had been what I was there for? Was I their next victim and he was prepping me?

"Yeah, 'cause you usually prepare a virginal sacrifice with

incredible sex, Edie, Jesus!" I muttered to myself, but then I was soon adding to that after crying out in shock,

"Ah! Okay, so time to pick up the pace, girl." I said after I heard the crackling of the flames in the lanterns, making the glass in them now crack. This was when I started to run, needing to get out of this creepy house of horrors and escape this charade. Because seriously... what normal people lived here?!

I made it back to the door and threw myself through it and down the steps with a speed that even impressed me. I burst through the doors at the bottom and shocked the hell out of the guards who had tried to stop me the first time. Half of me was now grateful they hadn't managed it and the other half of me wished they had!

God, but the sex.

"*That's it, just keep thinking of the sex, Edie,*" I whispered to myself as I pushed my way through the crowd, briefly looking up behind me at the VIP area I had been trying so hard to get to. Well, now after Jerry's warning and after what I had seen in my mystery man, then I was starting to think that the owner of this club wasn't entirely human! Shadowy figures were barely seen up there, but I swear I thought I saw one of them staring right at me and shake his head, telling me no.

Oh shit, could that be him?

I swear, but I nearly became rooted to the spot ready to obey. Ready to run back to that room as fast as I could, because that was how deep I had let this guy get into my head. Well, if he only knew the shit I was in, then he would think twice about wanting to get mixed up with me, so there was that.

Yeah, I was doing him a favor by running. Unless his idea of making a meal out of me had been literal and I was currently like fast food running in the wrong direction?

"*Oh God,*" I whispered to myself, I had never been so torn.

96

Because deep down, what I was doing just felt wrong... regardless of who or what he was. I just wished I could have told him that, so he didn't think badly of me. Despite what had happened at the end of our time together, didn't he still deserve an explanation? Christ, but I actually stopped at this point, and turned around before shaking my head, knowing it was a bad idea and then continued on towards the exit.

So, without being brave enough to look up at the VIP area again, I pushed my way through the rest of the club until making it through the doors. Then, I looked to where I had parked my car. I'd parked it at the back of the parking lot in hopes that when the place had all closed up for the night, I might have got away with sleeping there. But as for right now, the place was pretty well lit at least, so I could get to my car without incident. But as for sleeping here, well that wasn't going to happen now. No, my only hope left was that my car would at least start, or this getaway was going to end pretty damn quick! But then I saw that fancy black car of his and the moment I ran past it, I heard the door opening.

"Miss?" I stopped dead, knowing I just got my one opportunity to tell my mystery man what I wanted to say.

"*Jesus, Edie, you still don't know the guy's name!*" I hissed to myself, feeling ashamed that I had slept with him... okay, so not much sleeping involved but I had shared something with him, and I hadn't even known his name!

"Oh Deke, hey, hello again. How are you? Good...? Good, that's good," I said stumbling on my words, making the big guy smirk.

"Are you alright? You seem to be in quite a rush, and flushed at that," he said, giving me the once over and seeing my hands fisted in the overly long sleeves of my sweater poking past my jacket. I also kicked the toe of my sneaker on the gravel, as was a habit of mine when I was nervous, this was when I realised how cold my feet were. In my rush to get out, I'd forgotten to put my socks on...

Then again, there had been no time for trying to find them.

Christ, there had barely been time for a bra, and well, no panties to speak of after mystery man had torn through them like paper.

"Erm, yeah, I'm peachy. Oh, so I saw your erm... boss... anyway, can you tell him something for me." I asked, still walking backwards, and he frowned at both my actions and my words.

"You saw Wa..." he started to say, but I quickly interrupted him, needing to get my words out, and quickly, in case mystery man had been the one to see me running and was on his way down here himself.

"Yeah, you know the hot... I mean the guy in the back of the car, anyway, he didn't give me his name, but I'm Eden, he knows that, so if you can just tell him that Eden said..." At this point he took a step closer to me, and I took two back.

"Why not come and sit for a moment and tell me, or better still, why not wait so as you can tell him yourself?" he said in a voice that was low and coaxing, as if he was trying to lure me into a false sense of security.

"No! No I can't... I'm sorry, I just have to be somewhere is all," I stammered out, which again was another nervous habit of mine, one his boss now knew all about... seeing as that was all I seemed to do around him, like some bumbling idiot!

"And you're sure you will get there, are you?" he asked, nodding to my piece of shit car that deserved far worse.

Nope, definitely not.

"Yeah, of course," I said lying my pants off... oh, okay, maybe stay away from any puns where clothes are leaving my body. His disbelieving raised brow said it all, along with his crossed arms... Jesus, what did this guy eat for breakfast, dumbbells?!

"Look, can you just tell him that I am sorry, that he was, it was... very nice," I amended when I was granted another eyebrow raise, knowing it felt as if I was committing a sin by describing our time together as just nice. Something I have no doubt I would have been punished for had he heard me. But then I didn't want to give this guy the wrong impression of me.

"Eden, come with me and you can tell me all about it in the car. It's cold out, don't you think?" Deke tried again, and I shook my head and told him on a rush,

"I have lots of layers, so I'm good and besides, this won't take long as I..." I paused, closing my eyes against the hurt, knowing he had teased me about those layers not long ago. I swallowed down an emotional lump that seemed to clog my throat as tears threatened. Then I looked back at the main doors, as if I could feel any moment he would burst through them looking for me.

But then nothing.

The disappointment was like a lead weight in my belly making me just want to make it to my car, so I was free to cry. Fuck! But my life... it was like a never-ending self-pity train that just wouldn't stop long enough for me to get off. Well, no, that wasn't strictly true as my hero had stopped it for me. Doing so if only for a one perfect moment together. And what was I doing now but jumping back on the damn thing out of fear?

"Eden?" Deke's voice brought me back to my reality, and with my eyes closed I told him,

"Please tell him... it's not him, it's me, and I just can't get him wrapped up in my mess of a life, that wouldn't be fair you know... please tell him, that I will... I will never forget him," I said as if he might understand but when I opened my eyes, I could see his kindness had swapped for concern.

"I think you should come and wait in the car, Eden," he said more forcefully now, and I took another step back and jumped when his phone started ringing. Well, it definitely wasn't mine as that sucker had been sold on eBay to pay my last month's rent. Of course, the moment he looked at me and answered his phone by saying,

"Yes, she is here now," was when I turned on a heel.

"Okay, well time to shoot, bye Deke!" I shouted, and then started walking in a fast way that made it look as if I needed the toilet and was going to take a shit the second I got in my car!

"*Understood.*" This was the last thing I heard Deke say before distance got in the way and I was fishing my keys out of my jeans pocket ready to make like the jittering wind, as thanks to this shit engine, that's what happened whenever I hit the gas.

Of course, rattling of my bones was the least of my problems when this weird ass night just hit the fucked-up o'meter one more time!

It started when a sports car pulled in front of mine, and the same two of Gomez's goons got out making me jump as they slammed their doors.

"*Oh no… Jesus no, don't do this to me… not now!*" I muttered, holding the door open and wondering what my chances were at getting in it before they caught up to me. This option was answered as being zero when the door was slammed shut from behind me. It was then swiftly followed by being grabbed, spun around and pushed up against the car with a painful thud to my back.

"Hey, there's Jimmy's little bitch!" one of the goons said, who I knew was called Marco and was the shorter of the two. He had a mean looking scar running down the centre of his temple as if he'd had a bottle smashed over his square looking head at one time.

"Yeah, where you been hiding your sweet ass, you been running from us? 'Cause you know our boss doesn't like it when his commodities go running off," the other one said, and he was the one I was most scared of. This was because Rocco was bigger, meaner looking, and had made it clear he wanted to fuck me and let me work off some of my debt that way. I still remembered his grabby hands on me when bruising my ass, back when he pushed me up against my cubicle in my place of work.

He was big, but not exactly fit with it, as he had a beer belly that overhung his trousers in a way that if he had been a woman, you would have thought he was eight months pregnant. He had a shaved head, with a landing strip of hair down the centre... that he must have mistakenly thought looked cool and anything but the ass end of an ape. His ears were big, and he wore a pair of shades that were too small for his big head, and therefore always made me focus on how they dug into his wrinkled head at the sides. He also had a kind of biker thing going on, with the patch covered leather vest he wore over his shirt that was no way ever going to zip up over that food baby he had growing in there!

Just the sight of them both made me close my eyes as if this would help. But then I heard the clicking of fingers in front of my face and I knew I wasn't just going to wake from this nightmare, which meant I had no choice but to face my fate. The bad guys had followed me here.

"Man, you are one dumb bitch if you thought you could cut and run," Marco told me sniggering.

"Teach her a lesson," he added and before I could ask, Rocco punched me in the stomach, making me cough out as I doubled over in pain. Jesus, but it felt like the asshole just broke a rib. I knew this had been his intention when Marco bent over a little so he could tell me,

"Bitch, what did we say we would do when we found you again…"

"Bre…ak… mmmy… bon…es" I gasped out, making him chuckle and say,

"Fuck, right, now you got our boss' money, or do we need to break more?"

"Be a fucking shame, she's got a great fucking body," Rocco said suddenly, making me wish I was the size of a beached whale that was one fart away from blowing this asshole across the parking lot!

"Maybe we should take this somewhere else, Rocco, looks like one of the locals is gonna try to be a dickwad hero." Hearing this had my head snapping up to find Deke storming his way over, at the same time taking off his jacket like he meant business.

"*Oh no, please no,*" I muttered despite the pain.

"Don't worry, I will take care of this big fucker, he can crack his knuckles all he wants, it ain't gonna matter when I put a fucking hole in his head." My gaze snapped to the gun Rocco was pulling from his jacket and I totally panicked even more.

"N…no… please, I… I will come with you, just don't hurt him," I pleaded, now trying to get back up from being winded and using my car as leverage to do just that.

"Well, that depends on how good of a liar you are, as I suggest you start talking before I fuck your friend up here," Marco said, making me nod, and then I tried to start laughing the moment Deke could hear, saying now,

"Ha, these guys, they crack me up with their play fighting… it's okay, Deke, I know them, it's all good. Thanks though, you'd better go," I said, trying to tell him with my eyes to leave but his gaze only turned more deadly as he took in the situation.

"Yeah, dickhead, you heard what our little bitch said, we are all close and shit, so beat it!" Marco said, putting his arm around me and biting his fingertips into my shoulder, making me wince as I tried to fake a smile. Deke looked at my face and then to Rocco with his hand inside his vest. I just hoped this meant that he got the message and didn't want to risk his life for me, as I was already a hopeless case and not worth another life taken in return.

"It's okay... *it's okay,*" I said quietly, trying to stop the tremble of fear in my voice or the tears that had yet to fall that were clinging to my lashes. I also held out my hand, showing him my palm and telling him to stop, despite being unable to keep it from shaking. But I just needed to let him know that I didn't want him to get hurt... *not because of me.* I couldn't bear knowing that if this was my last moment on Earth, I would die knowing I had caused another to lose his life.

I couldn't have that weight upon my soul.

But then I had never been the type to be granted wishes and this day, well, it was just like any other. Because Deke didn't listen to my plea, to my prayer or to my wish. No, what he did do was demand that they let me go.

Then he took a step forward, and I cried out as I knew then it was to be his last step taken.

Taken with his life as he was...

Shot in the heart.

CHAPTER II
FORBIDDEN FRUIT
WARD

Gods in Heaven, I had taken a human.

I had broken the law. And fuck me, but I had never felt better! Because the truth of what just happened felt as though it had been written in stone by the Gods themselves and what I had just done, well it felt like the complete opposite of wrong. It felt as if I would have been breaking the laws of Heaven by walking away, as no other action had ever felt so fucking right in all my years walking this realm. I felt at peace, centred, and whole.

I felt as if I had just claimed what was always mine to claim.

Eden was mine... My Gods' Paradise.

Fuck me, but she couldn't have been any more perfect and my whole vessel itched to get back to her, to take her again, over and over, just so she knew without a shadow of a doubt who she belonged to! Of course, she had her insecurities, most of which I had heard spoken as an adorable monologue in her mind. And well, I hadn't been able to help myself in reacting to them, despite her worrying that I was some sort of mind reader.

But then, of course she would, for it wasn't like she knew who I really was.

No, unfortunately that particular truth would have to wait until I could be assured she would not be able to run from me. Until she had been firmly situated in my life and therefore, I was assured I could control the outcome of such a discussion. I also knew that, despite my dominant nature, I would have to take certain things slow with her, for she needed to be protected, which included her fragile mind. Because there was still a lot about my girl I didn't yet know. Like the reason she was living in her fucking car for that matter, a thought that had me near fucking murderous!

My Fated One didn't sleep in fucking cars, she slept covered in the most expensive sheets, in the highest luxury and finally wrapped securely in my arms. She also didn't wear five fucking layers just to keep herself warm! Gods alive, but watching her strip each layer from her delicious body had been near fucking agonising, and nothing short of torturous. But then I had tried to go slowly for her, and I knew that I would have most likely scared her had I just done as I had wanted and started ripping clothes from her like a wild animal. So, I had commanded her to strip for me, and despite her nerves she had impressed me as she had done as she had been told.

She was a natural submissive and this pleased me... *immensely.* But then, she was born for me so it was hardly surprising that she would be such a perfect fit to my dominant ways. In fact, it was said that most Sirens were known for their submissive natures and well, they were said to be intended for the most powerful of the King's Enforcers, who were as I was... dominant fuckers who liked to get what they wanted and took it by force if anything stood in their way.

And nothing would stand in my way of claiming my Siren.
My Eden.

Gods, but just her name alone was utterly fitting and made my cock harder every time I spoke it, for she was my fucking paradise! Every shy and unsure look had tugged at my heart and dragged a new emotion out of me I had never felt before. I wanted to care for her, treasure her and tame her all at the same time. Because there had been a fire there and I had tried pushing for it, but she had held back. However, I knew why, as at this current time I still intimidated her, too much for her to challenge me. Something that for now would only serve its purpose and for a time, I would allow this as she didn't yet know that she would become my equal.

Of course, in the bedroom she would remain my slave, but her body would benefit from this as I would grant her a world of pleasures of the likes she had never known. I would make her sing out to me just like that small taste of what I had heard so far, and by the fucking Gods, I was already addicted!

It was as if she had been calling out directly to my soul, and the strength of my own release because of it had been beyond my wildest and most sinful dreams! Incredible hadn't been the word strong enough, for I had never known such a feeling had been possible to achieve. Now, had I known what I had been missing out on then I would have made it my private mission to find her sooner, spending every spare second searching for my lost Siren. But unfortunately, until today, I hadn't even expected to be deserving of one. Of course, I hadn't lied when I told her I was not a good man. Fuck, but I wasn't a man at all! But then I had lied when I told her I would have walked away should she wish it.

No. Fucking. Way.

No, instead I would have simply taken things slower and allowed her the time to trust me before making her mine and claiming my Siren the only way you could... making their souls sing for you as you fucked your fated essence into them.

It had been fucking heaven, every Gods be damned second of it.

"Fuck!" I hissed, and paused in my steps at just the memory of it before I realised the poor girl didn't even yet know my name! Well, there would be time for that but for now, I knew I had to face the King and explain what I knew.

She was one of the lost Sirens and she was mine.

It was the only explanation possible and that meant technically she wasn't entirely human, so as for our laws, then come the summer solstice, this would reveal whether I had broken them or not. But I feared not, as I knew deep within my soul and dark heart that she was a Siren, for no other explanation was possible.

Yet, for the one being on this Earth above the power of my own, then this was the only time of year that I could prove my claim true. For she would only be able to reveal her true self or not on this day, yet she would need the help of a Supernatural to do it, which was no doubt why it had never happened before. Also, her powers of persuasion didn't seem as if they came naturally to her. But then, seeing the strength of light in her soul, I doubted she had ever broken a law in her life! But fuck me, how she had sung naturally for me when finding every orgasm by my cock.

Gods alive, the things I wanted to do to her, it was a fucking minefield running wild in my mind. Because every fucking word out of her mouth had called out to me, meaning only one thing…

She was my Fated and no one could deny this claim, not even the King of Kings. It would also mean that he would have to grant me that time to prove this or risk the wrath of the Gods themselves. Because she was the one the Gods had fated to be mine. Now, if by some colossal and hellish fuck up, I was wrong, then that would mean come next year, my life would be forfeit and I would find death by my King's hand. As for Eden, her memories would be stripped, and she would have no knowledge of me even existing. But that was not going to fucking happen as I would have been prepared to go to war before anyone thought to take her from me!

So, with this in mind, I walked back into the VIP area only shortly after abusing one of the many guest rooms Afterlife had to offer, and well admittedly, that hadn't been all I had abused, as my little Siren had cried out for me so beautifully when tied to the bed. Fuck, but I was getting hard just thinking back to how well she had taken me, but damn, I needed to be careful with her. I had never lain with a human before and despite what she may be at her core, she was at this moment still as human as they came.

Meaning she was far more delicate than my own kind.

But by the Gods, how I had wanted to completely dominate her, and fuck her into a sexual oblivion. And there was still so much more for me left to discover, as that little bit of sass when in the bathroom when calling me bossy was one I relished the sight of. After all, I may have demanded a slave in the bedroom, but I was far from interested in having one in life. I wanted Eden to be my equal and not have her actions ruled by her fear of my reaction. I wanted her to be herself and not solely what she thought I wanted of her. She was perfect as she was, if not a little thin, but I knew this was no doubt because she hadn't been taking care of herself as much as she should have. Or should I say, capable of doing as I knew she must have very little in way of money.

Gods, but that thought broke my fucking heart!

Like hearing her craving a cheeseburger as I carried her up the stairs. Of course, this had also come with her giving me an unknown insight to her sexual history, that had sounded dire at best. Something I admitted I was a bastard enough to be thankful of, as I wanted my girl as addicted to me and my body as I had already become addicted to the whole of her.

Body, mind and soul.

She was to become my everything.

Because something unexpected had happened, for she seemed to become the light to my darkness and in that, I felt fucking powerless to her. Yes, I may have dominated her body, but she had quickly dominated my heart and made me a slave to her. Fuck, but I was falling fast and wondered if this was how it was always meant to be? Was this what all the Kings and their Chosen Ones were to experience.

Would the King of Kings also fall just as hard and fast?

Just as, would all Sirens make slaves out of their Enforcers?

I fucking found myself needing to adjust my damn erection before approaching the King's table at the thought of being chained to her. Admittedly, a very different sort of thought for me to experience, and no doubt it would not be the last with Eden in my life.

I retook my seat and masked my features along with my rampant thoughts of a particular cute strawberry blonde who smelled like summer, dreamed of cheeseburgers and fisted her hands when nervous.

"Problem solved?" Vincent asked with a curious eye directed my way.

"Not as of yet, which is why I must depart back to my hotel for a few days," I replied, trying not to give anything away.

"Anything we can aid you with?" The King's brother asked, this time after first shooting his brother a knowing look, no doubt trying to get him to focus his mind. One that most definitely seemed elsewhere, which was unlike him. This made me question if he too was preoccupied for the same reason... had his Chosen One finally showed herself?

"Nothing I cannot handle at this present moment." At this,

Dominic Draven rose from his seat and in a stern tone that was far more than the request it sounded, he told me,

"Join me, Ward." At this I bowed a head in respect, and followed him over to the edge of the VIP where we stood against the railings that looked down over the entire club below.

"I have sent word informing Malphas I require his presence and wish to speak with him. He will be here tomorrow," he told me, making me nod before asking,

"How do you intend to play it?"

"I am open to suggestions," he said surprising me.

"Malphas is a sly son of bitch, always has been, and has made no secret of his greed for an increase in power and seeing as he commands armies in Hell, what more he fucking wants is beyond me," I said, as Malphas was a president in Hell and therefore was slightly untouchable, even for the King of Kings.

"In this we both agree," he replied in frustration, something he rarely showed, adding to my suspicions of his Chosen One having made her appearance. Yet, knowing of the dangers a girl like that would face, then I didn't blame him for being cautious. Although, how frustrating that would be, I was only just now starting to understand, as it happened to me the second I left her on the side of that fucking road.

"But, I will say this, be cautious, my King, as from what I hear… his obsessions in the old pagan rituals and their Gods have only increased with time," I said, making Dominic turn his back on the club beyond and lean his large form against the railings with a fold of his arms.

"Yes, I confess to having heard the same thing, but it's what his dealings with Lucius are, that concerns me more." I nodded, understanding this, seeing as Lucius was basically the son of the Devil and was believed to become Dominic's equal in power if he wasn't already.

"Then my suggestion is this, keep your meeting vague and

let him talk himself into a hole. Let him talk himself into the lies he usually weaves and that way when the time comes for you to confront him, you will not have the word of spies to use against him, but the word of your hearing." The King nodded in a way I knew he was going to take my advice.

"Anything else to report in your ever-growing sector?" he asked as a way of moving the conversation from the shit stain Malphas.

"Other than that asshole Gastian throwing his weight around again and pushing for Spain to become part of his sector, nothing but the odd rogue here and there, something I hope you will find me no slouch in dispatching." At this he raised a brow and commented,

"Your power has never been in question, Warden Za'afiel," he said speaking my full name and making me nod out of respect.

"You think I should have someone take his place and reappoint a new Enforcer?" he asked, and I had to say, it felt good knowing he respected me enough to want my advice.

"That is, as ever, your call, my Lord, but as I said before, I just know that he has been linked to the Lega Nera, which you outlawed for a reason." He released a sigh and said,

"Then your word is good enough for me. Leave it with me and I will start looking into his replacement should I find his reasons lacking."

"And I will be at the ready for your call, should you need that extra hand in punishment," I replied, reminding him of his promise, making him smirk and damn, it was a darker grin than even I had. But then, he wasn't the world's most dangerous being for nothing. Poor little human, was all I could say and very much like my own would soon be, for she had no idea who she had handed her soul over to. And no doubt neither would the King's Chosen.

"You're a good man, Ward," Dominic said, and I lost all thoughts of pity for our fated humans, knowing now the time had come.

"My Lord?" I questioned, having my veins filled with fucking Hell's fire the moment he said this, knowing there was no going back now.

"I would hate to be the hand of Hell clipping your wings for any reason that has to do with a lustful mortal temptation when tasting what humanity has to offer and it be nothing more." I released a sigh and answered truthfully.

"Should that moment ever afflict me it would only ever be for something more, significantly so, my Lord." He granted me a knowing look and I swear I thought I saw the hard bastard grin, before he nodded down over his shoulder at the dance floor and said,

"In that case, my suggestion to you is go and solve that problem of yours before she goes running off into even more danger..." My gaze shot to the sight of Eden pushing her way through the club and I gritted my teeth and hissed a curse, giving myself away,

"*Fuck*"

"...Oh, and the next time you walk into my VIP after dipping your cock in the forbidden, do me a favor and shower first, that way I can ignore your law breaking a little easier," he said before walking back to his seat and making his point.

He knew.

But of course, he did. He wasn't the most powerful being on Earth for no reason! Fuck! Well, fuck it, I was taking that as a green light if ever there was ever one! But first, well it looked like my little Siren needed to learn another simple rule to follow...

Never run from the one who owns your soul.

I shook my head at her the moment she took pause to glance

behind her up at the VIP. I knew she saw me when her eyes grew wide like that little doe, I had named her. Yet my silent warning wasn't enough to get her to stop completely, even if at the very least she did take a moment and took a step back, making me believe for a few seconds that she might return to me.

A cruelty she would pay for, and a punishment she would receive by my hand in the bedroom as soon as I was physically able. But fuck me, my girl was an enigma. One I would do all in my power to discover, starting with why she was here in the first place and most of all, why my Siren was hungry, cold and homeless. Something that infuriated me when I heard her mind speaking of it in a barrage of thoughts from what I knew was an overactive mind. One I knew the best way to silence was to simply accept what was happening to her.

Her doubtful and questioning mind was what I knew was a defense mechanism and one I would soon take control of, eradicating her need for it. With first my hands, then my tongue and lastly a cock that was near throbbing to be back inside her.

But first, it was time to recapture my beauty. Which was why I turned on a heel and, no surprise, found Vincent standing there. As for his brother, well, he had disappeared into the belly of Afterlife which would act as his colossal home for the time he was here.

"She doesn't know what she is, does she?" he questioned, as clearly it was like Dominic had said, every fucker in the room could smell one of the forbidden on me. Not that I gave a fuck, as I could fight every single one of them and win, something the brothers both knew. I was the most powerful Angel here, other than Vincent, and the Dravens would want that power kept on their side. It was why I suspected I still kept my head now, for my own people would have gone to war in revenge of my death.

Fuck yeah, it was good to be an Enforcer and ruler of my

own domain and I spoke not only of the one of mortal's realm, something Vincent knew better than most. His brother may have been my King but as for Vincent, then he was at truth more of a friend.

"No, and neither will it be confirmed until the Summer Solstice, something I care little for as she is mine," I admitted. Vincent then slapped me on my back and said a simple,

"Be careful, my friend, for do not forget you have enemies and those... well, they only have power over us when they prey on those we care for. As we are all just now starting to discover," Vincent said, looking towards the massive doors that lead into their private home. Doors his brother had not long walked through.

"So, she has been found?" I asked, knowing not many would get away with asking, but like I said, I was a special case for I wasn't like most other Enforcers.

"Sophia seems to believe so. Which means take care, for it will not be long now until that catalyst affects us all and if your mortal and first of the lost Sirens called to you, then I am now inclined to agree with our sister's instincts." I nodded, before clasping my hand on his shoulder and telling him,

"Then I hope the next time we speak it will be a greeting that offers you all my congratulations." His grin said at all before admitting,

"As do I, Ward, as do I, for I feel as though very few deserve it more than my brother... company not withstanding of course," he added with a smirk, making me laugh. Because wasn't that the fucking truth. Everyone believed that being ruler over an entire realm would be easy and mean they lead a privileged life. But they would be fucking wrong.

I knew this, as ruling over Europe was hard enough and rarely offered much in a way of a reprieve. Now, if I had my Fated One to stand by my side when doing it, well, then that would have certainly made my existence more meaningful, enjoyable, and exhilarating. For even in that one moment shared together, I had never felt as alive as I had done. Not even fighting on the battlefield could be compared, and fuck me, I did so love a good excuse to feel the heavy weight of a sword in hand, before slicing into my enemies.

"Go, my friend, go and take care of your little runaway," Vincent said, seeing now that I was clearly eager to leave, which was why I nodded, and departed after a show of respect for my friend and another King in his own right,

"My Lord."

After this I left down the main staircase, this time no longer caring if I was making a show of it for those in the main club, because time was running out, and all I could be thankful for was that her car was a piece of shit and would be easy to catch up to, should she even manage to get it out of the fucking parking lot. Which was why I was pulling my phone from my jacket and ringing Deke.

"Have you seen the girl?" I asked, knowing he would know instantly who I was referring to, especially seeing as I'd had him search for her like a man obsessed. But it was of little wonder, as she was the first female I had shown any interest in other than filling my bed for the night, and because of this, Deke knew who she was to me. He would know what she meant to me and just how important, as nothing would be more so in my life ever again.

"Yes, she is here now," he answered, making me close my eyes a second longer than what was needed as I released a relieved sigh.

"Good, keep her in your sight until I get there. Five minutes."

"Understood," he replied. But then, before hanging up, he

let loose a growl of annoyance, and I stopped dead just before reaching the last step.

"What?!" I snapped, making Deke tell me something that made me feel as if I had just fallen into Hell itself!

"I think your girl is on the run and not just from you... and fuck, Ward, but whoever it is, well I would say they just found your girl."

"Fuck! FUCK! Keep her safe, at all costs, you got it?" I roared making those around me flinch back, taking the threat of me seriously.

"You mean kill the fuckers if I need to, yeah I won't have a problem with... fuck!" he shouted, cutting that sentence off, and I started running through the club the second I heard it.

"What happened?!" I demanded.

"The fucker's just punched her!" The second he said this, I swear I nearly erupted into my other form right then and there!

"*They are dead!*" I said in a dangerous tone the moment I heard this. No one touched what was mine and lived, but by harming her, oh they weren't just dead, they were going to roast in fucking Hell, and I would be the hand that held that fucking torch! Oh, I may have been an Angel, but I was as far from Angelic as you could fucking get, and I had enough connections in Hell to get me exactly what I wanted!

Revenge.

"Not unless I kill them first," he said, as he hated an injustice just as much as I did. But then, we would be, seeing as it was in our dark veins and the whole reason behind our fucking existence!

"*Fuck!*" I hissed again, changing direction, and seeing now a side exit that would get me out there quicker. It looked to be behind the bar area, and one that meant not crossing the dance floor and a whole fucking club of people that stood in my way! So instead, I avoided the mass of people, and without saying a word to anyone behind the bar who would have questioned what the fuck I was doing, I controlled their minds. Doing so enough to get them to back the fuck up and not get in my way. Then I ran out of the back entrance that led to where the garbage was kept, and vaulted over the railings to the steps that led down and ran for the parking lot.

Then I heard a sound that had the power to strip me of my will to move, for what it could mean?! A single gunshot fired, and my blood turned to fucking ice! As I had slammed to a stop and for the first time in my long existence, an emotion overwhelmed me.

One so foreign it almost took me to my fucking knees!

It was nothing but...

Stone Cold Fear.

CHAPTER 12
ANGEL OF DEATH
EDEN

"NO!" I screamed the moment Rocco fired the gun, and hit Deke square in the chest making him go back a step. How he didn't just fall to the floor I didn't know, but what confused me more was when he didn't seem affected by it at all. Well, that's not strictly true, because if I was to add an emotion to him being shot in the chest, then I would say he seemed pretty pissed off by it. I knew this the moment he looked down at his chest, seeing the black hole in his clothes that was smoking the edges.

"What the fuck?!" Rocco muttered in disbelief.

"Was that a fucking blank?!" Marco snapped, and I agreed that it must have been unless the guy had a bulletproof vest on. Well, whatever it was, I didn't want to chance it happening again, as I was pretty sure a bullet to the head wouldn't have been one he would survive. which meant the moment Rocco raised his gun again I just acted.

"DON'T SHOOT HIM!" I screamed as I threw myself into him sideways, so he lost his hold on the gun, making it shoot wide and miss Deke this time.

"Dumb bitch!" Rocco shouted and backhanded me, hard

119

enough that I felt my lip explode and I tasted blood as I landed on the floor with enough pain I cried out. Deke snarled like a wild beast and charged the guy, moving so quick it was like the guy had just been hit by a fucking freight train! Rocco literally flew backwards through the air as if he had been lassoed around the waist and yanked back by a speeding truck!

As for Marco, the second I heard the sound of choking I turned away from the spot I think Rocco had landed and back to Deke, to find him dealing with mafia goon number two. Something he did with frightening ease as he currently had him by the neck and lifted off the ground with one arm. Jesus, but who was this guy, a fucking superhero?! But then I heard a strange sound behind us as if the ground was cracking in the distance. After this, came a darkness that start to seep along the floor as if a blanket of fog had fallen, making it roll along the ground like a wave of vapour snaking through our feet.

This was when I felt it.

A hum of power that had me gasping for breath as if all the air had been suddenly sucked out of me. Something that was even more painful due to struggling to breathe with a broken rib. But then it suddenly disappeared as if all I had needed to do was think of the pain, and the desperate need for breath left me. Though it was the next overwhelming feeling to assault me was one that had my whole body shaking.

It was of course…

Stone. Cold. Fear.

Oh, and this fear came with a voice, one so deadly it felt as if the Devil himself had just stepped straight from Hell and into this world. There was such a raw, dangerous depth to it, that I didn't think it possible to have been created by a human being! No, that would have been impossible! But then, just how many times could I question whether or not my mystery man was human or not. Because as soon as a dark sinister figure approached and made his first claim, I knew then that it wasn't my mind that had been wrong.

Because I wasn't crazy. And as for my hero, well…

My hero wasn't human.

"*Unhand my kill, for vengeance is mine!*" This demonic command came from the shadowed figure walking closer towards us from the shroud of darkness he himself seemed to have created. Deke let a choking Marco go and my eyes didn't stray from the sight. No, that's because they were glued to where the disturbing voice had arisen from. Something I only saw fully when Deke turned side on to take in the man behind him.

No, not a man but more like some dark lord who was now emerging from the shadowed gates of Hell!

An Angel of Death.

But no, it just wasn't possible! It couldn't be him and yet there, right in front of me were the same wings that had belonged to my mystery lover! Only now the rest of him had also completely changed, as the Angel part of him now looked totally consumed by the Death he looked ready to inflict!

A darkness I realised was attached to him and covering his form like a living cloak that moved with him, with the veil of a hood casting his handsome face in shadow. As for what I knew first hand was an incredible body, well now it looked even bigger than before, as hints of plated armour of the likes I doubt any human's eyes had ever seen before, looked to be forged over every muscle. It was matt black and looked more like it had been made out of stone than metal, however, the details were lost to distance and that looming darkness he commanded. It also looked as if he had two spiked horns of stone rising straight up from where his neck met his shoulders that looked part of the larger plating that curved into two more spikes facing outwards.

He looked like some Hellish warrior on the warpath, and I was beyond terrified. Especially when he barely even glanced at the man choking for breath on the floor who looked five seconds from passing out, and to be honest, I wasn't that far behind him. Especially when the warrior of Death nodded to where the other guy had landed, somewhere now lost in that darkness. This meant he was silently telling Deke without words to go and fetch him his other kill, as clearly, he would not go unpunished either. Deke nodded once and left, walking through the blanket of darkness as if he were walking through a pair of curtains that closed behind him.

But after this, there was only one place he had his next sights set and that was firmly on me. Now, if I thought I was panicking before, well now I was near hyperventilating from it, as he started to walk closer to me. This was also when my instincts finally kicked in as I started scrambling backwards trying to get away from him. And despite the pain, I was left with no other option but to hug an arm around myself, holding my damaged ribs as I tried to put more space between us. But then he paused at the sight and tilted his head to the side as if he couldn't understand why I would be afraid of him. But then his huge wings ruffled as if he was frustrated, and I watched as he released a defeated sigh as if he finally understood why...

I was human.

He was not.

Well, as for this petrified human, I continued to scoot backwards like a lost crab scrabbling for water. However, all I found was the side of my car, which I was now plastered against as if this had any chance of helping me! Of course, it didn't as he continued to walk closer to me, now doing so slowly as if trying to appear unthreatening. He even held his hands out a little as if surrendering something and if he thought this would help, then he was fucking wrong! It would have been laughable had I not been close to pissing myself out of fear!

I just had to get out of here and leave him to his kill in peace, maybe then he would let me go and forget about me. Which was why I started to struggle to my feet, but before I could even gain an inch in height, he suddenly cut the distance down to nothing.

"ARRH!" I shouted in fright as his booted feet were right in front of me, and I felt as if I had no choice but to look up at him. But then what was I supposed to do exactly, try and ignore the enormous wings behind him or that thick fog that seemed to move with its master in mind. This close up, it even looked as if each feather was coated in its essence, like some smoked vapour clinging on to each length.

"Eyes, Eden." That different, hard voice suddenly spoke, making my head snap up from his wings, finding him now looking down at me from an even greater height. Christ, but he was like a fucking giant! And as for those black eyes of his, they looked consumed by death until they started to swirl with the comforting ones I was used to. This made a bright golden amber shine through as if he was calling forth that other side of him for my benefit. This meant after a second or two I was once again staring into those stunning brown eyes that looked more human and were easier to keep contact with. At least without being controlled by the fear of what staring at them could do to me.

Yet as he gazed into my own with that hard disappointed edge seeping away into one far more comforting, I felt myself finally take a breath. Then, as he lowered down to one knee in front of me, the rest of him started to make its way back through. Now showing a human body beneath the armour as it seeped back into the shadows he now kept behind him, so all that was left was the man I had made love to who still had wings at his back. But despite knowing he had done this for me, the moment he got close I still couldn't help but flinch back. He rumbled a displeased growl, and held up a hand again in an easy gesture before telling me,

"Easy, my little one, for I will not hurt you." I knew when he spoke that he had even tried to soften his voice, and I had to admit that looked difficult to do in this form. I swallowed hard and almost choked on it, making him notice and tell me,

"Take a deep breath for me." I did as I was told, too afraid not to, but then again, I tried to tell myself that he hadn't hurt me so far, so maybe reacting like this wasn't the best way of thanking him for that fact. Then again, I was only reacting rationally, as I didn't think many people in my situation would have been readily accepting of what this man appeared to be. Yet knowing all this, I still needed to show him some trust as it was clear he was trying desperately to earn it. Something I had to admit, I couldn't fully express just how much I appreciated right now. Not because I didn't know what to say, but because I didn't seem to have the ability to speak in that moment.

However, what I did have the ability to do was remain deadly still when he reached out towards my face and not flinch back like I had done. Jesus, but even his skin looked as if it had been overtaken by some sort of smoke, as if it was moving underneath his skin and seeping out of his pores every time he moved.

But even with how dark and ominous it looked, he was still so gentle with me, that I couldn't help but lean into his touch as if it had the power to soothe me and keep me protected. The pad of his thumb ran so gently over the cut on my lip, making me smell the fresh blood now on his skin. God, but how could something so dangerous and deadly looking be capable of such a tender, gentle gesture?!

And speaking of dangerous, that lethal sound rumbled from

his chest as if he was furious and then he closed his eyes, and whispered a growl,

"They made my Siren bleed."

I opened my mouth ready to say something, anything, if it would offer him comfort in return, because something inside me didn't like to see him distressed or in pain. And obviously seeing me after I had recently been struck was doing something to him. So, I reached out slowly, ready to touch him, even in the way he appeared now as this frightening, dark angel who looked made for killing, not for granting miracles. It was a feeling, an impulse that I didn't fully understand, yet one that couldn't be denied. One I didn't want to, even if I had tried. Even if I had the will, I knew nothing in that moment would have stopped me. So, I reached out and just as I was about to touch my dangerous hero, something violent happened.

"I… it's… LOOK OUT!" My voice ended up as a scream the second I saw a flash of movement behind him. Marco had obviously found the discarded gun and was now firing it at my Angel's back. But I reacted instantly as I reared up, about to throw myself in front of him to save him from being hit. However, it didn't work this way as he wrapped both arms around me, catching me the second I moved. Then he turned me away the same time his wings became solid, creating a barrier between us and the flying bullets. He then struck out with one of them and I saw a flash of light, like something was striking metal before this snap of movement ended up knocking Marco off his feet and backwards through the darkness.

After this, he held me to him and the intense look he gave me stole my breath, as I shuddered in his arms that were banded around me protectively.

"You… you tried to save me?" he asked, and even with the heavy weight and roughness of his otherworldly voice, I could still hear the astonishment in his question. I fisted the hem of my jacket in my hands, and looked down as I told him,

"Of course I did… you're still…" I paused, not knowing if I could say it and well, it wasn't surprising when I felt my chin being taken in his grip before he was using his hold on me to force my eyes to his own.

"I am still what, *tell me, my Siren.*" I swallowed hard before deciding it was time to be brave in sight of this side of him, because would I have been really ready to take a bullet for someone I didn't care for? Meaning that despite whatever or whoever he was, I still cared about him…

I had still fallen for this Angel of Death.

So, I told him,

"*You're still… my hero.*" At this, I watched as he closed his eyes as if savoring the sound of my confession.

"You know not what that means to me, Eden," he told me affectionately, now caressing the back of his fingers down my cheek. But then, as if our moment had always been destined to end, the sounds of men's screams penetrated through the command of his dark fog.

I watched him release a sigh as if this was very frustrating after our tender moment had been severed and reality had set back in. Something that included the reminder that I had run from him and clearly this was something he was less than happy about. I knew that when he looked down at me and said,

"I would ask you to wait here for me, but that didn't go so well the last time." His voice was cutting, telling me how pissed off he had been to find me gone and how disappointed he was that he couldn't trust me. I opened my mouth, but nothing came out like I wished it would. Then the darkness split, and Deke walked back inside it before jerking his head to the side. It was as if he was telling my Angel without words where he had dumped the two men that now had to deal with the real face of death. I knew this when he released his hold on me and stood back to his full height. Then, with every inch gained the veil of his darkness flowed back over him, creating once more the figure I had seen when he first emerged. His demonic looking armour was back, and those spikes looked even deadlier this close up.

"Take the girl back to the car and wait for me..." He paused, and his eyes turned completely black once more. Then, before he looked towards where the two thugs that were out of sight beyond his darkness, was the first time I was granted the same face of death.

Because this time, that dark hooded veil of his no longer hid the face of the man I was falling for, as it was,

The terrifying skeletal face of the Bringer of Death.

This was when he promised in that Hellish voice of his,

"This won't take long."

And this was true, as he said it himself...

"Death waits for no man."

CHAPTER 13
EDGE OF DARKNESS

After this, he walked away from me and straight through the blanket of darkness, disappearing just as Deke had done. And speaking of Deke, the moment he started to come closer I freaked, making me act quicker this time. So, I found my feet and started running around my car, getting lost the moment I was faced with the endless depth of the back fog. Jesus Christ, it was everywhere, as if it had the power to cling and swirl around me, as if responding to my body. It was like a living entity that wanted to cage me in, tightening around me in a way that had me locked inside.

"Please! Let me go!" I pleaded as I twisted and turned in the substance that, thankfully, was one I could at least breathe through, otherwise I would have been screwed! But then I heard the terrified screams behind me and I turned quickly, towards where they had come from. Good God, but they had sounded beyond petrified, as if they were facing the Devil himself and he had the door open to Hell ready to toss them inside for an eternity of torture!

It also sounded as if they might have been experiencing some of that torture right now, and by the hands of my mystery man… hands that had been oh so gentle with me. Hands that had also brought me more pleasure than I knew existed, than I knew I was even capable of experiencing. He had touched me as if I had meant everything to him and now, well, I knew that those same hands were capable of so much more.

They were capable of death.

One tortured scream later, and the next one came from me as hands grabbed me, suddenly appearing through the fog as if from nowhere.

"Got you!" Deke said just as my body was suddenly pulled backwards through the cloud, and then my world turned upside down as I was hoisted over his massive shoulder like a sack of potatoes. Man, it fucking hurt thanks to my broken ribs, something I knew he had no clue about.

"AH!" I shouted in surprise before my fight or flight instincts snapped into gear, despite it hurting even more. I tried in vain to escape, squirming to get off him despite the long fall and hard landing I knew would face me if I fell, as the guy was huge!

"Calm yourself now, girl, we won't hurt you, but I will tie you up and gag you if you force my hand." Hearing this, I instantly stilled, knowing that if I had any chance at escaping then being tied and gagged would only render this a mission impossible. No, I had to be smart here and play the good little captive and then, when their guard was down, I could run. Now just how far I would have to run to get away from them was the biggest question of all, as right now that was anyone's guess.

This thought was cut short when the frightened screams of the thugs were swiftly cut down from two to one and then after a last desperate cry for mercy, there was one more scream before an eerie silence descended. This made me jump when the sound of a car door was opened, and I was being slid off Deke's shoulder and dumped into the back seat of their fancy Maybach.

I cried out in pain again, making him frown in question before telling me,

"Now, sit tight, he won't be long." Then he slammed the door shut and I jumped again thanks to my frayed nerves. This, combined with my fear of them both, made me feel like my backbone was beyond repair! Because what in Hell was happening to me…? I didn't know, but I knew the 'Hell' part was definitely an important factor in that sentence.

However, at least I was no longer consumed by that Hellish dark cloud I had been stuck in, now feeling slightly safer in the car, despite what that most likely meant for my future. Meaning that when Deke got into the driver's seat, I almost tried to see what it would take for him to drive away. But then, yeah, that's right, I was broken, and literally everything I owned was either on my body or in that rust bucket currently consumed by darkness!

Talk about jumping from the frying pan into the fire… make that 'Hellfire'!

"Are you alright?" At this, my head shot up and I looked into Deke's eyes staring back at me through the rear-view, one I noticed didn't have a crack in it like mine. Seriously, it was so much easier to dislike villains when they didn't come with a handsome face or a caring, easy smile.

"Far from it, but hey, thanks for asking," I replied with a surprising bite to my words, but he surprised me when he started laughing.

"Good, that's good," he seemed to say to himself in an amused way.

"What's good?" I asked, unable to help myself.

"Having someone with spunk to challenge him… he needs that and from someone other than me."

"Well, that spunk won't be coming from me, as I don't particularly have a death wish. Besides, I don't even know the guy's name!" I complained, making him smirk before he actually turned around to face me after placing a large arm along the back of the seats.

"Firstly, death wish or not, sweetheart, he would never harm you."

"Oh right, just order my kidnapping… yep, upstanding guy, that one," I muttered sarcastically, making him chuckle.

"Well, even without it being easy to see what you are to him, he only harms those who deserve it. And as for you and that bright shiny, clean soul of yours, well, I bet you would just fall over yourself to help some old dear cross the street and beg them to let you carry their bags." At this, my mouth dropped open and I made a noise as if to answer, but then paused. Because I knew I had no argument to voice, as he was totally right… I totally would and yep, *I totally had*. But then Mrs. Penny was in her nineties with a bad hip and no family left. Plus, her barky little Pomeranian, Mr. Binky, would have been strong enough to pull her over, as she must have weighed the same as a fold out chair when ringing wet!

"Yeah, that's what I thought," he commented on a laugh, making me frown. But before I was given the chance for a comeback, he took the wind out of my angry sails and told me,

"My point is, he would feel sickened even by the mere thought of hurting you or…"

"Or?" I asked, when he paused to look back through the window at the darkness that was only now starting to evaporate.

"…Or become murderous and deadly to any that did think to harm you," he answered, making me suck in a quick breath, one that hurt my ribs.

"But why? I don't understand, he barely even knows me!" I argued and he chuckled again, before looking back at me to answer me face to face.

"Yeah, well I think that is about to change." He ended this

by putting the privacy screen up between us, and I would have questioned why when suddenly the door next to me opened making me scream in fright. Something that was ignored, as my mystery man appeared and was currently folding his large frame to get inside. Well, I was at least grateful to see that he was back to looking human once more, so yay for small mercies.

He gave me a quick look and, still clearly in the height of his raging 'Angel of Darkness and Death' anger, snapped,

"Is there anything in that heap of shit car of yours that means anything dear to you?" I swallowed hard, and for some reason the question made me want to cry. I wanted to answer that it only contained my whole life or at least what was left of it. Yet I was too embarrassed to say that. Too ashamed of what my life had become. And with one look at me he knew.

He knew it all.

This was confirmed when he said in a stern tone that clearly demanded an answer,

"I know you have been sleeping in it, Eden, and are homeless, so answer my question, is there anything in there that is of sentimental value to you?" I finally let a tear fall, and swiped at it angrily before telling him in a tense tone that felt as if it had the power to snap my vocal cords,

"No... it's... *it's all gone.*" He nodded once as if he understood this, and I was just thankful in that moment he hadn't pried too closely into that statement. Thankful that I hadn't been forced to tell him that I came home one day to find my place ransacked and pretty much everything I owned was burning in a trash can. Photos, mementos, letters, cards, and anything that had ever meant anything to me had been turned to ash. Meaning that right now, in this very moment, I had never hated my stupid step-brother so much and only now really realising it. Because at the time I had only ever blamed the thugs who had done it.

But in reality, it was Jimmy's fault.

It was all Jimmy, and he was the reason that all I had left of my mother was a scorched picture in my wallet of us together and a plastic heart I had given her for Mother's Day one year. I had made a braided necklace to hang it on for her to wear. I'd wanted to bury it with her as she always wore it, but in the end, I just couldn't do it. It felt as if it was the last piece of her I had left. So, I had selfishly kept it and I had felt ashamed of doing so ever since. It was irrational, I knew, but I just couldn't help myself. I needed to blame myself for something, and it was hard to punish an illness no one had any power over.

And speaking of power, the man sitting next to me pressed a button that must have activated an intercom, as he said,

"Let's go." This was when I fisted my hands to try and get them to stop shaking but when that didn't work, I sat on them instead. I wanted to scream and shout, to tell him that he couldn't just take me like this. But then I knew my words would have meant nothing. Because in reality, that was exactly what he could do and well... *he was*. Now, what I wanted to know was why... but admittedly, I was just too afraid to ask.

As it was times like this that made you realise the truth about yourself. Because sure, in the comfort of my own safe space I would do what most people did. I would shake my head at the TV screen whenever the lead female did anything stupid or acted weak. I would roll my eyes at the book I was reading when the girl needed to get a backbone. Okay, so sure, she had just been faced with some vampire, demon, werewolf shifter or Hell, even some ancient highland warrior set in the past... it didn't matter, because it was always the same, no matter the circumstances. We all wanted to think that we would be brave enough to handle things differently than those fearful characters. Or just the opposite, believing we could be as strong as half of them whenever they kicked ass and put a large powerful man in his place.

But this wasn't fiction.

This was real.

And in this real world of mine, I was just a human girl, who was scared shitless. And you know what, I didn't blame myself and was actually stunned that I hadn't just crumpled in a tearful mess and begged for mercy. Not after I first had to face two thugs who I was pretty sure were just sent to kill me, and then faced with a man I had not long ago made love to then to find out he wasn't even human! Yeah, okay, so if anyone wanted to take a shot at being braver than me and acting any differently, then hell, they were welcome to take my place!

Because right now, I just wanted to wake up from this nightmare and even if that meant freezing my ass off in my car, then so be it. But then, I also had to remember what that meant and if these two hadn't come along, then I would most likely be digging my own grave by now, like hitmen made them do in the movies. Okay, so Beavis and Butthead had hardly been John Wick but still, I shuddered to think of what they would have done to me.

Fuck me, talking about confusing! I didn't know whether I should be trying to throw myself from the car or thanking the guy for saving my life! And speaking of the car, it had left Club Afterlife behind us and was now travelling through the arch of trees towards the main road. I looked back one last time to see the last of what remained of my past now sitting there looking pathetic. I also noticed there wasn't a body in sight, making me wonder what he had done to them both. But then, did I really want to know? Another shudder wracked my body and I winced at the pain it caused.

"You're injured," he said, making me flinch a little at the

sound of his voice bringing me back to reality. So, I shook my head a little and mumbled,

"*I'm fine.*" At this, he growled, making me shift further away from him, but well, this he didn't like all that much.

"Gods, girl, there is no need for you to be so petrified of me, I am not going to fucking hurt you! Now come here!" Again, I nearly choked on my own spit. Oh yeah, 'cause shouting at me like that was going to fucking help!

"Hey!" This ended up being my response, as he took matters into his own hands by closing the distance between us and taking my head in his hand, framing each side of my face.

"Ssshh," he said, making me snap,

"Did you seriously just shush me?" At this he smirked and after getting closer, he said,

"*Again... Ssshh.*" Then he kissed my nose, completely shocking me at the sweet and playful gesture. Jesus, I needed my head examining, and not by this guy but by a professional! Because despite everything I had just seen, I was now wishing he would just kiss me again and my heart pounded in anticipation. Talk about Stockholm syndrome, I would have won a damn pageant had they had one!

But then he ran the pad of his thumb over my lip and the second I sucked in a hiss, I knew kissing me wouldn't be on the menu. Something my confused mind should have been thankful of.

It wasn't.

"That bastard split your lip," he said, making sure to keep his voice low, and I knew this was for my benefit as clearly he knew how close to the edge of insanity I was and didn't want to scare me again.

"Are you injured elsewhere?" he asked, making me shake my head knowing it was best he didn't know about my ribs so, as my hand started to move to where it hurt, I stopped myself.

"No," I told him on a whisper, but his growled response made my head snap up.

"Never lie to me, Eden, for I will know *every time.*" I swallowed hard at his gentle threat and when he patted his lap, he added an order to it.

"Now come here, my little Carino." I shook my head a little before he released a sigh of frustration telling me,

"If you do not do as you are told then I risk hurting you when I take that decision out of your control." He then nodded down to his lap where he clearly wanted me, and I gave him wide eyes telling him I was afraid. But then his gaze gentled a little and what he told me next quickly became a deciding factor to do as I was told.

"This way, I am giving you the choice, for I will not be happy if I pick you up and cause you pain... and be warned beautiful...

I am on the edge of darkness here."

CHAPTER 14
VENGEANCE AND FEAR

"**I** *am on the edge of darkness here,*" he growled out, and I had to say I didn't fancy being locked in the car with the other terrifying side of him on show. So, wisely, I shifted closer to him, and he helped steady me as I raised a leg up and over to his thigh, trying to hold back showing how much it hurt. Then, once I was sitting astride him unable to hide from the handsome face of his, he started to remove my jacket. I froze, tensing instantly making him coo down at me, given that he was still taller than me, even like this.

"*Easy now*... allow me to be gentle with you and I will reward your trust in me... now hold still," he said, and I had to say it was nice... okay, more than nice and definitely swoon worthy. Especially considering the size of him and now knowing the immense unearthly power he possessed. Yet, seeing how gentle and caring he could be with me was the polar opposite of what I would have expected, which had me questioning, was something deeper going on here? Did it have something to do with what Deke had said, about who I was to him?

But even as I tried to question this in my mind, I had to admit it was difficult to think of anything but the feel of him whenever those large, strong hands of his were on me. This even more so when they were being so tender. Like when he gently rid me of my jacket and then did the same with my sweater, making me shiver the moment his hands ran softly up my sides.

"Are you cold, my girl?" he asked, and I shivered again, only this time it wasn't due to his touch but more his words when calling me his girl, doing so in that deep and affectionate voice of his. I nodded making him remind me,

"Remember, Eden, I will always want your words."

"I am," I answered this time, making him smile as if pleased with my quick compliance. Then he reached for the intercom again and without taking his eyes of me, said,

"Raise the heating, Deke, my Siren is cold." I blushed at this because forget about the car's heating, his passionate gaze had power enough to warm me up, along with his thoughtful words. Deke answered with a brief,

"You got it," before we were alone again and as for my mystery man, he went back to his task of discovery as soon as he heard the gentle hum of the vents start.

"You and your layers, sweetheart." He chuckled to himself as he started to lift them all as one so he could assess the damage for himself and the moment he did, all humor fled him as he hissed a cursed,

"*Fuck!*"

I closed my eyes and held myself still when I felt his fingertips run gently along my ribcage.

"Gods, but I could kill those fuckers all over again!" he snarled angrily, making me tense and it hurt doing so, something I tried to hide.

"Easy, sweetheart… ignore my outburst and focus on

keeping still, for I do not want you in pain, which I see that you are," he said excusing his reaction, which I admit, was nice.

"This is most likely broken... does it hurt when you breathe?" he asked softly, and I nodded. But then with a knowing look, I quickly added a small,

"Yes." He instantly looked touched that I had remembered his rule and I was rewarded with a sweet kiss to the forehead, making me blush. Then he sat back and nodded down at the swollen area before telling me,

"This will need to be looked at." This was definitely said as more of an absolute, which had me worrying for another reason. Meaning I was now forced to tell him in an embarrassed tone,

"I don't have medical insurance." At this, he growled in annoyance before snapping,

"You don't fucking need it!"

"But..." It was at this point he simply started to talk over me, adding in a stern tone,

"Nor will you want for anything, not ever again, for you are mine to take care of and that means in every way... but we will get to that in a minute."

"Erm... I don't..." I would have liked to have pointed out at this juncture that I still didn't even know his name, but it was a bit difficult when he was steamrolling over me and my thoughts.

"Now, if the pain worsens or if it becomes harder to breathe you need to tell me immediately," he told me with that hard edge of authority coming back and when I opened my mouth to speak again, he raised a brow that told me there was only one thing he wanted to hear.

"I will tell you," I replied with a sigh, making his features soften and I suddenly couldn't understand why every time I pleased him, it made me feel all warm and gooey inside, especially when he ran the backs of his fingers down my cheek as if in silent praise that I had obeyed his rule. But then he ran those same fingers across the cut on my lip, telling me without words that he was pained to see me hurt, and that tenderness shot straight to my heart.

Jesus, I was falling fast and again, I had no real clue as to who this guy was! It was crazy, insanity and bordering along the realms of being utterly ridiculous! But then I also knew that what I was feeling couldn't be ignored, as every second I spent around this guy only strengthened that connection. One I could feel getting stronger with every caring, gentle touch or every tender word spoken. He was wrapping me up in his spell as if he were wrapping me up in his wings, doing so by making me feel something I hadn't felt in such a long time…

Safe, protected, treasured and above all, cared for.

It was all-consuming!

But because of all these things, there was also a part of me that, admittedly, was terrified, even though it wasn't of him hurting me physically, as it was abundantly clear that thought sickened him. Even Deke had told me that. And I wasn't blind, as here I was, sitting astride him, those large powerful hands I knew had the strength to tear men to pieces now handling me as though I was a precious breakable doll of his. No, it was the power he was gaining over my heart that frightened me, because I really didn't know the full depth of what was happening here. I didn't know why he felt this way for me, and if it was possible it could change at any minute. Whoever he thought I was to him could end up being proven wrong, making me question where that would leave me and my heart?

Unsurprisingly, the next words out of his mouth had me questioning my sanity once more.

"I am furious you left me, but lucky for you, I am furious at those who did this to you more," he said, with those incredible brown eyes of his glowing brighter as his fury grew.

Then he re-covered my injury, removing it from his sight as he rolled down my layers and doing so far more gently than I would have thought possible given the depth of anger in his voice.

"I... well, you see I... erm." Again I tried to get my words out as he looked at me expectantly.

"What made you run from me, little Doe?" he asked, this time in a gentler tone I knew was purposely used to draw out the truth from me. I swallowed down the guilt he made me feel and told him,

"I saw you... at the end of... erm... you know, when we did... stuff." At this his gaze softened before he smirked in amusement, then he mimicked,

"Stuff?" This was when I forgot my injury and said,

"Yeah, you know..." Then I rolled my hips over his lap and moaned thanks to the pain it caused me, making him suddenly grasp my hips in his firm hold and lock me down to him.

"Oww," I muttered, and he gave me a reprimanding look but one that was still gentle.

"Sweetheart, I remember every second of our time together and don't require any prompting on your part, especially not when doing so hurts this delectable, and very fuckable body of yours. Fuck, but it's hard enough with you sitting upon my lap and recreating the memory." I couldn't help but blush again at this as it was nice to know I had affected him just as he had affected me during our time together. A time it seemed he wanted more of.

"Which is why it is most likely safer if I move you back to your own seat, despite how much as it pains me to do so," he said tensing his hands at my hips at the thought. Which was why I frowned a little, before asking,

"Why would it cause you pain, surely having my ass sitting in your lap so long is what will make your legs go dead and lose feeling." At this he laughed, but when I winced he stopped instantly and replied,

"Oh, you have no idea what I want to do to that sweet ass of yours and having it sitting in my lap for endless hours is only one of them. And trust me, sweetheart, there is no chance of anything of mine losing feeling around you... *hard as a fucking rock,*" he said, muttering this last part to himself and making me turn away, shy at the thought that I could do that him. But when I looked down between us, he took possession of my chin and raised my head back up, so he had my eyes. Only then did he speak once more, telling me his thoughts.

"However, the pain I spoke of is both the loss of having you in my arms... *momentarily*... and also in seeing the discomfort moving from me will bring you." I released a deep sigh that couldn't be helped, as Christ, but he was intense, and not exactly afraid to tell me his thoughts or how much he cared for me. It was crazy seeing as we had only met each other a few hours ago at best. Yet the way he was talking, it was as if he'd spent years loving me!

It was as if this guy didn't say anything he didn't mean, and every word was said with purpose. Like the way he had emphasised the word 'momentarily' as if warning me that letting me go wouldn't be for long. I had never known anyone like him, let alone been intimate with someone this intense. But then I had to remember he wasn't exactly human, so maybe that was it. Maybe all of his kind were the same... unless... *he was the only one?*

Oh shit, I really didn't know anything at all!

Talk about way out of my depth here, I had never even been to Sunday school! So, what did I know about Angels? There were the books of course, and I think people who read Angel cards and see signs in rays of light and feathers and stuff. Had I unknowingly channeled an Angel, or did you need crystals and essential oils for that?

At this, I felt a slight shaking beneath me and when I looked back up, I saw he now had placed a fist to his mouth. I frowned in question as I saw him biting it and looking close to tears at trying not to laugh, no doubt so as not to hurt me.

"Err… you… okay?" I asked tentatively. To which he let go of his fist and used it to hold up a finger telling me to give him a minute. Then he rolled his lips inwards before needing to bite them, as it looked as if he was dying to burst out laughing. That was when it all came crashing back to me. All those times I had questioned if I was speaking my thoughts aloud or asking myself if he could read my mind!

"Oh no! No, no, no… please… oh please don't tell me…" I said, making him swallow hard before wincing in a teasing way. Then I groaned and threw my arm over my eyes and moaned,

"You can read my mind, can't you'?" At this I felt my arm being removed as he sat up closer to me. He then continued to move my arm behind my back before clamping it there at the base of my spine with his palm shackling my wrist. I also noticed how he did it slowly and cautiously, no doubt in case it hurt me. Something that didn't, being as it was on my uninjured side. After he had me locked in place, he got closer to my face before telling me softly,

"Fuck me, you're endearing."

"That's not an answer," I snapped before he threaded his free hand through my hair and used it to hold me still as his lips descended over mine.

"Yes, my Siren, your sweet thoughts are mine… *just like the rest of you!*" He growled this last part before his kiss claimed me just like his words did and I gasped in surprise. But then when both his hands tensed around my hair and wrist, I knew he did so to ensure I wouldn't move as he dominated the kiss. It was as if he never forgot about my injury, not even for a minute, despite him obviously wanting to kiss me. Something that made my toes want to curl, it felt that good. I found my hands fisted in his t-shirt, holding on as if any minute I would fall out of this dream. One I no longer considered a nightmare, but instead one I never wanted to wake from.

But as it grew more intense, I knew he was wrestling with himself on trying to continue being gentle with me. I knew this, as seconds later his kiss grew less urgent, and I had to say that both sides had the power to undo me and unravel me at the seams… his soft and gentle and his rough and demanding.

In fact, I think I would have melted into him had he let me but his hold was one I now knew was done for that very purpose. It was to hold me steady so I wouldn't accidently hurt myself as he kissed me, something I most definitely had the power to get lost in.

But then he tore his lips from mine, and I sucked in a quick breath that hurt, making him place his forehead to mine and whisper,

"I am sorry, forgive me in my weakness." It was such a touching moment that I was brave enough to raise a hand to his cheek and whisper back,

"Please, don't ever be sorry for kissing me." At this his rumbled growl had me nearly pulling away, startled and about to question what I had done wrong, or if I had crossed some unknown line or not. But then, the moment I did move, he gripped my wrist harder, and his hand released my hair and took hold of the back of my neck instead.

"My sweet Siren is too good to me," he muttered before releasing me, and telling me sincerely,

"But you are never to fear me, Eden, even when I react in such a way, for it is not done in displeasure… *never."* At this I nodded telling him I understood, although I wasn't sure I could ever promise such a thing. Not until I understood more about him... *what he was*. As soon as I thought this he nodded once and agreed.

"Fair enough, sweetheart." This brought me back to the reality that he could hear my thoughts and I was a little mortified, something he saw straight away.

"Don't worry about it." Then he lifted me over to the other seat as I muttered,

"Yeah, easy for you to say... ahhh!" This ended in a cry of pain making him look pained himself.

"It's okay," I replied quietly, as the thought of him feeling guilty didn't sit well with me. But then he started shaking his head at this.

"It's never okay, do you understand?" he said sternly, and when I looked down to avoid his intense gaze, his reaction was to lower his face to try and gain my eyes again, telling me,

"Eden, tell me you understand that."

"Okay," I whispered, making him nod once, telling me,

"Good girl, now tell me why this will never happen again." I frowned at this and replied honestly,

"I don't understand. Why would it..."

"Because you will never run from me again, despite what you see," he said, making me avoid his stern gaze.

"I was... I admit that I was..."

"Frightened of what you saw in me," he answered for me, and I felt ashamed to admit it aloud, despite knowing it was justified. But he already knew the truth and like that rule he continued to remind me of, he wanted my words.

"Hey now, look at me, my little Carino." I did as I was told and looked into those thoughtful eyes, their amber depths now telling me so much more than his words did... *he wasn't angry*.

"I understand, Eden, I do... which is why, even though I am furious it happened, I know I must find patience with such

147

things. As you are right, there is still much you do not know and until such time you do, I also know that I must earn your trust, which I will endeavor to do. For you will see for yourself that I mean you no harm, despite you believing I have taken you against your will." I swallowed hard and tucked my hair nervously behind my ear as was a habit of mine. This, before giving into another which was to fist my fingers in the material at my long sleeves.

"So, you are kidnapping me?" I braved asking, and his quick reply surprised me.

"Yes, most definitely."

"But… but how do you think that's okay?" I asked in shock, making him smirk as if this conversation, along with my question, amused him.

"After what you saw back there, would you have come with me willingly?" he asked making his point.

"No," I answered honestly.

"Then that is why," he replied in an easy way that was disconcerting considering what we were discussing.

"So, you're not going to let me go?" I asked testing this now.

"Absolutely not," he answered without taking a beat, and making me near choke on a breath.

"And you ask me to trust you?" I commented, making him chuckle.

"I am not asking, sweetheart, for I will demand it from you, along with your promise that you will never run from me again." At this, my mouth dropped open in shock and he tapped underneath my chin in a playful manner, grinning as though he was having a great time. Seriously… *was this guy for real?!*

"You can't demand something like that," I told him with a shake of my head.

"We shall see," was his cryptic answer and I decided to push.

"I don't understand... why are you doing all of this... why me, why do what you did back there... why...?" He cut me off with a stern look and a rumble of words.

"Because you are mine and I protect what is mine," he stated sternly, as if his word was law, and I shivered because of it.

"*Yours?*" I questioned, and it sounded high pitched even to my own ears.

"*Mine,*" he said with a certainty that frightened me, but it was one I knew was for my benefit again, as he tried to get me to understand he wasn't playing around.

This was serious.

"And that means that I will never let anything happen to you and I will kill anyone who tries to hurt you again... *ever!*" he stated firmly, only adding strength to his claim by growling out that last word.

"But you can't just go around killing people!" I shouted, making him smile before saying a condescending,

"That's cute you think that, beautiful, and you can go right ahead and keep thinking it if it helps you sleep better in my arms at night, but the reality is, I can do what the fuck I want if it means protecting you." Naturally, his reply startled me yet again, enough to shriek,

"Oh my God, you're serious!"

"Gods, not God... and yes, I am fucking serious... besides, I would be surprised if a good girl like you has more than one dumb fuck like Felix Gomez as an enemy." At this my hands flew to my mouth in shock, and I shuffled back so I could see him better, and was thankful he allowed it, despite wincing because of the pain. I also allowed my mind to skim over the bit about Gods, filing it away to question him another time, one that seemed to be adding to a great big pile named 'you're fucked, Edie!'

"You know about Felix Gomez?" At this I saw a tick in his jaw as it tensed, before he gritted out,

"Yeah, I know about that fucker and soon he will know about me. But we are not talking about that waste of a vessel right now." Waste of a vessel? What did he mean by that?

"But…" I tried to argue but he quickly put a stop to it.

"No, Eden, we will discuss all about how you got yourself mixed up in that shit, but right now, I want to get you somewhere comfortable so I can get you seen by a doctor and you can rest, because you may not feel it, but you're gonna crash, babe, and that adrenaline is only going to keep you going so long." My eyes widened at this and I shamefully had to admit my moment of weakness where I focused on how good it sounded when he called me babe.

"But I don't even know your name!" I argued, making him grin at me this time and Christ, it was so breathtakingly handsome, even when I was still slightly terrified of him, I wanted him to kiss me!

God or Gods, either way I was still crazy!

At this my answer came first by him hooking me around the neck so I couldn't pull away, then he held me still as he came closer, before kissing the side of my lips gently, avoiding my cut there, then he kissed his way to my ear when he finally told me…

The gift of his name.

"My name is Ward, Sweetheart… *Warden Za'afiel.*" I sucked in a breath at finally getting to hear his name, as if now I owned a little piece of him too. But then this was when I made the mistake of asking him what it meant, making him reply,

"It translates as my purpose here on Earth, as it means I am a Warden of the Gods' Wrath." I released a surprised sound in the back of my throat, and he pulled back before looking me in the eyes as I forced out my next question, knowing that I was quickly moving past the point of no return.

"And what… what does that mean… what… *what are you?*" This was when his grin got bigger and with every single ounce of pride a person could possess, he told me,

"I am your fated Angel…

An Angel of Vengeance and Fear."

CHAPTER 15
DARKNESS REVEALED
WARD

Fear.

I swear the emotion was still clinging to me like some foreign entity.

It was strange experiencing a new emotion after all this time, believing all my firsts were long ago dried up. It made me wonder what others there were to discover. I was already questioning myself on the level of my obsession, that had only built in its intensity these last few hours since meeting my Siren. Meaning that I was now asking if this was what falling in love was exactly.

What was next... *jealousy?*

Well, when it came to Eden, then I gave it a fucking hour and I would be tearing someone's head off... *again.* Of course, the first had been for the offence of touching my girl and terrifying the shit out of her. But then this had brought me to the next emotion on the list of firsts for me to experience, and that was one that admittedly left a bitter, dark taste in my mouth...

Guilt.

Which meant that by the time I had finished torturing those two wasted souls and sent them to the only place they deserved to be, I was an unsettled fucker when getting in the car. Soon to be a pissed off one when I heard my Siren, my fated one cry out in fright at just the sight of me. It had been like a lash to the heart, and one I tried not to take personally. Because could I really expect anything else, considering what she had been forced to witness? Well, there was one thing, and that was my plan at going slow and easing her into my world was well and truly fucked!

No, instead I had been forced to throw her dead center into my darkness and into the very core of my being... *the essence of my Vengeance and Fear.* It had swirled around her as though it had wanted to consume our fated little Doe, clinging to her as it too felt the connection, the pull and need to reach out and touch her. It had wanted to play with her, protect her and dominate her all at once.

But that side was just as much a part of me as the vessel my soul had forged with. Something she would come to understand in time... *I hoped.*

Hope that had most definitely bloomed the moment she had rocked me to my core and shocked me like never before. It had been a blinding moment in time, like some divine being had just been dropped from the metaphorical heavens above and tried to save my life... despite what she knew what I was. Now why would she have done that? Why would such a golden soul like hers want to save a bringer of death like me?

Of course, she hadn't known exactly what I was, but just the sight of me would surely have been enough? This had me questioning if it was an action bred from some fated compulsion or just how Eden herself felt for me? Perhaps a bit of both, but even with what little I knew of the girl, I was still inclined to go with the latter.

Such a pure soul.

In fact, I was still torn between being furious or in utter

shock that she would put herself in harm's way for me. But then when I had seen that cut on her lip, fuck me but my darkness had roared in fury!

No one made our girl bleed.

So, of course, my darkness had not wanted to leave her when I had to deal with the two destined to die—who both had a look of terror on their faces, a sight I was pleased to know would carry them to Hell. My darkness had latched itself to her form, only releasing her when it recognized a friend, my second, and allowed Deke to take her.

In fact, it had been the only reason I had dispatched the assholes a lot sooner than I would have liked, as preferably, suffering for days at the very least would have been more my style. But then, my darkness had pushed for me to hurry so we could get back to her. Which proved just how much she had affected that side of me, as usually it was this sort of shit that we lived for. The need to instill fear and extract vengeance. It lived in the very core of us both. The Yin to Eden's Yang. The pure light and pure darkness, never to merge but always to coexist as one and the same.

Now, all I needed to do was convince my fearful little Doe here to see it like that. But then even in my darkest form, she had still claimed me as being her hero, something I would never forget for however many more millennia I had left in me. Which was why I told her the truth, for she truly would never know what that had meant to me.

Of course, I would have liked to have been given a shred of that same faith now, for she was back to looking terrified of me. Which was why I was trying to give her space and time to get her own thoughts together as we travelled back to the hotel. Perhaps something I should have given her from the start, and unfortunately something my still heated anger wouldn't allow fully.

My once cold, hard and unfeeling heart had thundered in my chest when seeing that single tear of hers fall, watching the way she swiped at it angrily. It had tugged at a piece of me I never knew existed, cutting deep and making me flinch when I finally pushed hard enough for her to answer my questions. Something I only received when I destroyed her pride and told her that I knew. That I knew she was homeless and sleeping in her fucking car!

A fucking furious fact that made me want to know every detail as much as it didn't. Of course, I had tortured the name I knew I needed from the two fucks before ending their miserable existence. Because I recognized two disposable goons when I saw them… my own world had enough of them.

Felix Gomez.

Or should I say, *a soon to be dead Felix Gomez.*

But then this hadn't been the only name I had received from them, and now I very much wanted to know who this Jimmy was. This knowledge gave me another new emotion… jealously.

Was this the name of the shit stain that had gotten Eden into all of this in the first place? Well, if it was, then I didn't care who this person was to her.

He was currently spending his last few days on earth as a dead man walking. Now, if this was an ex-lover of hers, then I was not going to lie, I would merely class this as a bonus. As for her meagre possessions, well I would make sure that my girl wanted for nothing. For she didn't know this yet, but I was one of the richest men in all of Europe, and this was a fortune she would soon find as being one she too could claim. Whatever I possessed, was now hers as well. As was the way with any who were blessed enough from the very Gods and the Fates that commanded them to find the other half of their soul.

It was a struggle having such distance between us, even if it was merely the space between two seats. I could feel my other side beating like a drum against my vessel, begging me to let it come out to play... *Specifically, with her.* A fact that left me gritting my teeth knowing now that he too would want a piece of her, because by right, she was his as much as she was mine. As neither of us could claim her without the other.

I had tried to concentrate on listening to her thoughts, but it had been difficult as her pain was clouding my ability. Which was when I informed her that I knew, making her flinch at even the sound of my voice, something I growled at. In turn, she shifted further away from me, finally making me snap out an order, allowing the dominant side of me to take over. I wanted to hit myself upside the head, forcing myself to rein it in and take her confused and terrified mindset into account. One that was more than justified.

Which was when I took the matter into my own hands, quite literally, framing her face with both hands and telling her to hush. At this, she finally awarded me with the tiniest slice of sass, that I swear had my darkness craving to take a bite and taste it for himself. However, instead of giving into him, I gave into my own mad impulse, because the cutest fucking sight in the world warranted it, and I kissed her nose playfully.

Madness... sheer fucking madness, as I was one of the most fucking feared Angels of my kind, for fuck sake, and here I was being playful with a woman... and it didn't include chains or a gag.

What was this little Carino doing to me?

Of course, this playfulness ended the second I asked again if she was hurt, and she lied to me. My darkness growled. Which was why I warned her never to do it again, letting her know as gently as I could that I would know if she did. I tried to remind myself that she was merely scared and after what she had just seen, then it was unsurprising to know that she didn't trust me.

Which was why I needed her to come to me willingly. Besides, I had been on edge, fighting with myself so I didn't just grab her to me, which was what every instinct in me was roaring out to do. The only thing that kept this compulsion at bay was knowing that somewhere on her body, she was hurt.

Which was why I warned her about my darkness and how close to the edge it was. A threat that was certainly one she took seriously enough to act to prevent it. I would have laughed at her reaction, had the time warranted it. But with my girl hurt and in need of healing, then my amusement was overwritten by concern. Which was when I realized it was another foreign emotion for me as I didn't recall the last time I had felt the need to concern myself for another. My loyalty was reserved only for the people under my rule and for my King who I served willingly. But now that had all changed.

Now there was Eden.

My Siren.

This meant that, for me, nothing would ever come before this fact, and its profound knowledge settled deep and rooted itself within the very core of me. Of course, that core also cracked a little the second she flinched when I tried to rid her of her jacket, making me realize just how gentle and patient I was going to have to be. Something made even harder when I realized the frustrating truth...

I couldn't heal her.

This only added to my slip up of an outburst, knowing the second I saw her red mottled skin that I had killed them far too quickly. But then I also knew the importance of getting to my girl exceeded my time spent on revenge. So, I had hurried and now, fuck but I wished that I'd had the two fuckers transported to a warehouse I owned so I'd have their sentence waiting for me to deliver and what's more, to be able to take my time fucking doing it!

Fuck, but my gentle actions became such a contrast to my murderous musings, for if my girl had known, then she would have been even more fucking terrified of me.

But then they hadn't just made my girl bleed, they had...

Fucking broken her!

CHAPTER 16
FEELING HELPLESS

My broken little Siren.

I knew it the second she told me it hurt her to breathe, as I could tell with the way she was holding herself. Something that infuriated me beyond madness, because I knew I couldn't heal her. Because this was an internal wound and unless she drank my blood, then she wouldn't heal. If it had been an external wound, placing my blood over it would have worked.

Of course, I could have forced the issue, but then after what she had just been through, then I didn't think having me slit a vein and forcing her to swallow my blood was going to help either of us right now. No, all that would do would add even more trauma to an already traumatized mind. And well, lots and lots of sex was out of the question with her in so much pain, as that was the only other way to get my essence into her. But then, that could take months... fuck, but even years, I just didn't know!

Which was why I told her that I would need to get it looked at, something that incensed me, as her next fear was expressed and prompted by a fucked up, irrational concern. Something

161

that made me grit my fucking teeth as she admitted that she didn't have medical insurance. Fuck, but I wanted to howl at that statement, knowing she was breaking my fucking heart... one that felt as though it had started to beat for the first time since my existence!

Hence why I couldn't hold myself back when I snapped out my reply, telling her she didn't fucking need it! Gods, but how didn't she get by now that I was going to provide for her? That she would never want for anything, ever again! That she was mine to take care of. Well, with the way her beautiful light green eyes widened when I told her this, I would say it was pure disbelief, for she clearly didn't know any of these things.

I forced myself to find even more patience, knowing this was most likely going a million miles an hour for her. She was still human. At least until the time came for her to accept her Siren side, something she could now do since she had finally met her fated.

And I couldn't fucking wait for the day!

I had to keep reminding myself of what this must all be like for her, which was why I asked her what I wanted to know most of all...

Why she had run from me?

Admittedly, I had my suspicions, but I wasn't certain. Not considering that sometimes I had no clue as to what went on in that mind of hers. It was a bit like dealing with a newly Fallen. It would take time knowing how to block out others from knowing your thoughts, and it was the same when being able to detect others like yourself.

Although, the difference with Eden was that she had no clue she was even doing it. Like when I could hear her adorable and endearing inner monologue playing out in her mind. Something that gifted me with those sweet little insights into her personality and past experiences. Her likes and dislikes.

However, when her mind was as confused as it was now, then it was nothing but a faint shadow of emotions, without the words to back them up. It was how I knew she was in pain. Just like I knew she was confused, scared, distrusting and, what I was most impressed with, *she was a little angry.*

When she confessed to seeing me in my other form at the end of making sweet fucking love to her, then I could understand her reasons for running. However, this memory of our time together combined with her sitting on my cock, was like my own delicious torture. One I knew I had to stop before I ended up hurting her, something I did when I couldn't help but kiss her. But before that, had come yet another endearing moment of inner rambling, where she asked herself what she knew of Angels. Fuck me but I swear, I'd never experienced the near crippling need to try and stop myself from bursting into a fit of laughter!

Gods, even my abs hurt!

I'd had no choice but to put a fucking fist to my mouth just for something to fucking bite on! She was… *too… fucking… cute!* Of course, this was when she had guessed it, and looked utterly mortified to know that I had been able to access her thoughts. Which was why I couldn't have helped my reaction as I kissed her, no doubt hurting her lip. A kiss that felt as dark as it did delicious, as I could feel her lips coated in fresh blood, something she seemed not to have any clue about.

Which was why I finally forced myself from her, begging her forgiveness, but then she had raised one of her delicate hands to my cheek and whispered the sweetest words I think I have ever heard uttered to me,

'Please don't ever be sorry for kissing me'

Fuck me, but I swear if I had been standing, her words would have had the power to bring me to my knees. My reaction couldn't be helped, one she had taken for the wrong reasons, as my darkness was also affected. But of course, she would come to learn that a growl or demonic rumble from that side of me shouldn't ever give her cause to worry or fear me. Something I explained, which then led on to having to admit that I was kidnapping her, something that made me hide my smirk in regards her reaction to this.

She was naturally outraged and that in itself was fucking adorable. Which, admittedly, was why I pushed for more, quickly getting addicted to her cute little reactions. Like when she asked if I was going to let her go, her adorable rage when I told her *absolutely not* was why seconds later, I found myself chuckling.

But I hadn't been merely pushing her buttons when I told her that I would demand her trust, even if I withheld the simple fact that I would be patient in this need. And why? Because I needed her to understand she couldn't run again. I couldn't risk her getting away from me and straight into the hands of those that would wish to hurt her. Running foolishly from my protection and into danger.

Of course, my mirth came next, in the form of her jaw going slack as her mouth dropping open in shock. I allowed myself to smirk this time and playfully tapped her under the chin. But then she pushed at me to give her more, so I gave her the stern truth…

She was mine.

But then I knew I would have to give her something more, like my fucking name, as she still had no idea who I was. Something I found amusing, seeing as she was clearly getting more and more frustrated with this fact by the passing minute. But then I guess it had been done a little out of revenge, for making me wait so long before she trusted me with her own.

However, now was the time, which was when I not only gave it to her but also something profoundly more…

My very reason for being.

For I was a Warden of the Gods' Wrath.

Something that was better she knew now than receiving yet another bombshell further down the line. So, I told her not only my name and the title gifted to me by the Gods that created my dark soul.

But more importantly, who I was to her...

Her fated Angel.

CHAPTER 17
KIDNAPPED
EDEN

Kidnapped.

I couldn't believe it.

I just couldn't believe how this had all happened! At what point had my already fucked up life reached a whole new level of fucked up? A level that was labelled as not even human! What had I walked into when stepping inside that club? As it certainly hadn't just been a rich powerful man who I had been hoping to convince to take pity on me and help.

No, what I had found had been so much darker.

So much scarier.

Deadlier.

I cast my eyes nervously to that darker, scarier... deadlier side that felt... well, *as if it had found me*. However, when casting my gaze to the side and doing so in hopes he wouldn't notice, I swallowed hard when of course he did. That strong jawline tensed the second he saw my look of trepidation. The fear I couldn't seem to let go of. But then again, I doubt anyone in my situation could blame me for that. Not after what I had just seen. Something I was at least thankful he was giving me the time to process. Although, just how much processing I was actually doing I wasn't sure, as I wasn't convinced it was helping. In fact, I think it was doing the opposite as since he had stopped talking to me, I had nothing to focus on but the fear.

Because I didn't know this man. This dark Angel of Vengeance and Fear that he had claimed to be. I mean, come on! What the Hell was I supposed to do with information like that?! It was like finding out some guy you had a one-night stand with was actually an assassin and lucky for you, you didn't just end up being collateral damage or even a way to pass the killing time.

But as for Ward, someone who had finally informed me of his name, he genuinely seemed to care for me. Of course, this also worried me, as he was… well, to say the least… *he was intense.* A fact that I found almost as confusing as much as the whole, 'Supernatural' persona thing. I mean, if he had told me I would have been backing away and trying to find out who was best to call to get the crazy guy some help then I wouldn't have believed a word.

But that was the thing. Because he hadn't just told me.

He had shown me.

Something that had been absolute and cemented in my mind as being real. Unless I was currently living out some outer body experience or currently drugged out of my eyeballs in some mental institute, eating paint chips from my window frame and stealing checkers from the rec room to stuff in my socks to use as a weapon. Although, wouldn't I have been better trying to tie strips of bedding together to make a rope ladder…? But then again…

Would I have been on the ground floor?

At this thought, I heard Ward suddenly burst out laughing, making me jump as the silence had been cut. I shot him a glance, to see how damn handsome that smile looked on him, thinking now that the name really suited him.

Ward.

Or did he prefer Warden, I wondered?

What would a lover call him?

Jesus, Edie, get a reality grip, this guy basically admitted to kidnapping you and here you are wondering what he would prefer to be called by his girlfriend!

"Fuck me, my baby is cute," he chuckled, making me shoot him another look and this time, it was one of pure horror! Damn it! Why did I keep forgetting that he could hear my thoughts?! Oh yeah, I knew why, because it was freaking nuts and not normal, that's why!

"Please... please, stop doing that," I asked quietly, whilst hiding my shame and rubbing a hand on my forehead in a frustrated why.

"Hey," he said in a soothing voice, but I shook my head a little, telling him that I didn't want to acknowledge this anymore. But of course, this wasn't good enough for him.

"Eden, look at me," he demanded, this time making me release a sigh before doing as he asked. As, well, I was weak and pathetic clearly.

"Don't think that," he told me, making me frown in question.

"Doing as I ask isn't a weakness, Eden."

"No? Then what is it?" I snapped, this time wincing when I did because, well, I still feared him.

"It's a compulsion to be loyal to your Fated, and something I will only ever respect you for," he told me, making me even more confused.

"You keep saying that word, but I have no idea what it even means," I told him, being honest.

"You will understand it soon enough but for now, there is no need for you to concern yourself with the details. Just know that there is no shame in your thoughts, I find them delightful and endearing," he told me, making me wince for a different reason this time.

"Oh goodie, that's what I was going for when thinking private things," I replied sarcastically and without over-thinking it for once. Something that made him raise a brow in surprise as he clearly thought I was a submissive type. And yes, I clearly was, but I still had a backbone, and one that would show when the time was needed and yeah, that time was now!

Fuck my fear!

"You think I am underserving of your thoughts?" he asked, shocking me.

"They are my thoughts and unless I choose to voice them, then no one is entitled to them, deserving or not," I replied, making him shrug his shoulders and say,

"Fair enough." I granted him wide eyes in shock, as I hadn't been expecting him to agree so easily.

"Does this mean you will stop?" I asked in a hopeful tone that was dashed the second he turned, smirked and said,

"No."

"Great... good talk then," I remarked sardonically, making him chuckle as I turned back to giving the side window my attention once more.

"Oh, and I prefer Ward but as a girlfriend, as you put it, then I guess it would be your choice," he said, making me remark,

"Great, Pookie Snuggle Bum it is then." At this he burst out laughing and replied,

"Calling me that might be dangerous."

"Why, you gonna hurt me if I do?" I asked before I could stop myself, causing him to drop his grin pretty quickly. A grin that was soon replaced by a scowl of anger, making me flinch and realize I must have gone too far with that remark. I saw him then close his eyes and take a breath, as if trying to rein in his annoyance before he gritted out,

"Let's get something straight right now... I will never hurt you... *ever*... Now tell me you understand that." I folded my arms, sucking back the pain in my ribs when I did, forgetting I was still hurt. Then I gave him a few home truths.

"Look, just because you tell me to think something, doesn't mean I will just obey and deny my fears... fears I think even you can agree I have good reason to feel considering what I have just seen. And well, let's not forget that along with the title hero, you just added kidnapper to that, so you can see my predicament in trusting you." He looked to be taking this all in before throwing some truth back at me.

"Ask yourself, what would happen if I let you go, if I let you get back in that death trap you call a car and drive off...?" He paused to scoff before he continued.

"...That's saying that heap of shit you call a car would even start, so tell me, Eden, what was the plan after that?" I swallowed hard, knowing he had me, as my plans had pretty much been zero at that point.

"Yeah, that's what I thought," he commented the moment I turned away from him and ignored his damn logic. Because the truth was, I had no plan. Even if those goons hadn't been waiting for me, then it wouldn't have been long until they had caught up with me.

"Why would it be dangerous?" I asked after minutes had passed, finally turning toward him and trying to ignore the fact that we had reached the city of Portland.

"I would never be a danger to you."

"What, even if I called you Pookie Snuggle Bum?" I tested, making his lips twitch, fighting off a grin.

"I was referring more to my street cred, as let's just say that being known as a bad ass in my world kind of works in my favor," he teased, or at least I thought he did.

"Ah, and being seen with a girlfriend would ruin that I

171

guess." At this he growled low, making me jump a little before he slid over to me, crowding me in before hooking me around the back of the neck and getting in close. Then he ran his nose up my cheek and whispered,

"Eden..." I couldn't figure out if this was said in a teasing way or said out of exasperation.

"Now listen to me and listen carefully, as I will not always be so patient with you."

"Jesus, you call this patient!" I snapped, making him rumble my name again in what I was guessing was a warning of some kind. But seeing as this guy was clearly Supernaturally crazy, then who the Hell knew... well most likely Hell Edie, that's who.

"Eden."

"And when you lose that patience, what then?" I challenged.

"There are many ways for a man like me to get what he wants from the one he craves things from... or do you need reminding so soon of our time in that bedroom?" I shivered, which I knew he felt as he grinned against my cheek before kissing me there.

"I don't need reminding," I added quietly, making him chuckle and say,

"Pity." I released a quick breath before he continued making his point.

"Had you not been injured and in pain, I wouldn't have asked. However, until you are healed, I will refrain from physical examples of proving my point and rely on words instead." Again, I started breathing heavily, but then this was most likely down to a combination of things. Like the way his hold on my neck was alternating between squeezing and stroking. The hard possessive hold that reminded me who was in charge as well as a comforting, tender reminder that he cared for me.

But this wasn't the only reason I couldn't seem to breathe easy. As he commanded my space, making it his own and in it, he was forcing me to feel things for him. Like the attraction to his deep, soothing voice. The way my body tingled by being so close, wishing we were skin to skin. The heat I felt being generated between us was so powerful, it was almost electric. It was like the most attraction you had ever felt for another and having them so close, all you had to do was turn your head an inch and you would be kissing them, making all your dreams come true.

It was intoxicating.

"My patience lost will only ever manifest toward you in the form of pleasure gained or a bite of pain that you would beg me for… now that look alone tells me you don't believe me," he added when I shot him a heavy dose of disbelief.

"Why would I ever beg you to hurt me?" I asked incredulously.

"No one said anything about hurting you… no, the pain I speak of will be more like an addiction only I can give you," he replied confidently but then again, every word out of this guy's mouth was said with confidence. Hence why I pointed out,

"You sound very confident." This was admittedly snapped out, making him smirk before he lowered his lips to my neck just below my ear and as his thumb swiped across my lips, he whispered,

"You forget that I have tasted your desire before and oh my girl… it's fucking intoxicating!" He growled this last part before sucking my tender flesh and biting it, making me cry out as the pain morphed into pleasure, just like he said it would.

"Now tell me, Eden, just how wet would I find you for me if I was to dip my fingers inside of you…? For I already know how sweet you taste." I sucked in a shuddered breath, and he chuckled, taking this as my answer. Then he pulled back,

obviously knowing I needed it but then the next thing he said, I had to admit broke my heart a little.

"Besides, you're not my girlfriend, Eden, as the notion is fucking ridiculous." This time I pulled back and couldn't stop the hurt from showing, making his eyes widen as if he just realized something.

"Eden." He sighed my name, making me shake my head and say,

"No… of course… I mean, it was silly and besides, I didn't mean me… I just meant like other girlfriends, like what they called you… in the past I mean, but not me… this is… um… well… I don't know what this is but…"

"Gods, sweetheart, please stop," he said, moving back to consuming my space but this time framing my face with both hands.

"I am sorry, that was worded wrong," he told me, shocking me with his regretful tone.

"It's okay, I get it… I mean it's me and then there is you, and we are… are just…"

"…Perfect together," he whispered, finishing off my sentence in the very last way I ever expected him to. Then he kissed my forehead and was about to say something when Deke came over the speaker and said,

"We are here, boss." Ward released a sigh and after catching my eyes, told me,

"We will continue this conversation inside." I swallowed hard and said,

"It's really okay, I get it… I…"

"Eden, stop!" he demanded and when I did as he asked, he continued,

"We will be talking about this but for now, I would appreciate it if you could be a good girl for me and try not acting like my captive when we get out of this car… a screaming victim tends to attract human attention," he said in a teasing way that made me suddenly realize what this all was.

A way to get me to comply.

A way to control me.

Because what if all of this now was done as a way to stop the human witnesses from spilling the Supernatural beans? What if none of this was real but just words of manipulation? A way to use my clear attraction for him as a tool?

Oh God!

I could have gasped as the realization hit me. Jesus, what a fool I had been but then... *what if it had all been real... Every word?*

I just didn't know! I was so confused by everything he said and by my own mind trying to warp it all into being too good to be true. But fuck, what was I even thinking, because how the hell was this something I could class as being too good?! And really, I need to stop it with all the 'Hells' as for all I knew, that type of thing could be quite insulting. Jesus, I just didn't know... oh, maybe Jesus was the same thing? Oh God... but that was another one! Of course, by the time the car stopped, Ward was chuckling again, only this time he continued to do so whilst unfolding his large frame from the car as he got out. And as for me, a plan quickly formulated.

Because well, there was only one way to find out.

Because he was right.

I was a victim.

And now...

It was time to scream like one.

CHAPTER 18
BAD GIRL

I took some quick breaths, in and out, in and out again, with the last coming out more like a pant. Which meant that by the time my door opened, I launched myself out of the seat and out the car nearly falling.

"Whoa, careful... hey!" Ward shouted the second I twisted out of his way as he tried to grab me, making me run. Of course, he could have caught me but we both knew if he did, he would have ended up hurting me.

Damn him for keeping his promise and making this harder. Because I wanted to run from the bad guy, not someone I was clearly falling for.

Fuck, Eden, the guy just admitted to kidnapping you, what else do you need to make him the bad guy?!

So, with this in mind, I ran and only stopped when I was close to a bunch of people that had been out partying for the night. They all gave me funny looks, and one even asked me if I was alright.

I instantly looked back to Ward to see him slam the car door in anger but instead of coming to chase me, he simply folded his arms and leant back against the car, not taking his eyes off me... *very disappointed eyes.*

"Miss? Are you alright?" the man asked again, and it was at this point that Ward held up a hand to stop Deke, who looked seconds away from retrieving me himself. Then Ward looked down a little, mouthing something at him I couldn't detect before coming back to me and shaking his head, telling me no. Which was when I got what this was...

A test.

One I knew I failed the second I opened my mouth and screamed as loud as I could. And his reaction...

He sighed.

Then he shook his head as if he was nothing more than disappointed, and I had to question why I was feeling so guilty. Was his control on me already so deeply ingrained that it was making me question my decision? Question that I was the victim in this, and one that was merely frightened and trying to run back to my own freedom?

Could I really be blamed in that?

"Hey, are you okay...?"

"Just tell us, do you need the cops...?"

"Yeah, because we have a phon...?"

Three different people all started speaking to me at once but never got to finish, making me gasp when they were suddenly cut off. I glanced back at Ward to find his eyes narrowed and staring hard at the group, making me soon realize why, as their own eyes had glazed over. Then, before I could question their actions, they turned abruptly and started walking the other way. I looked around to see that others along the street had suddenly started doing the same.

My astonished gaze snapped once more back to Ward, to watch as he merely unfolded his arms and then motioned with his hand for me to come back to him. However, I just started backing up and shaking my head at him as I felt my whole body shaking with fear. I then watched him sigh again, as if disheartened by my defiance, before shaking his head and looking down at his feet. It was as if I was forcing him to make a decision he didn't want to make. Which was when I really started to get scared, so I backed away, now doing so with only one thought...

What had I done?!

So, I said the only thing left for me to say, having a feeling that he would hear it even with the distance growing between us.

"I'm sorry... so sorry..."

However, he ignored this lame apology I had tried to make, instead nodding to Deke, which was the last thing I saw before I turned around and started running. Something that was fucking painful, as breathing heavy was bad enough but actually trying to move quickly was torture. Despite the pain, I carried on, pushing past the people that had tried to help and who now moved like zombies to whatever destination they never intended to go.

But then that was the power of Ward.

He could control them.

But then why didn't he control me?

Naturally I didn't wait around to ponder this, I ran and pushed past the pain. Which meant that by the time I rounded a corner of what I assumed was the hotel, I finally braved looking back, now gasping for air and needing to hold a hand to the wall so I wouldn't collapse like I felt like I was close to doing.

But then I peeked around the corner and screamed when I saw the thickest dark fog now filling the space I had just ran through. So, I turned quickly and would have run straight into a solid body, had someone not grabbed the tops of my arms to prevent this and, no doubt, further injury. I looked up and saw that it was Deke, making me quickly start to struggle out of his hold.

"Lasciala andare," a deadly voice said in another language from behind us. A voice I knew belonged to Ward, and I gathered it meant for Deke to let me go as he released me a second later. Which was when I made the mistake of turning around and facing the darkness he commanded. One that now parted as Ward's dominating presence stepped from it and into view. On instinct, I cried out, stepping back and putting myself against Deke as there was nowhere else to go.

I was trapped.

"Please... please stop!" I said, holding out a shaky hand toward him. Something he focused on and narrowed his eyes at as if the sight physically hurt him. Which was why I quickly said,

"I'm sorry... I am so sorry, but I can't... I'm not the one you think I am... I don't mean to make you angry... I just can't go with you... please..." I mumbled, making him release some of his anger with a sigh before nodding to Deke behind me, as if telling him to let me go. I sucked in a quick breath in shock.

"You're... you're letting me go?" I whispered in astonishment. I turned to watch as Deke left but then, by the time I turned back again, Ward had cut the space between us to nothing, making me cry out again. Then I was forced to watch as his darkness started to seep closer, now bellowing around us, as if it were creating some kind of barrier between us and the rest of the world.

But just before I could ask what was going on, he wrapped an arm around me, taking care with my injuries as he pulled me into his tall, hard body. After this he collared my neck with a large hand, something I was getting used to by now as it seemed to be a thing with him. But I felt his thumb under my chin, forcing my head up so I couldn't hide from his intense gaze. His eyes seemed to penetrate my very soul for the power they held, making me start to lose myself in their amber depths. Like liquid gold that was heated and near glowing as the power hummed from him like charged lightening.

"That's where you're wrong, Eden," he told me, with his once smooth voice now having a dangerous edge to it. One that told me how close to the edge watching me run from him had caused him to be. After this, he leaned closer to my ear and whispered words that were nothing short of what felt like an eternal vow…

"I am never letting you go, my Siren."

Then, as I sucked in a shuddered breath, he pulled back and told me,

"However, I am sorry for this next part as I was hoping to do this without… well…"

"With… without… what?" I forced myself to ask, unable to stop my lips from shaking. He placed his thumb on them, and whilst giving me a tender look, one that was also underlined with something more, something that painfully looked like remorse, he answered my question.

"Without taking away your free will." I cried out in horror as I thought back to what he had done to those people, turning them into compliant little puppets and doing whatever he wanted with them! I started shaking my head, feeling tears form and making him cup the back of my head, cradling it to his chest as the first of my tears slipped free.

"Ssshh now, don't fear me. Don't fear what I will do, sweetheart… what you made me do… Ssshh and sleep now… Sleep my love… sleep and ease your mind… *sleep for me,*" he said, and I couldn't help but let those soothing words swim around in my mind, growing in their intensity before, seconds later, I could do nothing to block out the gentle command.

I closed my eyes at the same time I felt my head fall back,

181

blindly looking up at him. I felt my hair being stroked from my forehead as he cooed down at me,

"That's it... there you go... I've got you... I've got you now...

"My bad girl."

CHAPTER 19
GREY CLOUDS

"*That's it... there you go... I've got you... I've got you now... My bad girl.*"

These soft and tender words were all I could hear as I let my mind fade into darkness, feeling completely surrounded by all that was him.

All that was Ward, my dark Angel of Vengeance.

After that came mere snippets of what must have been dreams that barely made sense. A combination of hushed, soothing words hummed in the background like an eternal echo and I felt as if my body was being moved. But as pain tried to penetrate the fog that I felt buried under, his voice would simply chase it all away again. A voice that promised me care and protection. A voice that promised me comfort and affection.

But ultimately...

A voice that I knew was controlling me.

And where did that voice take me, but back to a place that I felt most comforted by... *my mother.* It was as if I was sitting back in my childhood home, on a couch I knew, surrounded by the familiar scent of my mother's cooking. Her humming to some song on the radio she didn't know the words to but letting the compulsion take her to try and sing it anyway.

All the colors of my childhood were bright and near blinding, they were all so wonderful. The vibrant swirls of blues and turquoises on the rug in front of me that I was currently kicking my toes into, getting lost in my thoughts as I often did. I used to sit on that rug as a kid and pretend I was sat in the ocean as it reminded me of the days my mom used to take me to the beach. It had been our favourite place to go together as Nags Head beach was only about an hour's drive away.

We would sit there for hours, staring out over the water and talking about all the adventures out there just beyond those blue waves. All the places we would heartbreakingly never see together. But then that was the beauty of dreams... *they were free.*

So that's what we did together. We would sit there and be free to dream all those impossible journeys we would never take. We would be free to dream about all the sights we would never get to see, and dream of the new food we would never get to taste. And, unbeknown to me at the time, but in the end, the only dream I was left wishing for was one more day with my mom. A dream of just the two of us sitting at that same beach, with the only destination I cared to reach for being her hand on the sand next to mine and at the ready for me to take.

But those days had been when my world had been filled with what seemed now like a kaleidoscope of color and my dreams had been shared with my mother. Hours lost to the sea and the two of us making shapes in the sand with our fingertips.

It had all been so bright.

But then one day it had all just... *gone.*

My bright days were no more, as if the sun had dimmed the day my mother had died and if I were honest, my dreams had died right along with her. After that, I never saw the ocean again. My beach days were no more, and I continued my life in a muted state of dull colors. But now, as I looked down at my younger feet, the ones my memories had obviously taken me to, I couldn't help but wonder where the color had gone and why that rug made me want to see the ocean again.

Because in truth, I knew that my mom would have been devastated to know that I had carried on in this gray world of mine without ever once going back to our beach. That I had, for a long time, given up on my dreams of ever seeing the world and discovering exactly what it was beyond those waves. And if I were really honest with myself, then that's why it had been so hard helping Jimmy out, knowing what I was really giving up.

A chance to finally make my mother proud. So that she may look down on me and instead of seeing the gray cloud hovering over my head, there would be a bright beaming light shining on a life of color. Which was why that money I had saved would have most likely gone toward a trip. A way to finally discover another beach, only this time, across an ocean and beyond those waves we had longed for. To at long last get the chance to turn our daydreams into at least one person's reality.

My own.

"I must still be fighting off this virus or something… so maybe we give the beach a miss until next weekend… maybe we go for…" I flinched the second my mother's voice dragged me away from the swirls on that rug as I suddenly felt as if it were being ripped out from beneath me. Because I knew what was coming next. The sound of my mother's gasp before the echoing of glass smashing on the floor. After this, the sound of me screaming out for my mother as she collapsed to the floor, me turning suddenly and skidding on that rug as I ran to her. A rug that from that day onwards remained rumpled up and was never straightened out again. Just like that next weekend at the beach…

185

It never came.

"Eden." I heard his voice suddenly and the memory started to float away around me, making me wish that it had come that little bit sooner. Just before where I knew I would have been hugging my mom after getting in from school. That would have been the comfort I needed. But perhaps that had been what Ward had been aiming for when sending my mind back to this place. Back to a memory he must have mistaken from the start as being a good one and the reason it had been there to begin with. Little did he know the reason it was one burned to my mind was because it was the start of a series of events that would mark the beginning of the worst days of my life. The beginning of when my childhood ended.

The day my dreams died.

Was that why his concerned voice was now once more trying to lure me away? I knew that it was, as every time I tried to fight against my memories to take me back there, doing so like some torturous loop I wanted to punish myself with, there was that voice pulling me back again. Until finally the images of my mother in pain faded away, and I found myself instead standing on some exotic balcony staring out over what I knew was most definitely a foreign land. It was stunning and unlike anything I had ever seen before. Old, whitewashed stone buildings nestled among narrow streets lined the edges of a rocky valley that led straight to a clear view of a turquoise sea.

"Relax and stay, my girl." I heard his voice again when I flinched after I felt a pain pinch my arm, making me even look down at myself in my dream-like state. This was to find a bead of blood pool on my skin as if I had just been pricked by something I couldn't see.

Yet again, there was that soothing voice behind me and the gentle fingers along my skin, which I couldn't see.

"Easy, my Little Carino, all will be well, just give it time." I

frowned and turned suddenly, expecting to see him standing there sharing this dream with me, one he seemed to have forced me under. However, all I saw was some grand ballroom cast in darkness. That, and a single door that stood in the center of the room like some silent beacon calling out to me and begging me to walk through its threshold. It was as if it had just been placed there for me and me alone. Almost as if it was my only way out of this dream world.

Yet, before I could make a run from Ward's control and toward what I knew would be my exit from this exotic world he had built for me, I would feel myself being pulled backward, keeping me rooted to the comfort of the ocean beyond.

Imprisoned and captured, locked to this secret paradise for as long as he wanted me here. So, I waited, and each time something new appeared, like a chair for me to sit in or a drink for me to sip, I would still try each time to move toward that door. However, it was only when the sun started to set, casting a gorgeous display of reds, pinks and oranges over the water that I was finally given more freedom. And with that freedom, I would make it further and further into the ballroom.

Then, as darkness finally fell, I was able to get close enough to actually reach the handle, turning it and stepping through the bright light that beamed through the opening. I cried out as I started to feel myself fall, knowing now how Alice felt when falling down the rabbit hole. This, before landing onto a bed of white and the bright light started to blind me enough that the only way to get away from it was to close my eyes. Something that seemed to have the opposite effect in the real world as this was when I was opening my eyes back in reality.

But unfortunately for me, that reality meant being faced with the fact that I still held the title of captive and Ward still held the villainous title of kidnapper. Oh, and my situation had just gone from bad to worse in a what felt like a dreaming heartbeat.

This was thanks to three reasons. The first being that I was now in a bed wearing what I could feel was just a t-shirt and from the size of it, then it wasn't much of a guess to know it was most likely Ward's. The second was that both my hands seemed shackled to the headboard, and any hope at running again was now labelled as mission impossible.

Now as for the third, well this was what worried me the most as my eyes shot to the point of pain on the inside of my elbow the moment I tried to resolve the second problem by pulling on my arms.

Because that's when I realized, I wasn't just a captive any longer.

No, I was now so much more.

I was now on the menu!

CHAPTER 20
THE MAGIC BLOODY REMEDY

"What the fuck!?" I shouted suddenly when I saw the IV sticking in my skin, with what was clearly blood being fed either from or into my arm, I couldn't yet tell which. Movement caught my eyes as a body shifted in a nearby seat, as my panicked voice had quickly alerted someone to the fact that I was now very much awake.

"Easy, Eden," Ward said, making me flinch the second I heard his deep voice.

"Don't, *easy* me! What the hell is this?!" I demanded to know, wondering now what had been done to me or had he had a doctor look at me and it was worse than I had first thought? But no, it couldn't be, as it wasn't as if I had been losing blood, unless there had been some internal bleeding. But then if that was the case, why wasn't I in some hospital somewhere? I yanked on my arm again making him quickly rush to me, taking hold of my arm just below my shackled wrist.

"Stop struggling or you will hurt yourself," he warned, making me shake my head at him before gritting my teeth.

"Let me go!" I snapped, trying again to pull my arm free and making him sigh.

"Eden, just calm down."

"Calm down! Are you for real right now?!" I shouted, unable to believe he had just said that. This was when he looked as though he was trying to gain patience, meanwhile I was at zero with that shit!

"I just woke up to find myself shackled to a fucking bed with half my clothes missing and a fucking IV sticking out my arm… oh Jesus, is that my blood you're getting…? Is that why you picked me… do I have tasty blood or something…? Like some rare wine for you to tap… oh fuck, that's it isn't it?!" I said, rambling and panicking as I tried to pull my arm free.

I only stopped moving when he growled above me, emitting a dark, Demonic sound. I knew now that his time of trying to find patience was clearly at an end. But then he must have seen my fear and instead of making the scary sound again, he took a deep breath.

"Fuck no! Gods Eden, do you really think that of me, that I could fucking do something like that?! Did you even listen to a fucking word I said in that car?!" he said as if I had just insulted him in the worst way possible. But this was when I lost it even more, and I did this by what I thought was making a good fucking point.

"People fucking lie, Ward, and well, this isn't exactly looking good for you, buddy!" I shouted back, shaking my arm and making the shackle rattle against the bed to emphasize my point. At this he closed his eyes and dragged a frustrated hand down his face before taking a step back. Then he turned around to face the window of what I could now see showed a city beyond the glass from high up in some fancy hotel suite. I mean, Jesus, who was this guy and what did he do for a living? I could have fit my old apartment in this place five times over! The cost of staying a few nights here was equivalent to all my debts, I was sure of it!

"Okay look, I will undo the cuffs, but you have to promise me you won't run again," he told me after he had taken his needed minute to calm down.

"Oh yeah, sure thing," I said sarcastically, making him grant me a pointed look.

"Eden, this is not a game."

"Yeah, I kinda got that when I was forced into a car with a crazy Angel of Vengeance and Fear, which by the way, I am totally getting the title now…" I said, pausing my rant to wave my fingers up and down to indicate his body before telling him,

"…Then I was kidnapped, being told that I am yours now, given no choice of anything, ran from you, caught in your dark, creepy cloud and then woke up to find myself as the next BLOOD VINTAGE IN YOUR COLLECTION!" I screamed at him, making him suddenly move, now looming over me and making me scream again, only this time in fear. Then he took a deep breath and with only an inch between our faces he told me calmly,

"First, you're forgetting the part where I saved your life and second, sweetheart, if I wanted to drink from you, I would do so straight from the delicious source, not drain you from a fucking tube!"

"Oh my God, you are crazy!" I commented unwisely, making him smile.

"Only for unruly little Sirens who continue to try and run from me, then yeah, sweetheart, that has the power to drive me fucking crazy," he said, looking me up and down as if I was now his new favourite tasty treat and well, with this IV sticking out of my arm drawing blood, then who knew, maybe I was.

"And for the record, that IV in your arm is there to heal you, or did it not yet occur to you to question why you are no longer in any pain?" he asked, and this time there was nothing playful about it.

191

But before I could reply, the door opened, and a man walked in who was clearly a doctor. This big ass clue was thanks to the stethoscope I could see in his hand and the fact he had that professional doctor look about him. Although, he also looked a bit young for a doctor, so maybe he was still in training. But then one look at the extreme luxury I was currently held captive in, then I doubted Ward was the type to cut costs by getting an unqualified medical intern in who was trying to make a buck on the side.

He suddenly cleared his throat awkwardly as he shot Ward a look. Meanwhile, my captor smirked before nodding for him to go ahead and approach me.

"I assure you, Miss, I am fully qualified and have been for quite some time," he said, making me gasp as realization hit and I felt my cheeks get warm. I then closed my eyes and groaned, mouthing to myself,

'This can't still be happening.'

"Erm… let's see how our patient is doing, should we?" The mind-reading doctor said in an uncomfortable tone, whereas Ward looked anything but uncomfortable as a knowing grin played on his lips. That was until I nodded toward the doctor and said,

"Can we at least have some privacy?" Ward dropped this amused look pretty quickly and just folded his arms, as if intimidating me with his size was now the aim of the game. Then, in that commanding voice of his, he replied,

"No."

I rolled my eyes and started muttering to myself about how I wished there was such a thing as a captive union so I could class myself now on strike. Something this time he didn't laugh at, and clearly, there were some benefits to having my pissed off thoughts read.

"Well, I have to say, you're looking better," the doctor said, after once again clearing his throat and no doubt trying to break the tension in the room.

So, I ignored the positive side of this and snapped,

"Yes, and I must look great shackled too!" At this, Ward's eyes started to burn, making me quickly look away as I knew what that look promised... *Shackles were definitely going to play a further part in my future.*

"Ah well yes, Mr. Za'afiel thought it best so you wouldn't hurt yourself, seeing as you made getting your IV in quite difficult." I flinched at this and couldn't help but quickly look to Ward, who simply nodded at the doctor, telling him something without words. Something I understood after the doctor started to release my arms, making me wince as I lowered them.

"Now, let's have a look to see how those bruises are looking should we...?"

"No!" Ward snapped suddenly, making the doctor look back at him.

"There is no examination needed. I have checked her over and she is healed. Now just remove the IV as she doesn't need any more of my blood," Ward said, shocking me enough to gasp, making him finally glance at me. However, he still looked hurt and tense because of it.

"Yyyou... *you healed me?"*

"As I said I would," he stated sternly in reply to my stuttered question.

"With your blood?" I added, making him merely nod before looking down at his own arm, pulling down the sleeve that had been rolled up as if at the ready to have more blood drawn from him if I had needed it. I had no clue as to how his blood could have healed me, but only that it did and now, well simply put, I felt like a complete bitch. Because there he had been, trying to heal me, and I had accused him of horrible things. But then again, I had woken shackled to his damn bed, so I wasn't totally out of line with where my mind naturally went to.

In fact, I was so lost in my emotions that I only just realized the IV had been removed, but before the doctor could tape some gauze over it, Ward was suddenly there, moving him out of the way. Then I watched in shock as he licked his thumb before swiping it across where the IV had been.

"You may go," he said sternly, and he did so without taking his eyes off me. I swear I was close to squirming under that hard gaze of his and now wishing that the doctor would do anything *but* leave. Hell, I would have faked a seizure if it would have stopped him from leaving me alone with Ward. But then the second I heard the door close, I knew that chance had passed.

"I have to say, Eden, you're making quite a habit of running from me," he said in a dangerous tone that told me he was once again on edge and well… *I now knew why.*

"Can you really blame me?" I asked, making him raise a brow before responding,

"That depends."

"It depends?" I repeated in a surprised tone.

"Yes."

"On what?" I asked with a little shake of my head.

"On what made you run this time," he replied, making me look down at the covers just to escape his intense gaze. But then I heard him sigh before I heard the sound of furniture moving and my gaze shot up, catching a glimpse of the impossible. This was in time to witness as a chair from over ten feet away suddenly slid along the floor toward him.

"Holy shit!" I shouted in shock, and I couldn't help but shift back as he simply took the seat that was now at my bedside.

"How on earth did you…!?"

"What made you run, Eden?" he asked, interrupting my

disbelief. However, my eyes were rooted to the chair he'd just moved and suddenly his face was inches from me, making me shriek out in shock before he hooked me around the neck and told me,

"I am a magician and if you tell me why you ran, I will pull a fucking rabbit from my hat." My eyes widened in even greater shock, and the first thing that came out of my mouth was what finally had him grinning.

"But you're not wearing a hat." At this he shook his head a little before tightening his hold on the back of my neck so I couldn't retreat as he kissed my forehead. Then he gave me back my space and retook his magical seat.

"You're not a magician, are you?"

"No, I am not," he replied.

"Shame, I always wanted a rabbit as a kid," I told him, making his lips twitch again as if he was fighting off a grin. Which was when I decided it was time to be honest.

"I ran because I thought the only reason you might have kidnapped me was so that I wouldn't go running off telling people about you or your kind... whoever you people are," I told him, making him looked shocked... shocked and now angry once again. Because it was clear that even though he could read some of my thoughts, it seemed not all of them made it through. Which now had me wondering how I could hide the rest from him.

"And all that I told you in the car... I gather meant nothing to you?" he snapped, making me flinch before sighing this time.

"I just thought it was a way to control me," I admitted with a shrug of my shoulders.

"Control you?" he questioned as if the idea was a foreign concept, which was a bit laughable all things considered.

"Yeah, you know, tell me you like me, make me feel special and stuff so I do what you say and am more compliant, that type of thing… obviously this is all before I knew you could become puppet master with the click of your fingers," I told him, and this time his reaction was to laugh, but even I knew it was a sound bred more from disbelief than hilarity.

"Oh, my girl," he sighed.

"What?" I asked when he said this, knowing there was obviously something big I was missing here. So, I argued my point.

"I mean come on, Ward, just look at me." At this he stopped looking amused pretty quickly, and suddenly he was up out of his seat. And what followed this movement was a predatory action, as he lowered himself down on top of me before suddenly yanking me under him, moving at impossible speeds and making me cry out in surprise. Then with that intense side of him firmly back and dominating the space above me, he pulled the sheet from between us and scanned the length of my half naked body. Then, with glowing eyes of amber, he told me on a growl,

"I am looking… and sweetheart…" he paused before some other side of him spoke next, and it equally terrified me as much as it turned me on. But either way, I knew one thing for certain…

I was fucked!

Something he confirmed seconds later when he finished his sentence in a Demonic growl of words…

"…We both fucking adore what we see."

CHAPTER 21
NO BROKEN BONES GETTING IN THE WAY

I gasped, a sound that ended up getting swallowed whole the second he took advantage of my mouth opening in shock. He kissed me, and the moment his lips took possession of my own I simply melted into him. Every muscle that had been tensed out of fear instantly relaxed to the point I felt myself give over total control of my body to this man. This huge, muscular man that dominated my every thought and every sensation as soon as his lips touched mine.

Oh, but who was I kidding, he did all that by simply being in the same room with me! Something I knew made him dangerous because I was falling for someone I still didn't know, and what I did know mostly terrified the living bejeezus out of me!

I wanted the time to process this. Time to weigh up the good versus the bad and make a list in my head, despite knowing that at the moment it would definitely be heavily on the side of bad. But then, with the way his hands were skimming up my sides taking with him the material of one of his own t-shirts, then it was hard to even remember my own name, let alone his.

An embarrassing thought he heard.

"Oh, you will remember it alright, especially when I have you screaming it over and over again," he told me with a growl of words, making me moan when his hands tightened their hold either side of my breasts, teasing me with his possessive strength. But then his words finally penetrated, and I sobered up enough to tell him,

"You need to stop doing…" This plea was abruptly cut off the second I found the t-shirt being whipped over my head.

"Ah… you did that on purpose," I accused, giving him a pointed look he actually chuckled at before leaning down to kiss my nose, telling me,

"Fuck me, you're so fucking cute." I groaned at this, despite the sweet declaration making my insides turn mushy.

"That's not a very compelling argument on your side," I pointed out, making him kiss his way to my neck, and I swear I had to bite my lip to stop from moaning aloud at how good it felt. I then felt his grin against my skin before he started to speak against my neck.

"Oh, I disagree… wholeheartedly in fact, as I think it's very compelling." I smiled at this as the obvious humor in his tone was infectious.

"How so?" I hummed in reply, wanting this teasing between us to continue for as long as possible. Like this very moment had the power to erase the reasons we were angry with each other. Had the power to tip the scales on that ever important good or bad list. Although admittedly, his hands had that power too.

At this he pulled back so he could look down at me, taking a full minute to do so, by which point I was most definitely squirming under his appraisal.

"Because, my beautiful little Carino, and one who is most definitely very deserving of the name… *you distract me like no other,*" he said, pausing to get closer and making me melt again when he ran his nose along my jaw so he could whisper this last part in my ear. I released a deep and dreamy sigh before asking on a breathy whisper,

"What does Carino mean again?"

"It means cute," he told me softly, making me blush as he grinned down at me. Then I told him,

"Alright, so after that one then I admit, I would feel bad calling you Pookie Snuggle Bum." After this he threw his head back and started laughing, and my body shook beneath him thanks to the bed he was making vibrate.

"Fuck me, but my little Carino is funny," he said, making me grin big this time as even more of his gentle, tender words warmed my scared little heart... *despite most of them starting with the F word that was*. But I didn't care as I liked how passionate he got.

Speaking of passion, it was only then that I seemed to realize there was now only my underwear preventing me from being classed as fully naked beneath him. At this thought, I watched as he slowly looked down the length of me, putting enough space between us to do this before his knowing grin appeared as his eyes found mine.

"You know, sweetheart, I think you're right." Then after what was him clearly reading my thoughts, he rose up enough so he could drag his own t-shirt over his head, soon making me gasp for another reason... *he was utterly droolworthy, incredible.*

I couldn't help but gulp down my next swallow, fearing it would get stuck there and start choking me if I wasn't careful. I had never seen so many muscles on one person in all my life! But then again, I hadn't exactly been a picky person when it came to boyfriends. Personality had always taken a front seat with looks and body type taking the back. But as for Ward, well it seemed as though he was the complete package... *and oh so much more.* The more part, I had to admit to still being slightly terrified of, but even that was starting to take a back seat. Because it was like he said, he hadn't hurt me and had in fact gone to great lengths to prevent that from happening. Although I knew I still had to address the fact that he had controlled me outside the hotel, and for all I knew would again at the next given opportunity he felt needed it. Which meant that if we were to go anywhere from this point on with any kind of relationship in mind, then that couldn't be allowed to ever happen again.

Something I think he himself knew as he seemed to have regretted the act even as he was doing it. But then had I really forced his hand? Could I blame myself? I shook these thoughts from my mind, knowing I was once again losing myself to my own rambling thoughts, something he appeared to be giving me time to do. Until of course... well...

He didn't.

I knew my time was up when he sat astride me, raised up on his knees either side of my thighs. With only a pair of dark jeans on, he was a feast for the eyes. Especially with the way the sunlight poured through the large windows, casting a warm glow to his perfect, flawless skin. I could see every inch of that impossibly strong torso, one that looked as though it had spent more hours in the gym than not.

And as for the way he now watched me as I took in the beautiful sight of him, drinking in every gorgeous inch of his body, he no doubt knew where my mind was at. I was a woman starved of the privilege him being here bestowed on my lonely, lust-starved heart. I even found myself raising my hand as if an impulse to touch him had been so strong, it had overridden all the reasons why I knew I shouldn't. But I stopped because I wasn't brave enough to touch such perfection like his without first feeling as if it belonged to me.

Because a man like Ward belonged to no one.

But suddenly he snatched out, grabbing my hand and startling me, preventing it from falling back to the safety of my side. Then with it now firmly in his grasp, he raised it back up to touch the solid lines of his rippled, muscular stomach.

"Touch me, Eden," he told me, his voice thick with an emotion I couldn't detect.

Swallowing hard, I started to do something I'd wanted to the second I was awarded with the sight of his gorgeous body. I ran my fingertips gently along the hard lines of his muscles, starting at his very defined six pack, biting my lip as I did. When I couldn't reach up further, he shifted so he was sitting back against his legs, along with adding a little more weight to my own legs. But it lowered him enough that I could stretch out and reach more of him. I then ran my flat palm over his pecs, crossing over from one to the other and holding my hand over his heart, feeling it beat beneath my skin.

The heartbeat of an Angel.

As for his reaction to this bare exploration of mine, he closed his eyes with each movement before looking up as if he was feeling something as profound as I was. In truth, it was one of the most intimate moments of my life, getting to discover this God of a man. Which was why I couldn't help but speak, despite how embarrassed I was to do so. Because I needed to tell him my deepest inner thoughts… he needed to know what this moment meant to me and how I felt when my hands were on him this way. But more than anything else, I needed it to come from my own lips this time, not just as inner musings or heard as unsure ramblings of my mind.

Which was why I told him,

"You're… you're so… what I mean to say is, well I've never been or even seen… I…" I paused when I saw the soft, tender look he was giving me, before he said my name in that gentle way of his.

"Eden… you don't need to…" I closed my eyes and blurted out the rest before he could stop me.

"You're beautiful, Ward, that's what I wanted to tell you. The most beautiful, perfect man I have ever se…" I never got to finish as he lowered over me quickly enough that it stole the rest of the words, and he silenced me further by kissing them from me. And this time, his aim was simple…

He wanted to consume every single, last thought.

And he did.

Because his kiss had that kind of power over me. It made every unsure, wary, fearful thought disappear, evaporating like the fog he commanded and had no more use for. That once gray cloud above my head would lift, and the weight of grief upon my shoulders would float away with it, leaving nothing but the clear sight of Ward in front of me. Like some kind of dream I had not only allowed myself to wish for again, but one that I was starting to believe in more and more. A feeling that increased in strength with every kiss we shared, and the dream soon blossomed into hope that this could actually work between us. A seed nurtured to the point of becoming a blinding color, flowering the moment his lips touched mine.

That was the kind of power Ward held over me, and it was both exhilarating as much as it was utterly terrifying.

"You're the perfection and one I would kneel at willingly and beg for its return should you ever be cruel enough to take it from me!" He paused long enough to growl down at me feverishly between kisses. Because he gave me no chance to respond before his lips took over my own, tasting me and taking the kiss even deeper. Then when he felt me near gasping for breath at the intensity of it all, he stopped again to growl,

"This time there are no broken bones to get in my way!"

Then, before I could react, a thick black talon grew from the tip of his finger in the blink of an eye. Something he used to pluck at the center of my bra, making it burst open. Then, as I was still reeling from the shock of this, his hand snaked down to my panties to award them the same treatment. This actually made me wonder where this underwear had come from, as the last I knew I had been forced to go without after our first time together back at that strange nightclub Afterlife.

Had he put these on me to save my modesty with the doctor? I would have asked had the next thing from those gorgeous lips of his been nothing short of a declaration.

"Now there can be nothing between us... and this time, there will be no fear of what you may see... yes?" he asked, making my eyes grow wide as I made sense of what he meant.

"You... you will change again?" I asked with a little stammer at first, making him grin down at me.

"Don't fear it, Eden, for neither of us would ever harm you, but yes, I fear that now he has also had a taste of you, then keeping him from getting to play with you too would be another cruelty on my part," he told me, and this time not only did my eyes widen, my mouth actually dropped. Again, it was a look he relished in as it soon had him smirking.

"H-h-he... wants to... *to play with me?*" At this his grin grew bigger as he leaned down so as he could whisper playfully in my ear,

"Oh, most definitely." He chuckled when he heard me swallow hard.

"And erm... *will he play nice?*" I asked, whispering back as if this other side of him might hear me and not like the question. But then I shouldn't have been worried as Ward chuckled again and told me,

"I wouldn't count on it, sweetheart, not with all the deliciously devious things we want to do to you but don't worry, I can promise… *you will enjoy them."* Then he finished this with a wink and my face must have said it all, yet I still felt the need to back up my worries with words.

"I will?" At this I received my answer in a way that backed up his words with actions, as it was a vow spoken over my lips before kissing me.

"Oh, most definitely."

CHAPTER 22
PLAYFUL DARKNESS

I had to confess, the second he said this I would have voiced my panic had it not been for the fact that Ward was back to kissing me, and that tended to render me pretty speechless. Because the passion of this man was nothing like I had ever known before. It made me feel things that I could only hope were true, as the way he held me to him so tightly, so possessively, well it had me believing he was terrified of losing me. As if he feared someone was seconds from bursting in and trying to take me from him.

I would have been lying if I said it didn't make me feel precious and honestly, in a way I had never felt from another. It was as though I was something special to him and I still questioned why. Why this God of a man had picked me above all else. What did I have to offer, what did I have…?

"Eden… give me strength, girl, for I will gag this mind of yours with so much pleasure, you will think of nothing else… is that what I have to do?" he growled, and again I wanted to smack myself knowing he had heard my insecurities playing out in my head. Which is why I said in a small voice,

"If you want it to stop so badly then all you need to do is stop listening." At this he pressed his nose into my cheek and growled,

"Not ever fucking happening!" Then he fisted my hair and forced my head to turn into his lips so he could kiss me on that same growl. This was when things within him started to change, beginning when that dark side started to seep beneath his skin. It was also when his eyes changed, with swirls of black taking over the heated amber that had been there before it.

I sucked in a startled breath, but it was pointless when it was one he merely consumed, swallowing the shock straight from me when taking possession of my lips again. I was starting to understand that kissing was a big thing for Ward, and I couldn't help but wonder if it had always been this way or if it was somehow an effect I was having on him.

"I think that should be obvious seeing as I can't keep my fucking hands off you, why would you believe my lips to be any different?" he pulled back enough to tell me, making me blush because of it.

"Now raise your arms up above your head," he commanded quickly, shaking me out of my lustful fog.

"Erm… why?" I stammered out, and there was the briefest of grins before his handsome face turned hard and stern. This was when I knew he had flipped back into Dom mode and I was soon to discover there were now even more rules to follow.

"I am still being patient with you, so I'll let you off with a warning, sweetheart, but a man like me doesn't like to repeat himself or… *be kept waiting.*" He whispered this last part down at me, only an intimidating inch from my face. I swallowed hard, something he seemed to take great pleasure in, as that knowing smirk was back and only deepened when I quickly raised my arms up.

"Good girl," he praised, making me feel something deep

inside that shouldn't have happened when being treated like this. Making me now question what was wrong with me. What was wrong with me if just those two words were enough to make me want to do anything for this man? Because I knew I would become a slave to this master just to hear it again and really... *what did that make me?*

He seemed to snarl low at this as if something in him snapped when he growled down at me,

"It makes you fucking perfect for me... do you understand that, Eden? Tell me you do and say it now!" This demand was strengthened when swirls of darkness started to seep out from behind him, framing his dominating presence in an ominous shadow.

"I...I..." I stuttered quickly, trying to find the right words he wanted to hear.

"You... Gods, girl, but how fucking addictive *you* are! Now give me what I want and say yes to me... *say yes, I understand, Ward,"* he told me on another growl, against my neck this time, with his whispered command rumbled in my ear.

"Yes, I understand," I whispered back, making him suddenly bite me hard enough that I cried out in pain but not enough to break the skin. He released me and started to sooth the sting with his tongue before giving me reasons for his punishing actions.

"Did you forget something, sweetheart?" he asked in a tender, kind way that was the dizzying opposite to what he'd just done. I sucked in a shuddered breath and tried again, knowing now what I had forgotten.

"Yes, I understand, Ward."

"Good, now don't forget my name again and I will not find the need to punish you," he told me, before licking up the length of where he had held my tender flesh captive in his teeth.

"You see, I like to hear my name coming from those

kissable lips of yours and well, unless there is something in between them then I will demand they remind us both of whom now owns this delectable little body of yours… tell me you understand this too, Eden," he said, shocking a gasp out of me. But then all it took this time to get me to do his bidding was to grant me a pointed look.

"I understand," I said quickly, and at this he flashed his fangs at me, making me cry out in fear as he started to get closer to my neck, giving me a clear warning of what was to come once more. Which was why I hurriedly shouted this time,

"Ward! I meant, I understand, Ward!" Thankfully this meant that by the time he touched my neck, making me flinch when he did so, it was to kiss me there, grinning against my skin. Then he whispered,

"My sweet girl is good at learning… now time for a new lesson!" He ended this whisper by a louder statement before raising up above me so he was free to rip open his jeans. Jesus, but I swear my eyes bulged as they were glued to the sight of his large cock straining against his boxer-briefs, as if silently begging to be freed.

And freed it soon was.

"Keep your arms above you," he told me, his voice thick and heavy with the same lust I could see in his glowing eyes that were once again getting darker by the second. As for me, I naturally did as I was told, secretly getting a high from the dominant demand, despite the internal battle I still fought. Because half of me wanted to fight against him and refuse him his desires. But every look of pride he gave me in return for doing as he wished… well, in truth it felt like some kind of gift I was quickly becoming addicted to receiving.

So, I stretched out my arms and gripped onto the first thing I felt there, which ended up being chains, as the shackles were still attached to the headboard. In fact, I was sort of surprised he hadn't put them back on me if he wanted me to remain still beneath him. But the second I thought this, his smirk told me he had his reasons as he nodded to them before telling me,

"We have other plans for keeping you where we want you." I visibly gulped at this, something his eyes heated at as if he were feeding from my internal struggles and enjoying himself immensely. As if this was all part of his kink, making me wonder if he didn't in fact have a sadistic streak as he clearly enjoyed watching me squirm beneath him.

He grinned even more at this, and I couldn't help but snap,

"You're listening to me again, aren't you?" He raised a brow and gave me a stern pointed look, that I had to say was enough to get me to back down quickly.

"Hold on tighter," he commanded, in a harder tone this time instead of answering me and the second I did as he asked, he gripped my hips and pulled me down further, making me shriek out in surprise. After this he freed his cock and whilst rising up above me, fisted its impressive and intimidating length, pumping it a few times. I swear my mouth went dry at the sight as it was without a doubt one of the hottest things I had ever witnessed!

Although that thought was quickly replaced with another as he suddenly grabbed my ass with both hands and used his hold on me to lift half of me off the bed. I cried out again as he pushed his hips forward and thrush up inside of me, connecting our bodies in a way I had never experienced before.

"AHHH... OOOhhhh!" I moaned at the sudden intrusion, tensing my whole body before he lowered me back down and leaned over me, keeping himself rooted firmly inside me.

"Ssshh now, just give it a moment and relax for me... Gods, but you are so fucking tight... *fucking Heaven being inside you.*" He whispered this last part down at me after first placing his forehead to mine, and I had to say it quickly had my heart racing for a different reason. Because this level of intensity I had never experienced with a man before and combined with what his body could do to mine, well it made this game of losing my heart even more dangerous.

"Don't fear us," he said, and this time I questioned what he meant as I didn't know if this was because of what he had heard of my thoughts or what was still to come. But when those shadows around him started to flow over both of us, then I would say it was the second.

"Relax, baby," he cooed down at me the second I let go of the chains so I could grip onto his shoulders in panic. Then I stared wide eyed at the darkness beyond, and would no doubt have started shaking had it not been for Ward's hold on me.

"Look at me, Eden," he ordered, and this time it was done softly, and that tender lure of his words was just as effective as the authoritative command he used to also get his way. So, I left the shadows and focused instead on his amber depths that seemed to glow brighter the moment I did as he asked. Then I took a deep breath and nodded silently, telling him that I was alright as I forced myself to relax around him, and effectively losing my death grip on him.

"That's it, good girl... *such a good girl,*" he whispered as he kissed my hairline before he started to move above me, making me moan at each gentle stroke of his cock against my sensitive flesh he was seated firmly inside.

"You like that, beautiful?" he asked with a knowing tone, making me nod, but this wasn't good enough for him as he told me,

"When I ask you a question, I expect to be answered with words, sweetheart... now try again."

"I like it," I whispered shyly, giving him what he wanted and making him grin down at me.

"Good, now just remember that and use it to beat back the

fear." Before I could utter more than a squeak of alarm, he pulled back from me. Then he gripped my ass once more and lifted it up just as he thrust up inside me, this time making my gasp of panic turn into one of pure pleasure. I arched my head back as I closed my eyes and let out a long, deep moan, quickly feeling that deep erotic bliss grow and build within me.

It was the kind of pleasure that felt as if it had the power to tear you apart the moment you allowed yourself to free it from its sinful cage. You almost feared it as much as you craved it. You nurtured the feeling, allowing it to build almost until the point of pain knowing that it had the strength to reward you in such a way, you would likely remember it like no other time before.

But then it wasn't me that was nurturing it this time... no, it was Ward. And he wasn't simply asking, he was demanding, commanding and forcing it to build for me. That was what made me fear it so much, as I knew my own limits and this... well this felt close to destroying them all.

"I know you're close... you're so close I can almost taste it for myself... fucking delicious, this sexual essence of yours... *fucking addictive,*" he told me as his cock continued to piston in and out of me, stroking those nerves over and over again.

"Now open your eyes and show me... show me how I am the only one who can break you this way... show me how well you shatter around me," he commanded, doing so in such a way that I couldn't possibly deny him. So, I opened my eyes and the second I did, I came, screaming out with both the strength of my orgasm and the strength of my fear as the two strangely merged as one.

"WARD!" I bellowed his name as those shadows had formed a Demonic figure behind him and he was now changing into elements of his other side. This figure of death flowed through him and over me, and I cried out the second it touched me and covered my body with its dark desire. It was like igniting every single sexual nerve I had, and stroking every erogenous zone my body possessed. Like hundreds of hands all covering me and each time I tried to shout for him in panic, another lustful feeling would assault me, halting me trying to get away from him. No, instead of making me shy away from him, my back bowed into the shadow's touch instead of cowering away from it. I sought it out, pressing myself firmly into each sensation rather than trying to find a way to escape it.

"Yes... yes, yes, yes... God yes!" I panted over and over like there was some secret spell being cast over me, one that was strong enough to keep it going. But then as I screamed out as yet another orgasm swept through me like a tidal wave, I knew Ward must have been close to finding his own. Because this was when things started to change, and those invisible fingers became stronger and were being used to shift up my arms until they became shackles around my wrists.

"My turn," Ward said when his face burst through the shadowed essence of his other form. Then the flow of darkness over my body started to form hands that were used less for pleasure and more for restraining. Restraints that may have started at my wrists but certainly didn't end there. No, they also felt the need to frame my waist, ribcage, shoulders, neck and breasts.

In fact, I felt held down at every point other than where Ward held me by the hips. This was where he kept me exactly where he wanted me as he continued to power into me. Now doing so at such speed and strength that I was left with no other option than to pant and moan through it all, feeling another impossible orgasm build within me.

One that scared me more than all others!

Because I knew that it would replace the memory of all before it as being the strongest one yet, the one I wasn't ready to experience. I knew that when I felt the shadows flow over my stomach and down to where we were joining over and over again. Ward continuously pulled almost all the way out before hammering back into me again, hitting that sexually pure bundle of nerves of mine that felt as if it had the power to make me self-implode and cast me into an endless oblivion.

"Ward... Ward, I can't... I can't... I... please no...!" I pleaded the second I felt that dark touch of his start to stroke at my folds, caressing gently around my most tender flesh. Because I knew where it would eventually go, and I was terrified I would do as he wished and actually shatter around him.

"You don't get to make that choice, Eden... *I do!*" he stated firmly, making me cry out in both frustration and pleasure,

"NO, please!" He ignored this and instead made more demands of me.

"Now trust me and give me what I want," he ordered, and before I could ask him what it was that he wanted and most likely doing so in some mindless jumble of words, his smoke tensed harder over me. This quickly had me pinned to the bed so I couldn't struggle, at the same time the feeling of non-existent fingers found my clit. I started screaming his name as seconds later I was coming hard, feeling like he said I would...

Sexually broken.

"AHHH WARD! FUCK! NOOO... YESSSS!" But this was then drowned out by his own pleasure found. I watched as he threw his head back and roared at the ceiling with the Demonic looking presence around him pushing through once more. It echoed his roar with one of its own and mirrored his movements, extending outwards past his features as if his supernatural essence was trying to break out completely.

"FUCK!" I screamed this time in fear until that deathly face of his essence formed to one with more features like its host.

This was so it could look down at me, and this was when the
impossible kept on coming. As his darkness did something next
that left my mouth hanging open in utter shock before I
promptly passed out...

It winked at me.

214

CHAPTER 23
BRAVE GIRL KISS

"*Time to come back to me, beautiful.*"

The moment I heard this being whispered straight into what seemed like my subconscious mind, I started to come back to the real world. But when I did, all I felt was a surrounding warmth that I now seemed cocooned in. Of course, it was only when I opened my eyes did I realize why. Thus, making the water around me splash over the sides when I started thrashing.

"Hey, easy now, you're safe... *safe in my arms,*" Ward said from behind me as his arms tightened around my naked torso, tensing the harder I fought him and only relaxing when I stopped. This was because I realized I was safe like he said. Oh, and I was now currently sitting in the biggest bath I had ever been in, that was situated in the most amazing bathroom I had ever seen.

It was covered from floor to ceiling in the same light-gray tile that was strangely tranquil, which I guess was the look they were going for. The twin sinks framed either side of the door, which was mirrored sections held between swirls of wrought iron and looked more like sliding screen doors. This matched the large arched mirrors over the vanities that held white stone sinks and looked to be carved out of quartz. It seemed to be a running theme as this white stone was also what we were bathing in. It was a large oval space that was big enough to invite a small party to join us.

I looked around and couldn't see a toilet so gathered this must have been in its own separate space behind us both, as Ward was currently cushioning my body against his chest.

My very naked and wet body.

One he had his arms around, with one across my belly, his left hand resting at my hip, and the other across my heaving breasts, with his right hand stroking up and down my neck.

"How did I...?" I left that question hanging after my voice came out hoarse and well, from all the screaming I had recently been doing, then I couldn't exactly say I was surprised.

"I carried you in here after you passed out on me," he told me, making me ask,

"Then who ran the bath?"

"Magician, remember?" he whispered in my ear in a teasing tone that had me trying to hold in a giggle. So, I looked over my shoulder at him and teased back,

"Then you owe me a rabbit." At this he let his head fall back as he laughed, making my whole body shake seeing as I was plastered naked against him. I had to say I adored the sound of his deep manly laughter, and even more so knowing I was the one with the power to entice it from him.

"My little Carino is funny," he hummed against my neck at the same time squeezing me tighter, making me blush and grin ridiculously.

"However, I do feel as if I need to apologize for... well..." he paused, clearing his throat as if he felt awkward or could it be something else?

"Apologize for what?" I asked, trying to turn to face him when his hold on me tightened to prevent it.

"I fear I took you too hard, too soon," he admitted, and I realized what that pause had been for... *he felt guilty.* Which was why I braved touching him, reaching up and stroking the arm that was banded across my breasts. Then after clearing my own throat, I told him in a quiet unsure voice,

"You don't need to be sorry... I... well, I... *I enjoyed it.*" I pushed this last part out, even if it came in the form of a shameful whisper. I felt his growl vibrate against my back before he buried his face in my neck and kissed me there, before telling me,

"Careful, sweetheart, or you will tempt me to take you that way again, and sooner than your sweet, tight core may be ready for." As he said this, his right hand snaked down my belly until it was cupping that sweet tight core he spoke about, making me moan back against him. But then when he was about to remove his hand after making his point, my reaction was instantaneous as I shackled his wrist, preventing him from moving. Then, with this new found bravery, I turned my head and told him boldly,

"Who said it wasn't ready for you?" At this he growled even deeper, and to answer my challenge he suddenly had me crying out in pleasure as he thrust two thick fingers up inside me. Then, as he delved deeper, I arched my back against him at the same time his left hand came up to shackle my neck, collaring it in his large hand. It was such a possessive hold that I felt it only add to my arousal, heightening the act his deft fingers were currently playing against my nerves.

"Mmm... *undeniably ready,*" he stated with a growl of lust-filled words, this before he used his hold on my neck to grip my chin, using it to turn my head so he could kiss me side on. And when I came, screaming out his name, I did so against his lips, and he could taste my pleasure for himself.

After this he released me, pulling his fingers from my now sensitive channel and taking the time to reposition my relaxed body against his. One that felt as if my bones had been replaced by pie filling. He chuckled at this thought, making me mutter,

"That's gonna get real annoying." At this he laughed and leaned closer to tell me,

"Or continue to be highly entertaining." I hid my grin at his quick-witted reply and instead scoffed. Then I settled my weight back into his muscular body even more. I had to admit that with his arms around me like this, I had never felt so treasured. In fact, I wasn't even aware that such a thing was possible for an adult, as the last time I had felt so cared for had been when my mother had still been alive.

The moment this entered my mind he gave me a squeeze, and I knew it was yet again another thought he had heard.

"Tell me about her," Ward said, making me jerk a little in surprise.

"You want me to… to tell you about my mother?"

"Why do you seem surprised? I want to know all there is about you," was his easy reply, one said in a way that told me he thought I should know this was obvious. I laughed once and replied without malice,

"Then starting with a sad story or my childhood tales of woe might not be the best place to start."

"Perhaps you're right but if it is on your mind then I wish for you to find comfort and solace by sharing it with me, and therefore easing your mind of the weight." I released a dreamy sigh, wondering for the millionth time if this guy was for real!

"I think you have found your proof of that enough by now, unless you would like the reminder?" he replied to the unvoiced question, making me retort,

"You know if you keep this up then I won't need to speak at

all." At this he ran the backs of his fingers gently across my naked breasts and hummed,

"Now that would be a shame indeed, for I happen to enjoy the sound of your voice, no matter how dangerous it can be." I frowned at this before asking,

"What do you mean?" After this question I felt him tense at my back before relaxing again, but I couldn't help but feel as if he had forced himself to do so.

"Pay no attention to my words… now, you talk whilst I wash," he replied in a way that told me two things, one was that the conversation was over, and the second was that Ward was keeping something from me. But for now, I focused on the part where he said he needed to wash as he picked up a cloth that had been resting over the edge of the tub.

"Oh sorry, I should probably get out and let you do that," I said, reaching for the edge and leaning forward ready to get out. At this he tensed his left arm that was still around me and stopped me from going anywhere.

"That would defeat the object of what I am trying to achieve, seeing as I need your body here with me in order to wash it," he told me firmly.

"Oh, you meant me." At this I felt him smile against my neck before kissing me, nipping at my skin playfully before saying in a knowing tone,

"Yes, sweetheart, I meant you… now relax back and let me continue to take care of what is mine." I had to say his words definitely took hold and stayed with me, seeing as this hadn't been the first time he had declared such a thing. But my biggest question was the one I was most terrified of asking… *just how long would he want me for?*

"Eden." He said my name in reprimand, and not exactly wanting to go down that serious conversational road yet, I in turn quickly blurted out,

"I am a data analyst... or at least I was before... well, you know." I heard him sigh as if deciding whether or to let my thoughts go or not, when in the end I continued making the decision for him.

"I'm originally from Edenton, North Carolina but moved away when my mom died."

"Edenton?" he repeated, obviously not missing the significance.

"Yeah, my mom loved her town so much she named her daughter after it," I said on a nervous chuckle, especially when I had no choice but to be mesmerized by watching those strong hands of his start to soap up the cloth in front of me.

"A perfect name for you," he told me, forcing me to ask,

"Why's that?" At this he brought the cloth up to my neck and started to work his way down my body, answering me when he reached between my legs and what I was starting to think was one of his favourite places to touch.

"The origin of Eden in Hebrew means, place of pleasure," he hummed knowingly in my ear as he started to push the cloth through my folds, making me arch my back and moan at the contact.

"Gods but I love how responsive you are to my touch." I grinned and with my eyes still closed, I told him,

"I believe this time that response can be claimed by the cloth."

"Is that so?" he asked in a teasing tone, making me hum in return,

"Uh huh."

"Then fuck the cloth and fuck getting you clean!" he replied, quickly throwing it behind him and making it slap against the tiled wall. I shrieked in surprise as what came next was him tugging me around to face him and pulling me up against his body so he had full access to my lips, taking me in a kiss he seemed addicted to.

"Addictive is fucking right!" he growled down at me, before fisting my hair and using it to pull me back tighter against him after reading my thoughts yet again. But then something in me seemed to snap, like cutting some unsure little cord that had kept me tethered to that shy side of myself. I pulled back, ignoring his growl of disapproval so I could tell him,

"Yeah, well you're not the only one addicted!" Then I maneuvered myself so I could straddle his lap, keeping my weight on my knees either side of his thighs. Then, just as I was thanking some unknown bathroom designer that the bath was more than big enough for the both of us, I framed his face with one hand, tilting it back a little so I could kiss him. With my other hand, I reached back and the second I took hold of his hard length, I lined myself up enough so when I sat down, I could impale myself on his awaiting cock.

And this time…

It was his cries of pleasure that I consumed, with…

A brave girl's kiss.

CHAPTER 24
FRUSTRATIONS OF HUNGER

"You know I have a perfectly good set of legs," I commented on a giggle as Ward carried me from the bathroom now dressed in a fluffy white robe.

"Oh, but how could I forget, seeing as the memory of them wrapped around me is still featured firmly in my mind," he replied, making me blush as the same memory now started to replay in my own mind and well, for Ward this was like a double showing as he read my thoughts and chuckled.

"You're going to have to teach me how to stop you from reading my thoughts," I complained.

"Oh, am I now?" he answered in an unconvincing tone.

"Oh, come on, it's hardly fair," I grumbled again, making him grin, and damn him for how it made him even more handsome. Especially considering he now only wore a towel hanging deliciously low off his hips. But then I was half surprised he even bothered seeing as he was now walking me back to bed, and we both knew what was likely to happen there most definitely didn't need clothes. Although, after sex in the bath, this time bravely instigated by me, I had to wonder if giving my lady bits a break might not be a bad thing. Because let's just say that I was definitely feeling delectably used and abused down there, as every time I moved, I couldn't help but still feel the memory of him.

Christ, but even being slightly sore there was making me aroused and I had to wonder what this man was turning me into. Some kind of sex addict who now liked it rough and dominating. Because I loved it when he restrained me, collared me with his hand and forced orgasms out of me. Which quickly made me the kind of lover that cried out, not in horror but in pleasure, doing so with every bite of pain he gave me. And that's when I realized he had been right…

I would beg him for it.

"Your thoughts aren't helping here, sweetheart," he growled, making me smirk as he lowered me down on the bed. But before he could give me any space, I held him closer and told him,

"You're right, Ward… you reading my thoughts will be entertaining… *especially in public.*" At this he groaned, placing his forehead to my chest before muttering a comical,

"Fuck, I'm doomed." I chuckled at this, making him grin back up at me as if he liked the sound. Then I ran my fingers through his still damp hair and this had him growling for a different reason, now raising himself up above me so he could kiss me. Then I felt the hard tug of my robe's belt being pulled open, so I was back to being mostly naked against him.

My stomach chose that moment to make the loudest grumble that quickly made Ward freeze above me. Naturally I was mortified, and he knew it the second he pulled back. But then ignoring my now reddened face, he slowly looked down at my bare belly, one that I knew was a lot less squishy than it used to be. Which made me wonder when the last time I ate was and in all honestly, I couldn't remember. Most likely another pot of cheap noodles in some gas station but in reality, the days had long ago all started to merge into one. And as for the hunger, well that had been a feeling I had long ago grown used to.

Suddenly a deep and scary growl rippled from his chest above me, making me flinch this time. It was only when a burning pair of amber eyes came back up to look at me, did I press myself back into the bed.

"You don't know the last time you ate?" he asked in a deadly tone that again made me flinch, wishing there was now more space between us. Jesus, but he looked so angry I almost winced. So instantly I said the only thing I could think to calm him down,

"I'm sorry." At this, he shouted a curse, before hissing it again after first tearing his body off me,

"Fuck... *fuck!"* I swallowed hard and quickly reached for the sheet to cover up my nakedness, feeling ashamed and having to try and prevent my tears from overflowing.

"Gods, Eden!" he shouted after rubbing a frustrated hand at the back of his neck, making his biceps bulge seeing as he was still only wearing a towel around his hips.

"Please don't shout at me," I said in a quiet voice, I had always hated it when people did that. Of course, I shouted enough when the need called for it. But only when it was warranted, say like when waking up and finding myself cuffed to a bed. At this he looked at me and after only a second of watching as I wiped angrily at a falling tear, he released a heavy sigh. Then with a slump of his large shoulders he walked back over to me, sitting down on the bed side on so he could face me.

"Gods, Eden, but you're breaking my fucking heart here," he said softly, before grabbing me behind the neck and pulling me closer so he could place his forehead to mine. I had to say I was so shocked that I froze in his hold. I just couldn't believe how angry he had been, but then the second he saw how it affected me, I was amazed at how quick we was to comfort me.

"I'm sorry if I made you angry," I told him, making him pull back, and the look he gave me was shocked. Then he cupped my cheek and said my name in that lovely, heart melty way he usually did, before giving me oh so much more.

"Eden… sweetheart, I was not angry at you. Gods, but how could I ever be?"

"Then I don't understand why…" At this he placed his thumb over my lips, a pair that other than being kissed thoroughly, were no longer split or injured. Then he told me,

"I was angry at myself."

"Oh… but wait, why would you be angry at yourself?" At this he dropped his hand and instead of using it being gentle and tender with me, he used it to rake through his hair in a gesture anything but gentle. Then he got back to his feet and put space between us before storming over to the phone that was situated on a fancy sleek white desk.

"I want a selection of dishes from your room service menu to be sent to my room as soon as possible. Give me a selection of three from each course… a moment… Eden, what would you like to drink and do you have any food allergies I should know about?" I was still in so much shock it was only when he said my name again that I shook my head enough to respond.

"Erm, just a diet soda please and no, no allergies but anchovies are a hard limit for me." At this he smirked, and I felt the handsome grin even in my toes, for I loved that I had the ability to make him smile that way.

"A selection of diet sodas and not an anchovy in sight. Thank you," he said finishing the call, and I swear my mouth had started to water already at just the thought of what may come. Whatever it was, it was going to be real food and nothing from a packet or made from more E numbers than actual food.

It was only when I heard a chuckle, did I glance up to find Ward looking down at me tenderly.

"What?"

"Oh nothing… I just have a feeling someone is going to be putting themselves into a food coma before long." I grinned at this and just as my stomach rumbled, I patted my tummy over the sheet and said,

"And my empty belly will thank you immensely." At this he winked at me before he walked toward what I gathered was a walk-in closet. Something that was confirmed when he walked back out again wearing clothes, much to my disappointment.

Although, it also had to be said that Ward's casual look of worn blue jeans and a light gray tee was also droolworthy, as the material hugged his muscles in all the right places.

He soon sat down next to the bed, using the actual seat this time and sighed, as if this next conversation was one he didn't want to have. But then he also must have felt like he needed to, as it was clearly one we were going to have regardless. I knew this when he asked,

"I think now the time has come to tell me how this all started, sweetheart." I mirrored his sigh and tested him.

"And how do you know I didn't just do this to myself. You know, ruin myself with some, body rotting addiction and got myself into debt to keep it up?" At this he gave me a knowing look, giving me the type of answer I would have been a fool think of any other way than as a gift.

"Because it's you I face and even though I haven't known you long, I know enough to know that what you just described isn't you." I released a shuddered sigh and closed my eyes for a few seconds before telling him,

"Thank you, you don't know what that means to me because I swear during this whole ordeal, that's probably the first time I haven't been made to feel as though I deserved this or something."

"I find it hard to believe how anyone could blame you for anything, let alone the situation you found yourself in where it was bad enough to make you homeless." I swear this guy was making me melt yet again.

"And you know that all by just looking at me, do you?" I tested with a raised brow, yet still being sure to keep my tone light-hearted so as not to insult him. At this he chuckled, raised his hands in surrender and told me,

"So, I may be biased considering who you are to me." I started to shake my head, telling him without words that I was still far too confused about all that. Especially when not having the first clue as to what a Siren even was, let alone what one meant to him. But before I could voice all of this he continued.

"But Eden, even if you were the cutest fucking girl on the planet…" I gave him a disbelieving look and said,

"What, even in my many layers?"

"Too many fucking layers," he growled, and this time the sound made me chuckle.

"My point is, even from the first moment I saw you, standing by that roadside, something drew me in and it wasn't just a young girl in need of aid. I swear but I had never met anyone who took my breath away the way you did." At this my eyes grew wide and this time when I shook my head, it was in true disbelief.

"You don't believe me?" he guessed easily, making me look away because I couldn't bear disappointing him. Which was why what I did next was done so in a cowardly fashion, as I looked down at my hand and plucked nervously at the sheet. Jesus, but just what cotton thread were these, a gazillion? I heard his chuckle before I felt the bed dipping next to me. After this his hand came to my chin as he took hold and brought my face back around to face him.

"I will make sure they are in every bed you sleep in from now on if you like them that much, just say the word and they are yours in every home we own," he told me, and at this point my mouth hung open as though I no longer had the power to keep it closed.

"You're kidding... but of course you are... *right?"* I said on a nervous laugh.

"Do I look like the type of man to joke about something like this?" he replied sternly, making me gulp.

"No, you don't, and that's what's freaking me out," I replied honestly.

"I already told you that it is now my job to provide for you," he added, making suck in a quick breath before repeating his words,

"Your job?"

"My duty as your..." I stopped him at this with a quick shake of my head.

"Your duty... God, Ward, it's no one's job or duty to care for me, I am an adult for Christ sake and until all of this shit got dumped on my life, I was doing a pretty good job of it," I snapped, making him sigh.

"Eden, you are taking this all wrong..." I sliced a hand through the air at this and argued,

"No, I think you are. Look, I like you and I think evidence would show that it's a lot, like a Hell of a lot, considering we are having this conversation with me sitting in your bed naked, but..."

"But nothing!" he snapped back, this time as though this half-naked conversation was over... when it was far from it.

"*But*... I make my own way in life and I won't be like my

low life soul sucking brother!" I shouted back, emphasizing the 'but' he had interrupted first.

"Brother…" he muttered, but I ignored him as I continued on,

"I would never expect money from someone just because I'm in a relationship with them…"

"Eden." He said my name again but once more, I carried on.

"…Now, if you want to help me out by getting me back on my feet then that would be appreciated like you wouldn't believe, but it would only ever be as a loan…" At this he held up a hand,

"Eden, stop," he warned but I forced myself on, needing to get this all out.

"…And well, I won't ever say no to being protected like you did with… AH!" I shouted the second I suddenly felt my body being dragged under his, and soon his massive frame was caging me in from above. Then when I opened my mouth to complain about what he was doing, he quickly covered my mouth with his hand, holding all his weight up with one hand to the bed. I was so impressed by this I couldn't help but ask how long he could hold this pose for without even breaking a sweat or looking in the slightest bit strained.

"Sweetheart, you're cute as fuck but right now, I need you to do me a favor and stop talking… okay?" I nodded my head a few times, making him grin.

"Excellent… now I am going to take my hand away and you are going to be the good girl I know you can be for me and be quiet whilst I tell you exactly what is going to happen. Then you're going to take time to think about it and not argue… now, can you do that for me?" he asked, and I swallowed hard beneath his hand before nodding again, making his grin get bigger. After this he removed his hand and gave me a little more space, shifting his weight so it was once more between two hands. Hands that he had positioned either side of me, still keeping me contained.

"Now this low life soul sucking brother of yours, I'm gonna take a not so wild stab in the dark here and guess his name is Jimmy... correct?" I gave him a look of shock and was about to open my mouth to ask how he knew. However, after a single pointed look, one from what was clearly a man in pure Dom mode, I locked my lips shut and nodded a yes instead.

"Yeah, thought so... well that's disappointing as I gather I can't just kill him like I had planned?" At this my mouth opened and I frantically shook my head to tell him no. He sighed as if this truly frustrated him, making me realize that he hadn't been joking!

"Alright, I can see the panic building there so we will come back to that part." Oh Jesus, not something to look forward to, that was for damn sure!

"As for this fucking loan bullshit, I can tell you now, Eden, that shit is not going to fucking happen."

'But...' I mouthed, making him grant me another one of those 'you want to get punished?' looks and seeing how hot he was, then I was tempted to push it. However, I still wasn't brave enough, so I rolled my lips inwards, making him do a press up, lowing himself enough to kiss my cheek,

"My good girl learns quickly," he praised, making me squirm beneath him as again, arousal pooled between my legs.

"Now as to what will happen when we eventually leave this hotel. There will be no dating, no testing this out or boyfriend/girlfriend bullshit. I don't date, sweetheart... *I fucking claim.*" I sucked in an anxious breath but before I could worry about just how many 'Claimed' there had been before me, he carried on.

"Now, as for you, well you should know that you're not

231

only my first but more importantly you're *my only*. Which means what is mine is now yours, that is not up for discussion and definitely not up for fucking argument." Again, I was in total shock, thinking this guy was most definitely crazy, and it was a good job I couldn't speak as I was speechless anyway!

"Now, I get that this is a lot to digest, which is why you can take all the time you want, but I am just telling you now that no matter how much time it does take, it won't change the outcome." I started to shake my head at this, which he frowned at before continuing to make his insane point.

"Which means that the quicker you understand this, the better, so we don't drag this shit out." I shook my head again, again telling him no, something he this time grinned at.

"Fucking cute... now I get you're independent, baby, I really do, but the thing you have to understand is that what's happening now is gonna change that mindset, and here's why..." I mouthed,

'Oh God, there is more.' At this he chuckled and mouthed back,

'Fucking cute,' before he continued to voice his commanding words that were continuing to freak me the fuck out!

"I think you get that I'm rich, as I noticed you looking at the car, baby, and know you knew what that meant. Now this is not me bragging, only a way for me to inform you that it now means you're rich too. Which also means all the high thread cotton sheets you want and more importantly, about as far from living in your fucking car as you can get." I started to shake my head in earnest now, telling him without words I wasn't comfortable with any of this!

"It's happening, Eden, as I won't see my girl without, won't see my claimed without and absolutely refuse to see my Chosen Siren without anything but the best. For if I ever do, it will cut me deep and to the core. I won't like it and that shit will make me angry." At this I flinched back, and he frowned telling me,

"But you have to know that no matter how angry I get, that temper will only ever be aimed at you in the form of words, letting you know I'm pissed at you but that is it, Eden. That's as far as it ever goes, so don't ever begin to fucking fear that I would hurt you as I would rather cut off my own fucking hand than lay it on you in anger!" At this I mouthed one word,

'Punishment?' Now this was when he really smiled.

"When you get punished, sweetheart, trust me, you will do so screaming and begging but never in fear or pain, not unless it's the type of pain that's adding to your pleasure… pleasure that you have only had but a mere taste of." This time, instead of shaking my head, I was shuddering in the cage his intimidating frame held above me.

"Now, I want your submission, Eden, this is true, I will even fucking crave it and continue to do anything in my power to get it and keep it. And when I get it, well fuck me, my girl, the power you hold over me will be like no other." My eyes grew wide at this discovery, surprised that he would be so honest in admitting this exchange of power.

"Like now, it makes me want to worship at your feet for being such a good girl for me. But none of that means you are beneath me. You are not my slave, Eden, and nor are you my submissive in everyday life. You are my equal and always will be."

'I am?' I mouthed. He nodded once and continued to explain the dynamics of what he expected in our relationship.

"You stand by my side and get to make decisions. That being said, if any of those decision means it affects you in a way I don't like, then they won't get made… now, is that understood?" After all of this, I remained frozen as I let this bombshell named Ward crash over me and basically continue to blow my mind. But as for this delivery of life changing information, he simply grinned and lowered himself enough to whisper against my ear,

"It's easy, Eden, you've just got to nod your head for me, baby." At this I released a big sigh and braved shaking my head, telling him no. But instead of getting angry or upset, he simply grinned against the sensitive skin under my ear and then whispered,

"Then let the battle begin, for when I win... my victory will be all the sweeter... especially when..."

"You're screaming your Master's name."

CHAPTER 25
FOOD GLORIOUS FOOD
WARD

G ods, but I was losing my ever-loving vengeful mind! But then, could I really be surprised? I hardly doubted that when being gifted with a Siren by the Fates themselves, it was going to be an emotionally smooth ride. Fuck, but half of me wanted to chain her to my bed and keep here there with my cock firmly seated inside her. And well, as for the other half, that was simply to worship at her feet, surrendering myself to her as her slave. I was completely addicted and totally unashamed to admit it!

However, when it came to trying to get her to understand that I would be taking care of her from here on in, well I admit intimidation had been the main state of play. Because my sweet little submissive needed to learn what being with a man like me truly meant—quickly. Of course, I had told her that I would allow her time to process this, something she had been doing a great deal of since my last conversation with her. But this also didn't mean that I wouldn't do everything in my power to speed up the process.

Because I was eager to move past this stage and onto more important matters, like getting her on my private jet and back to where I now considered 'our' home. However, all I needed to do was convince her of this fact and we could be on our merry fucking way, starting our new lives together. Although, that wasn't to say that this reluctant state of mind of hers was the only thorn in my side, as I still had some loose ends to cut. And when I say loose ends, what I actually meant was, I still had...

People left to kill.

Now, as for the fuck wit, low life, soul sucking brother of hers, this would be a problem, as I saw her reaction when I spoke of killing him. Knowing now that this might be a hard limit for her, I would have to tread carefully in this regard. As for Gomez, well that fucker was mine to do with whatever I pleased. And what pleased me was to see that poor excuse for a gangster hanged by his own entrails. Or perhaps, I would simply rip out his own heart and place it in his hands, so that he could look down at his own blood-pumping ticking clock of death.

Yes, that sounded far more satisfying. And well, speaking of satisfying...

"Oh my God, this is soooo good!" Eden's voice brought me out of my vengeful and murderous thoughts, making me grin at her as it was clear she was enjoying her meals. Gods, but earlier I had needed to leave the room, as just watching her eat made me want to take her again, getting addicted to that hot little body of hers. One I wanted to feed as much as was needed, for it was clear she had lost weight. Her thoughts had told me as much.

I had growled and punched one of the mirrors just thinking about her sleeping in that fucking cold car whilst her stomach rumbled with hunger! But then I had wanted to kick my own ass the second I heard it growling and realized my vital mistake.

In truth, I had never had to care for a human before and my kind didn't have to eat as frequently as a mortal body did. But then, when her thoughts gave way to the truth of her prior situation, silently saying that she had been used to the feeling of hunger... well, then fuck, but I had wanted to fucking howl. A roar of pain and anger that resonated deep down within my darkness.

He was, after all, as addicted as I and just as obsessed.

She was ours.

However, that didn't mean we knew what we were doing here as it was clear my outburst had scared her, and she broke my heart when asking me not to shout at her. But then that crack in my dark armor evaporated to vapor when she said she was sorry. Gods, but I nearly crumbled at her feet and begged for her forgiveness. She was the sweetest soul I had ever come across and it was making me fucking crazy!

I didn't know how to deal with half the emotions she was dredging to the surface belonging to the shore of uncharted waters. Feelings I'd never experienced before and everything seemed raw, intense and ten times stronger than what they should do.

I felt... *sensitive.*

Fuck!

But what was to become of me?! Uncertainty was not exactly a feeling I had been used to before this day, but it was there now all the same. Gods in Heaven, but it was starting to feel like a fucking constant presence, as I questioned everything I did in regard to her. Was I being too rough, was I pushing too hard, or frightening her with my intensity? Of course, being able to read most of her thoughts helped in this regard, but then it made me wonder about the ones I missed. *What if they had been the most important?*

What if I was hurting her mind?

My only consolation in this was that I at least knew how she felt about me, both physically and mentally, for I knew my kindness was playing a big part when forming her attachment to me. To begin with, she kept questioning if I were real and this had nothing to do with the elephant in the room, which was of course, the darkness in me and who I was in my world. Something she seemed almost afraid of asking and as of yet, we were still to have that conversation. But then, since she decided to push my limits and run from me, there had been little time once she had awoken.

I also understood her dismay at waking to find herself shackled to my hotel bed and with my blood being pumped into her. Although even I had to admit being surprised at my own reaction to her bite of anger and seeing the way she had openly challenged me. Her fiery spirit was in there, despite obviously being a natural submissive. And seeing my reaction to it was one of interest, instead of the disdain I would have thought to find, then it made me realize how wrong I had been. My belief that I had once wanted a Siren to submissively stand by my side now just felt wrong. Which was why from that point on I realized I wanted her to challenge me. I would only take pleasure in her teasing me, pushing me and eventually giving me an excuse to punish her sexually.

It… well… *excited me*.

Something I will admit to not experiencing before, as fucking someone had only ever been a basic need for sexual release. But with Eden, then fuck me it had been so much more! It had been like experiencing it all anew for the first time. To engage in the act feeling solely connected to that one person had a power of the likes I had never experienced before. Every feeling was amplified to the point of pure rapture. A single touch became electric, as if there was now some sexual current running through my ancient veins. A pleasured look became the most beautiful sight, one rivalling all those before it that these ancient eyes had seen. The taste of her gasp against my kiss had been the greatest thing to pass through my lips during all my ancient lifetimes combined.

She had quickly become my everything, and I found myself terrified that someone would try and take her from me. Try to snatch this fated perfection from I, the keeper of her soul. For I had hopes of soon adding to the title as being the keeper of her heart also. But for now, well the fear of not getting that chance was growing the longer we were together. Making me question if this would be how the King of Kings would feel when meeting his own Chosen One?

Would he be equally as terrified?

For as long as I'd lived in this world, I had known Dominic Draven, and been a subject under his rule, doing so for all of his many names before this one. I had respected him and followed him with the kind of loyalty I would gladly sacrifice my own life for. But now? Well, I knew that my loyalty would first and foremost belong to that of my fated Siren. So, I had to question what of the King's loyalty to his people when his time came? What of his fear? Something he was known famously for not having.

Fear and loyalty that no doubt would soon both belong to another, if his reaction to that little blonde mortal in his club was anything to go by.

"I can't believe you ordered me so much food! Why not pull up a chair and help me, or I will feel so guilty wasting it all." Eden's sweet voice brought me out of my thoughts after entering back in the room, having long ago healed the cuts from my knuckles after first pulling pieces of the mirror from my flesh.

"Eat until your belly is full and don't fret about the rest," I told her with a wave of my hand, telling her I cared little about the guilt she spoke of.

"But what about...?" This was the point when I thought it

best to interrupt her, doing so by taking hold of her chin and using pressure there, so as to tip her face back up to meet my own.

"The only guilt I feel is unknowingly making you wait for it," I told her, making her frown in that adorable way of hers.

"I have a voice, Ward." She pouted, making me grin down at her.

"That you do… and you sing with it so beautifully for me when I am claiming you with my cock," I told her with a wink, excited for the reply I knew was coming. And she didn't disappoint when she gasped, giving me the opening I had also been expecting, tasting for myself the chocolate cake she had been teasing me with when humming her pleasure.

"Mmm, dessert never tasted so good," I told her when pulling back and licking my lips, making her blush. And therefore I accomplished easily what I intended.

I fucking loved her shyness.

Although I knew with time, it wouldn't last, so I vowed I would at least enjoy this part of her until such times changed. Because I wanted them to change. I wanted her to feel comfortable with me like she never would with another. I didn't want her to shy away from my crude lustful words forever but take them as a challenge… one I would always win when getting my way with her. I wanted her to revel in my compliments and accept them gracefully and with confidence. Something I knew she was lacking in, thanks to my insight of her thoughts. I wanted her to believe my words when I told her she was a fucking Goddess! I wanted her to own them and keep them within her forever, as I would never stop saying such things.

But most of all, I wanted her to have confidence when it came to touching me. To not question her desires to do so and feel as free to my body as I felt toward hers, as I was as much hers as she was mine. And well, considering how much her touch had affected me, when it finally had happened and due to some prompting on my part, it had been unlike anything else I had ever experienced. In short, it meant that I wanted her fucking hands all over me and exploring every inch of me should she so desire... and I hoped that she did, as her touch had felt like some mind-fucking drug!

Just like kissing her did.

Fucking addictive wasn't strong enough a word.

But then she replied, and I swear I nearly swallowed my own tongue for she was continually shocking the shit out of me, making me wonder if her shyness was going to live hand in hand with the fire she gave me.

"Then clearly, you haven't tasted everything." After this she looked down at herself to where she was now purposely spreading her legs. This created a delicious looking sight after her lascivious actions made her robe split and part like a curtain to the opening act. A show I very much intended to enjoy being a part of, for I looked back at her with open surprise, making her do the unbelievable. She winked at me and then gave me an order, as if I was the slave this time and by the Gods, for the first time in my life, I fucking wanted to be!

"Well, what are you waiting for, Angel..."

"On your knees, Handsome."

CHAPTER 26
CLAIMING MY LUCK

I swear I dropped to my knees as though she had the power of the Gods and just clicked her fucking fingers!

'Oh wow, I didn't expect him to... oh fuck!' Her thoughts spoke to me and ended just as quickly, doing so on a cry of pleasure as I gripped her behind the knees and spread her wider before doing as she commanded. And she was right.

I hadn't tasted everything.

It was like drinking from Heaven's cup after stealing a barrel of Bacchus's finest, who was also known as the God of wine and ecstasy! It was quickly driving me wild! Just one look up at her as she let her head fall back, gasping at the ceiling, had me close to fucking coming in my jeans like some adolescent teen. The way she gripped onto the armrests as if they would save her from my onslaught, for I wasn't as slow or teasing as I could have been. That's not to say that I wouldn't have liked to have been, but in truth, I was fucking lost the second she told me to get on my knees!

I was making a Gods be damned meal of her, I knew this! Because despite her small victory of being in charge, it was lost the moment I took over in all else, making her scream out her release after only a minute, no more. But I was far from done with her, as the second I felt her jerking out her release, I quickly thrust two fingers up inside her, making her scream harder as her soft heated flesh quivered around my intrusion.

Then, the second she started to try and close her shuddering legs, I snarled at her flesh, biting her inner thigh in warning to back off and leave me to my pleasure. She cried out again and spread her legs for me, making me kiss her to silently praise her for giving me what I demanded. After this I went back to my newly discovered craving, and this time had more of her to quench my thirst, as I lapped up her recent release.

Fuck me, but it was,

"Fucking delicious!" I snarled against her swollen little clit before taking it between my teeth and rolling it around, making her cry out and this time her hands went to my head. I grinned the second I felt her fingers curl into fists in my hair, and when she tugged I went fucking crazy!

"Mine!" I growled before sucking her back into my mouth like a mad man and with each small bite of pain she took for me, I felt my own pleasure rising.

"Ward, Ward... Oh God, Ward please... you have to stop, you have to before I... oh God... Fuck, fuck, fuck, fuck... AHHHH FUCK!" She screamed as she came again and this time, I knew it was much harder than the first. She started to pull on my hair with earnest, and I growled as I fucked her with my fingers through the orgasm I was still forcing from her.

Gods, nothing had been fucking hotter!

But it was time to show her who was in charge, so after ripping the rest of her robe down her arms, I growled,

"Hold on, sweetheart," before gripping her hips and lifting her up, keeping her spread open wide to my face as I rose to my feet. This left her naked in the air, quickly making her cry out in fright,

"Fuck! Ward, what are you...!?" She screamed again, making me chuckle against her soaked folds, dripping down into my grin. She was high above me as I walked her to the bed, appreciating the high ceilings one would expect from the most expensive penthouse suites a fuck load of money bought you. Then, as we neared the bed, I lowered her down before letting her drop without too much cause for worry, making her scream all the same. Then I let her bounce the once as I tore at my jeans, freeing my straining cock before was right back to devouring her.

"No Ward! I can't... nnot again! Please I... Ohhhh God yessss!" She ended this plea on a moan as I slowed my brutal tongue and this time, the pleasure I brought her was of a tender kind. This was before I rose up above her and as she was still coming down from the euphoric high, I thrust up inside her and cried out at the fucking bliss of it all.

Gods, but she was utterly made for me... *Every. Fucking. Inch!*

I didn't have to be a betting man to know this wasn't going to last long. Not after such a feast... Speaking of feasts, there was one last thing left for me to do to complete the claim, and it started to happen even before I could think to stop it. I was too close to the edge of darkness and seconds from bursting inside her, flooding her with my seed, when I heard her say my name,

"Ward?"

"I'm sorry, I can't wait my love... can't fucking wait any longer, my darkness... it... it... *it won't let me!"* I admitted the second it burst through and changed me into my true self. This meant that the first of her screams were shamefully ones that were terrified as my fangs extended and I forced her head to the side. Then, after the black soul of my Angel kissed its way up her neck, marveling in its fated heavenly prize, I sank my fangs into her flesh and drank straight from the source of that Heaven.

This was when her screams soon became ones of uncontrollable ecstasy, as I fucked both my essence into her and sucked her own straight out from her. There had not been a single, more erotic moment in my life than there was in this fated exchange that marked her as mine, once and for all. By the Gods, but if I had thought her release had tasted like wine from Heavenly Gods' cup, then her blood felt as though I was drinking from the powerful rivers in Hell, for it was just as addictive!

Thankfully she wasn't fighting me, nor was she trying to get away, for that would have enraged my darkness. No, instead her hold on me intensified and it made me wonder if she knew what she was doing. Did she know that she was clinging onto the part of me she was afraid of? Did she know that it was only the start of both our dark addictions and that her actions spoke only of craving me, as I craved her?

This was one time her jumbled thoughts weren't clear enough to read, as euphoria clouded her mind in nothing but a blissful fog. But then I knew what was coming as I felt her fingers loosen their hold on my flesh, where her little human nails had pierced the skin on my back. They slipped from my muscles and I felt her go limp beneath me, making me release her as she was seconds from passing out... again.

I quickly pulled my fangs from her delicate flesh, and sealed the wound, lapping up the last of any blood that remained on her lightly freckled skin.

"Fuck!" I hissed when she didn't move through any of this. However, before I could panic, I was surprised yet again when I felt her little hand come to my cheek, before patting me twice and muttering,

"Not yet, but give me an hour, Angel." Then her hand slipped and seconds later I was holding myself above her, with my mouth hanging opening in shock as she was...

Snoring!

I couldn't help it, but I chuckled quietly to myself before shaking my head, as it was clear the firsts in this relationship just kept coming. After this I let my forehead fall to the pillow next to her and cursed happily into the material.

"Fucking lost, Ward... *lost to this love.*"

After this I regrettably removed my still hard cock from her dripping core, making her moan in her sleep, and grinning because of it. I knew I had taken her again too rough too soon, especially since the last time. But at least I knew she had enough of my blood still left in her system that she would heal quickly. This meant she would wake and not find herself too sore as, yes, I was enough of a sadist to want her to feel me there even when I wasn't, but I wasn't bastard enough to want her in pain. Tender yes, pain... *fuck no.*

After this I pulled away, sitting back on my knees above her, just staring at the beauty that was my woman looking delectably fucked. I couldn't get the fucking stupid grin of satisfaction off my face.

Gods, but she had been so perfect and just continued to be so, no matter what I did. She was continually surprising me and for the first time, I felt a kind of lightness in my chest I couldn't fully understand yet.

I had never spent time looking down at a lover sleeping before but now... well, *I was transfixed.* My darkness inside me rumbled in contentment and knowing that I had to do my duty in caring for her, I couldn't help but grin sadistically knowing what I would leave her with. So, I reached down to my still dripping cock and swiped a bead of cum from the end with the pad of my thumb. Then, after leaning down over her, I kissed her cheek, enough to get her to stir, before smearing my dripping thumb across the stem of her lips, making them open enough for me. Then like some sick bastard, I quickly slipped it between her wet lips, leaving her with her own taste of me to savor.

I then gave her space, biting my own fucking lip the second I watched like a fucking freak as she licked her lips and swallowed that small piece of me down, getting a satisfaction from it. I even closed my eyes, looked up at the ceiling and shuddered as my darkness vibrated its approval inside me like a fucking cat purring.

"Ours," I growled like a Demon, quietly allowing him to push through, making me agree as I climbed off the bed and made my way into the bathroom.

"That she is, my friend… *that she fucking is.*"

Moments later, I was dressed and had finished cleaning our girl, despite being almost pained to do so. Yet I ignored my own wishes, knowing it would make her more comfortable for the night ahead, as she had slept most of the day away already and the sun had long ago set. I then covered her up, being careful not to wake her after first shifting her body further up the bed so her head was more on a pillow. Then I kissed her forehead tenderly before leaving her, as Deke was waiting to speak to me.

So, I left the suite, knowing I wouldn't be long and already feeling the loss of separation between us. It may sound pathetic but after sealing our bond by exchanging blood, then I knew the feeling would only grow stronger. This until the day that she finally was to gain her own powers as a Siren. But until then, the obsession would not leave me, strengthening to the point of near madness. It would be this way until my darkness knew she was capable of taking care of her own fated mortal body that she had been born into. Meaning that I would become near unbearable now I knew that every fiber in my being would need to keep her safe. A need that would intensify and push at me to exchange our blood each day to keep that essence topped up in her body.

"You do realize how hard it is to try and control the minds of an entire floor of humans, just so they don't call the cops with concerns of murder being committed above them, don't you?" This was Deke's first comment, making me smirk.

"And my girl would most certainly thank you for it, I am sure."

"Right... passed out, is she?"

"Yes, as a matter of fact she is, and thankfully not from fear at seeing me having to kill a load of mortals in uniform just for the offence of seeing her naked," I replied, making Deke laugh before muttering,

"Yeah, that would do it, and no doubt become a cock blocker for the future if ever I heard of one." I scoffed at this knowing that it was most likely true, as mass slaughter would definitely be a mood killer for a pure soul like Eden's. Besides, I didn't want her to think of me as a monster, but as we were already on the subject of murder...

"Did you get me what I seek?" At this my second in command smirked and told me,

"I did, and am just sorry that I will most likely be on babysitting Siren duty and miss out on all the fun."

"Then take solace in knowing that I doubt my darkness would have allowed you the pleasure, as this time, Vengeance is mine and mine alone." At this Deke looked disappointed and muttered,

"Always the lucky bastard." I chuckled and slapped him on his back before telling him,

"That may be, but just think of how many more of our kind you will have to play with now their master is off the board and taken by his queen." He scoffed at this and agreed.

"I guess there is that, although I am not sure offering up

your used seconds is what I would class as a consolation prize, but it would be fun showing up your failings in the bedroom," he teased as any friend would. I laughed and said,

"Coming from the man who just complained at having to control the minds of an entire hotel floor… good luck with that, Dickhead." He was the one to chuckle this time.

"Now, give me further good fortune and tell me I have someone close by to kill." At this my second's grin grew into one belonging to a sadist, just like me, and with glowing eyes, told me,

"Indeed, you do." I felt my darkness start to take over my host as excitement hummed beneath my human flesh, morphing it into something mortals would call unnatural. I added to the look of a crazed supernatural fucker who wanted revenge, when my darkness answered him. Doing so now as I looked back at my door, where a sleeping beauty rested away from her beast.

"Fucking lucky indeed."

CHAPTER 27
ROTTEN

"Um, well I have to give it to this Gomez, he's fucking inventive," I commented dryly into my cell phone to Deke, who had given me the address I needed. Hence why I now found myself in Southwest Brooklyn, in an industrial development that looked about as developed as Chernobyl.

But then again, it was a shithole for good reason and 258, 41st Street was just a front.

"And lucrative, as it's a cleaner way of getting his drugs to the runners." I had to agree, as I hadn't expected to be sitting on the roof of the tallest brick building on the street, now looking down at a food packaging factory. So, once I assessed it as being the right place, I moved closer, releasing my wings long enough to fly me down to the roof so I could get sight of the inside, thanks to the dirty skylights.

But after watching this hive of worker bees fill boxes full of fresh produce for thirty minutes, I knew what his game was. This then made me wonder how many of these fools knew they worked for a scumbag like Gomez, and that this was just a front for the drug cartel as a way to shift drugs without the DEA finding out. I would say all of them, considering the amount of security guards that were all carrying far more weapons than were needed to guard fucking food! But then I watched as some boxes were labelled differently and with my heightened sight, it looked like logos for food trucks.

"Perhaps not," I commented to Deke, who I had called once I was in position.

"What do you mean?"

"I am not sure he even uses drug runners. Gomez obviously isn't as old school as we first thought."

"Gotta give me more than that here, Ward," he replied, making me grin as I enjoyed frustrating him, poking at his own darkness.

"It looks as though he is using this food distribution plant as a way to send his drugs to food trucks, where his clientele obviously buy more than just a burger," I told him, making Deke hiss,

"That clever little fucker!" I had to agree, as it was the perfect front for getting his drugs around the country, but how none of this had ever led back to him yet, only meant one thing.

"That and the use of dirty cops," I told him, making Deke agree.

"That's a given considering he would need them for this to continue to go by unnoticed."

"Either way, check with our connections to see if the DEA have any wind of this operation," I told him, as the last thing I needed was fucking heat from the cops when I burned this entire fucking operation to the ground. But that wasn't the only reason, as I had a sneaky suspicion that wouldn't leave me.

"Why, what you thinking?" he asked, making me snarl my reply with only one name,

"Jimmy."

"Ah." I narrowed my gaze on the sight below, weighing up my options and essentially deciding if there were any clean souls down there that were worth redemption or letting escape my wrath.

"I will look into it but until then, what are you planning?" I grinned at this before answering,

"Time to eradicate some rotten food." Deke chuckled and told me,

"Damn and here I was thinking you were going to use a cheesy line, like time to take out the trash."

"You watch too many damn movies, Deke."

"Yeah, well you fucked up, as it would have been perfect timing," he replied, making me shake my head at him, despite him being unable to see this.

"Well, lucky for me I am working solo on this and therefore spared the shit one-liners from my asshole friend." He chuckled at this and said,

"Then I will let you go and have all the fun."

"That I will, my friend, but before you go, what of my Siren?" I couldn't help but ask, making him scoff,

"Sleeping so soundly that I almost feel sorry for you." I frowned before asking,

"And why is that?" At this I heard the grin in his reply,

"Because you're facing an eternity of peaceful nights shattered, my asshole friend," he replied, throwing back my own insult.

"How so?" I asked, of course, taking the bait.

"She snores like a fucking freight train, Ward." At this I threw my head back and laughed, continuing to do so even after he had disconnected the call. Suddenly my Vengeance was something I was eager to dish out quicker than usual, as all I wanted now was to be back to her so I could discover for

253

myself if Deke exaggerated or not. Either way, I bet she was still fucking cute!

Which meant that it was time to get this done. I watched as deliveries came rolling in, as even at this time of night, nothing would have looked amiss. Truckers usually drove nights and food plants like this one would continue to run 24 hours a day. Like I had said, it was the perfect drug front, seeing as produce was imported in from all over the world, which I suspected was how they got their drugs in the first place.

Now it was obvious I had just found their means of distribution, but I wouldn't stop until I found every aspect of Gomez's operation. Which meant that this was only the first place on what would no doubt be a very long list. I would have to hit where they cut their drugs and kill their cooks. I would then take out where they laundered their money, find any stash they had before burning it all to the fucking ground, just like any other business he owned. I would take everything from him and cut off any means for him ever making money again. This all before cutting the head from a defeated, desperate snake.

Because just outright killing him was far too easy and far too quick for my liking. He had taken everything from Eden and for that, he needed to know what it felt like to endure the same fate. Now, as for ordering the hit on my Siren, well for that, I would succeed where he had failed. Gomez would die, but not before I had extracted the full force of my revenge.

Starting with this part of his operation.

Thankfully for me, he had set up shop in New York city, which meant my stay in Portland would have to last a little longer than I first expected. As for Gomez himself, he was comfortably situated in some Upper East Side mansion that was said to be heavily fortified. I had grinned at the information, for I always did enjoy a challenge and liked my kills to be less easy. It made the hunt more enjoyable that way.

But this all meant that it had been a two-hour helicopter ride to get to where I needed to be, instead of the five-hour drive it would have taken me. Speaking of which, I eyed my entrance and dropped down from the rooftop, allowing my darkness to caress the mortal realm with its presence. Thus creating wings so it slowed my descent and placed me in the shadows of where I needed to be. Then, as the delivery truck stopped by the loading bay, I waited for the doors to open before I made my move.

I let my other form take hold and used my armored talons to aid me in destroying the lock before slipping inside. Thankfully, I had chosen one ready to be loaded so it was empty inside and ready for its next cargo. I had watched long enough to know the routine of the guards, seeing that whenever a delivery came or left, their involvement was to make sure this ran smoothly.

Not tonight, fuckers, I thought with a sadistic grin, listening out for the signs that told me I was only seconds from them opening the doors. I let the rest of my avenging Angel come to the surface, welcoming it as it washed over my mortal host, one I'd had for thousands of years now. It was literally my second skin for I had been first born in Heaven and well, as for now, I was about as far away from being Heavenly as you could get!

Something my enemies were about to find out.

I took a few measured steps backward, at the same time allowing my dark essence to seep from my back and shroud me in shadowed oblivion. I felt the power humming beneath my mortal flesh as excitement grew, just like it always did when I had justice to deliver.

"Hey, what the fuck happened here?" I heard from the other side, and grinned to myself knowing he was about to question a lot more than some broken fucking lock.

"Let's play," I whispered to the brother of my soul and who was my other self, just as the doors opened.

"I don't fucking know but it wasn't like that the last time I stopped," the driver said as light infiltrated the parts of the truck I didn't command.

"Well, I don't know how you can pick up a load... wait, what the fuck is that?" the guard said, now squinting inside before grabbing his flashlight and shining it my way. However, I made the bulb smash before it landed on me, ending my fun, as I so did love to terrify those that deserved it. In truth, it was what I fed from and right now, I knew I was about to get my dark fill.

And as the saying goes, it was the main reason I didn't just go in there all guns blazing. Because really, where was the fun in that and... *I was so very hungry for fear.*

"Fucking thing!" the guard said, hitting the now useless flashlight a few times as if this would help.

"Hey, what is that?!" the driver shouted, making my darkness shiver in anticipation.

"What you talking about?"

"I swear I saw something fucking move in there!" the driver complained, making me grin this time.

"Fuck me, Chuck, tell me you didn't pick up some fucking immigrant!"

"I have just dropped off in Chicago, asswipe, not fucking Mexico!" he complained as they both stepped inside.

"Yeah, whatever... look, whoever the fuck is in there, you'd better get your ass out here or I swear to fucking Christ, I am gonna beat your dumb ass until you will be begging for a fucking bullet!" the guard said as he pulled his gun from its holster and continued inside getting closer, until suddenly I made my move.

"AHHH!" he screamed the second my darkness roared silently out from the shadows, making it look as if he was being swallowed whole by a phantom. Then I allowed that dark side of myself to pin him against the side of the truck and after the driver ran off screaming, I walked through the fog created, and I told him,

"Christ can't help you here, but please… *feel free to pray, won't you.*" Then he continued to scream when he took in my Demonic looking form, no doubt asking himself if the Devil himself had come to collect his tainted soul. Because I knew instantly from feeding if a soul was pure or not. I knew the second I tasted its addictive evil essence if I was needed to punish him for his twisted sins.

For I couldn't punish those who did not deserve it. I was here to do the work of the Gods and unless there was a rotted soul worth extracting vengeance on, then I was forbidden to kill. I was a Reaper's King in my own right for I worked for both sides. It was my gift as much as it was my punishment.

I was an Angel of Death after all and well, what was the point of such a name unless I was able to rid the world of its sickness of evil. Like this shit-stain whose bones I had already started breaking, doing so for beating on his kids as seeing such was my curse. So, I broke the same ones he had broken on his sons, starting with his ribs, nose, moving to his limbs, soon getting drunk on that fear and pain like sipping down the finest cognac. After this I let his broken body slump down making him whimper in agony,

"W-w-why?" I grinned down at him and lowered myself to a bent knee, before raising his blood-soaked head up with the deadly point of my talon.

"Because, Richard MacGregor, your sins against your kin have made your soul foul to its core and I am here to cleanse the world of *its rot!*" I snarled this last part before slitting his throat and taking but a second to soak in yet another soul that fed my reason for being.

Of course, this moment was stolen from me the second a

wave of bullets erupted all around me. But it was no matter, for as I was bombarded with one bad deed after another, I grinned inhumanly as sin surrounded me and made this Angel of Death crave only one thing…

Vengeance and fear.

CHAPTER 28
GLUTTONOUS

After I left the broken pieces of the child beater on the floor, I pulled my mortal form back from the wall of darkness my other side had kept us both in. Then I walked casually from the lorry, stepping onto the loading bay now surrounded by bad guys and their guns.

"So, who here is going to tell me where I can find Jimmy Valentino?" I asked, speaking of Eden's fuck-up of a brother and the last piece of shit puzzle I didn't yet know where to look for. At this, all their guns clicked at the ready for firing, giving me my echoed answer.

"No one?" I sighed, cracking my knuckles and telling them before the first gun went off,

"Excellent." I moved with such speed they could barely trail me with their automatic weapons, as I snapped bone after bone. Meaning that within five seconds, all guns were now on the floor and there were seven men all clutching their broken wrists to their chests, crying out in pain. I had to say, the room quickly filled with the addictive taste of fear, and I sucked it back as if I was sitting and drinking at some hotel bar.

Of course, it also helped when the rest of the workers

started to run screaming from the building the moment they heard gunfire, as I suspected they would. I swear it was enough that I wouldn't need to feed for months, for the energy surge was like having a solar panel strapped to my chest being charged by the sun only a mile away. It swept over me in a wave, and I couldn't help but shudder as I absorbed every single cry, pleading for life.

But then, my intentions weren't just to merely kill every mortal here, only those who deserved it. And despite there being plenty with a rotten soul still left in the building, there were equally just as many of those that were merely trying to earn a living. Those who didn't fully understand what this factory truly was at its sinful core. Which meant that when I burned this place to the ground, innocent lives wouldn't become collateral damage.

After all, I wasn't completely heartless, I thought with a sinister grin, before stepping on one of the guard's hands as he tried to reach for his gun again, this time breaking six more bones to match that of his wrist.

"Now, let's try this a different way…" I started to say as I forced each of the seven men to their knees before me with just a thought.

"For the ones who give me the information I require, I in turn will promise not to break their legs, which means that when I set this whole fucking place on fire…" I paused, grabbing one by the hair and wrenching his head back so I could snarl down in a menacing tone,

"…*they can run from the flames.*" After this, well I almost smirked as I couldn't get any of them to shut the fuck up, finding out everything I asked, which included where they suspected Jimmy was hiding out. Of course, most of the information I knew already, as Deke was nothing if not thorough.

However, what I hadn't known was that Gomez had a favourite mistress. One that he used to meet every Friday night at an underground sex club in the city. I also hadn't known that Jimmy also used to date one of the waitresses there, and if he wasn't at his usual haunts, then if anyone knew where he was, she would.

"Very well, if that's everything, then off you go, cretins... NOW!" I roared, getting them into action and making them go scrambling off, scurrying like crabs upturned from a bucket. But then I got a distasteful whiff of a particular sin and grabbed one of the guards by the back of the collar, restraining him back.

"All except you!" I told him, making him yell out,

"But you said we could leave!" I grinned down at him before tossing him back through the factory, making him land on his back.

"That I did, but here's the thing, Johnathan Parker... *I don't make deals with rapists,*" I said, letting my eyes change before the rest of my dark side followed, making him scream at the sight of me.

"No! FUCK! What the fuck are you?! NO! Please!" he shouted as he tried to outrun me through all the workstations filled with boxes of food.

"Tell me, Johnathan, did they beg the same as you do now when you took them?"

"I...I... don't know what you're fucking talking about, man!" he argued.

"Tut, tut, and the sins just keep coming," I told him with a shake of my head, before he ran through a curtain of thick plastic, entering a cold food storage room. I had to say, I was enjoying this cat and mouse we played, as I rarely had the chance to play with my food. I even gave him a few seconds head start to make it more fun. This allowed him to watch in fear as my dark figure was outlined against the clear plastic. I knew I looked frightening.

Foolish little mortal, did he not know that I could hear his heart beating wildly and his breath shallow and labored? Although, to give him his due, I hadn't expected him to try and fight me as soon as I got near to the stack of boxes he was hiding behind. However, I grabbed the crowbar he had raised above his head ready to try and hit me with, snatching it and bending it as easily as if it had been made of rubber.

"Tell me, Johnathan, did they scream in fear as you do now, when you hurt them?" I asked, making him take a step back and shout,

"I haven't screamed yet you fucker... AAAAHHHH!" He ended this on a scream so piercing it would have hurt my mortal ears. This was after I grabbed him by the neck and was now cutting my talons into his flesh from the strangled hold. Then I lifted him up to eye level and asked him one last thing,

"Tell me, Johnathan... did you get off on watching as the last of their breath left them after you raped them, as you strangled the life from them... *after you stole each of their precious moments left on this earth?*" At this his eyes started to hemorrhage, and I knew he didn't have long left. But like he did with his own victims, I wanted him to see what they saw. Woman who had no other option but to turn tricks on street corners or addicts that would do anything needed for their next score, *lives he thought wouldn't be missed.*

I wanted him to see all their pain, so I covered his eyes with one right hand of the Gods, and I showed him. I forced so much pain and suffering into his mind that this time he was screaming not from his own, but from the nightmares of theirs.

From his own lifetime of horror.

That's when I killed him.

After this, I found what Gomez prized above all else, his

precious drugs. Then, after forcing my form back to that of a mortal, I gathered it all up in front of a security camara, wrote out my message loud and clear and then set fire to my handy work. This was so the flames written in gasoline on the floor told him my intentions, before setting alight a gangster's gold,

'U R NEXT

GOMEZ!'

I then walked out of the factory and released my wings as the whole place exploded behind me, obviously finding some gas line to help the flames along. Shortly after this, I was back on my private helicopter on my way to Portland. An arrival that couldn't come soon enough. Because despite my need for extracting vengeance, and feeding my very existence, I found a much greater need back at the hotel, fast asleep in my penthouse suite. Which gave me thought on the next places I needed to hit if I was to complete my plan of revenge so perfectly, and how best to do that was to enlist the help of loyal authority. Because in truth, as enjoyable as it was letting loose my darkness, it didn't quite feed my soul like my Siren did.

I had missed her.

Of course, it was only right I inform the Enforcer and ruler of the Northwest that I was about to create havoc in his city. And well, knowing of the ruthless big bastard, then he would only be happy to accommodate me in this, only if he could have a hand in it himself, no doubt. But then that was the bonus of having friends in high places, and the Wrath brothers were as hard and sinister as they came.

Kaiden Wrath in particular, who was the oldest of the two and held the title of Enforcer. But then again, he was the first son of Sathanas, the King of Wrath, who was not to be mistaken for the Devil himself. No, like many, he was just another ruler in Hell and lorded over this particular dark Demonic realm, becoming yet another right hand to Lucifer, Hell's God and King of Kings.

In short, he was one hard fucker who, like me, had his own fair share of enemies. Yet I was not one of them, as I happened to like the big bastard, being smart enough to want that kind of power on my side in a fight. And I would soon be walking to his council table and laying it all out for him. But first things first.

"Well, you look like you had fun," Deke said to me when I entered the suite, making him get up from the sofa after folding a newspaper in half. I shot a look to Eden in the bed, and he chuckled.

"Don't worry, your girl sleeps like the dead." I scowled and snarled at him, making him hold up his hands in surrender before correcting the offence.

"I mean, like the passed out living mortal she is. But I am serious, a mariachi band could have been playing and she wouldn't have stirred." I scoffed at this, walking toward her and when I was just about to reach out to her, Deke stopped me.

"Now, I am not one to come in between an Enforcer and his Siren, being that I like living and all, but I wouldn't be your friend if I didn't tell you that touching her covered in your recent kills' blood over you might not be the best idea... unless you want her to wake up screaming your name for a very different reason," he added when I paused to look down at myself. He was right, I was a mess. Thankfully I had come straight from the roof after jumping from the helicopter, and therefore hadn't had any run ins with any other mortals. As for the pilot, his mind had been easy to manipulate, making him believe he had already dropped me off at the helipad.

"You may have a point," I admitted. He grinned, to which I muttered,

"I'm going to have a shower, smug bastard." He chuckled and slapped me on the shoulder as I passed, telling me,

"Sound plan that." Then he retook his seat and unfolded his paper once more, still looking smug. But he was right, as I had been so focused on getting back to her, I hadn't even given my appearance a single thought. Hence why I showered in record time and was soon walking out of the bathroom for the second time with just a towel around my hips.

"Well, that is clearly my cue to leave," Deke said, making me grin this time.

"You can update me on all I need to know when you wake, unless there is something you wish dead, bloodied or burned to the ground before then?"

"Not quite," I replied in short.

"That's disappointing," he grumbled, making me smirk.

"I do, however, want you to look into a club in New York for me, one called, Staircase H, oh and set up a meeting with Kaiden Wrath and his brother, Helmer." At this he rolled his eyes and replied,

"Not that big fucker."

"The very same, and you would be a fool to ask me why," I reminded him, making him nod and save me the complaints. I think the last fight they'd had happened over a curvy little blonde both had their sights set on. If I recall, the result had ended with both being bloodied, and neither were fucked the way they had hoped by claiming what was between the Demon's legs with their cocks.

"On it," Deke said, before he looked over to my girl and told me,

"You might be in luck as the snoring ceased about an hour ago." He winked at me and chuckled as he made his way to the door, making me mutter,

"Funny fucker."

"Oh, just wait, asshole," he muttered back as he left laughing to himself. As for me, I quickly slipped under the covers and pulled my girl close, grinning to myself when I heard her whisper my name in her sleep. But then, just as I was settling down, feeling relaxed that all was right in my world with Eden now here in my arms, my sentiments were doused in ice water. This was when I realized that contented happiness had led me into a false sense of security, for Eden didn't only have my name on her unconscious mind.

No, she had another, and it was a name she shouldn't have known. Making me suddenly question everything.

Making me question her.

But mainly making me question what the name of my enemy was doing coming from her lips...

"Gastian."

CHAPTER 29
GRATIFICATION
EDEN

I don't know what I had been dreaming about, but whatever it was made me awaken with a start, instantly feeling a pair of strong arms tense around me.

"Easy, Little Carino, it was just a dream." I let Ward's voice surround me and I felt myself sigh back into his hold, feeling instantly comforted by it.

"More like a nightmare I think, but strangely, I can't remember."

"Then how do you know it was a nightmare?" he asked, and I grinned to myself before turning around so we were face to face. That's when I told him softly,

"Because you weren't in it." At this his eyes heated before he was rolling on top of me, keeping me caged beneath him.

"Good answer," he growled happily, and he was right, I was starting to understand the difference between the sounds he made. As this one definitely came under the happy, turned-on category and to know that I could do this to him quickly gave me my own high. But then I remembered I had been asleep for a while which meant that when he tried to kiss me, I turned my head away, denying him.

"Although, I must say, sweetheart, you ruin the blissful moment when you deny me like that and... I. Am. Not. A. Fan," he said, biting out each word before he was biting into my neck as punishment.

"Ahh... ahaa... Ward," I said as he held my flesh captive, making his point, both as a painful one as much as it was then an erotic one.

"Now, have you learned your lesson and will therefore give me what I want?" he asked, making me roll my lips inward, giving him his answer, but I chickened out when he went back to my neck and I shouted out,

"I haven't brushed my teeth yet!" At this, he let his head fall so that his chuckle was in place of his bite. Then he lifted his head to look down at me, telling me,

"Do you think I care for the flavor of toothpaste over that of the taste of my Siren?"

"That depends, do Siren's usually taste like they spent the night sucking on sandpaper?" I asked, making him laugh before he admitted,

"Alright, little Doe, point taken." Then he pushed himself from me and walked over to where there was a bar area with a fridge hidden in the cupboards below. The whole room was sectioned off into different areas, like an apartment would be, complete with living room and of course, dining room. This instantly made me blush at just the sight of that chair, remembering the sweet torture I had endured while sitting in it.

Ward retrieved a bottle of water and brought it back to me. Then after taking a long drink, I placed it on the bedside table before making a show of putting my arms behind my head and leaning back, telling him,

"You know, I could get used to this type of service." At this he stood next to the bed, looking down at me, saying in a teasing tone,

"Is that so, little queen?" I made a show of looking him up and down, licking my lips as I took in every delicious muscle on show, before purring,

"Most definitely." At this he laughed and shook his head at me, but I swear, was that him blushing? I quickly got up on my knees before him, keeping the sheet between us, telling him,

"Oh my God, you're blushing!" At this, his warm amber eyes heated a moment before he warned,

"I will give you cause to blush woman!" Then he bent, grabbed me behind the knees and pulled my legs from under me, making me fall back. He followed me down and soon had my wrists shackled in his large hands above me.

"Now I believe I am owed payment for services rendered," he told me, causing my playful response in return as I kissed his nose quickly, telling him,

"Thanks, Snuggle Bum." He growled at this, before snarling like some wild beast at my neck, soon threatening,

"I think someone wants to start the day with punishment." I froze at this and quickly said,

"No, she doesn't, and she takes it all back, Master and very manly Lord of all sex stuff." He chuckled again before pulling back from my neck and looking down at me.

"Yes, well this Lord and Master is hungry for his morning meal, so tilt your head for me now, little slave, and offer yourself up to feed me." At this I felt my eyes widen in shock, remembering what he had done to me last night. Yet as terrifying as it had been at the time, the pleasure had quickly cut through that fear and replaced it with euphoric bliss. Which was why I knew this was a test, as his glowing eyes said as much. Because this was Ward getting off on my reaction and seeing my internal struggle, for he held his grin in place until I slowly did as he asked. I offered my neck to him in the ultimate sign of submission. I was then awarded with his darkness growling over me, making me close my eyes in case it was that other side to him that I would soon see staring back at me.

"Mmm, what a lucky bastard I am indeed, for what a good girl I have been fated to own," he said, making me flinch when feeling his nose running up my neck instead of the feel of his fangs like I had been expecting.

"Now count to ten," he ordered, and my eyes snapped open, regardless of what I may see. I was left frowning in question before I was suddenly flipped onto my belly, feeling the burning sting of having my ass slapped.

"OWW! What the fu... OWW!" I ended this complaint the second time it happened making me realize that, yes, the unbelievable was happening. Ward was spanking me!

"Now, I told you to count, my sweet, fuckable girl, and well... *I only heard you complaining.*" He said this last part whispered in my ear from behind, making me gasp. So, he slapped me again and I forced out the numbers through gritted teeth,

"One... Ahhh... Two... *Fuck*... Three, three!" I shouted this last one twice just in case he didn't hear it the first time and he would be cruel enough to start over. Naturally, this made him chuckle as he rubbed his hand gently over the burning marks he had made and strangely, this was what started to morph outrage and anger into complete lust. And the bastard knew it too when I started to squirm, wiggling my ass as if silently begging for the next one.

"I see now that I will have to get more inventive with my punishments as I think... *my Siren likes my firm hand,*" he whispered before biting my earlobe and holding it in his teeth, then he sucked it in his mouth to sooth the sting.

"Now for the rest." This was my only warning as my whole body jerked when I was spanked again, making me holler out the rest of the numbers quickly and without the spanking.

"Aaahhh fuck! Four, five, six, seven, eight, nine… TEN!" I shouted, making him laugh before telling me,

"That's not how the game is played, love." I sucked in a quick breath at being called love and before he or I could think more on what that could mean, my head was pulled roughly to the side. Then before I could question why, he sank his fangs deep into my flesh.

"AAAHHH!" I cried out, first in pain, then in sweet, forbidden pleasure as I didn't know if I was permitted to come or not, but I was screaming out my release all the same. It was so strong, that I continued to ride the waves of gratification, getting off on the feeling of him feeding on me from behind. It was as if he was some wild beast that had jumped on his innocent prey. His arms banded around me so tightly that I was completely immobile, held in his grasp. It was like he feared me being ripped away from him as he made a meal out of me. He was a man addicted, and I felt myself getting lost in the same dark obsession.

But then, with each pull of his lips as he drank me down, I felt myself becoming fluid in his hold, meaning that he knew it too, stopping before he drained me dry. Then, while I was in this sleepy, relaxed state, I felt him pull his fangs from my flesh, making me shiver in his tight hold. After this, he leisurely started to clean up the mess he made, just as he had last night, making me wonder how my skin healed itself.

"My saliva has a healing agent along with my blood," he told me, reading my thoughts after rolling me around so I faced him.

"Does it also make me feel drunk and soothe the sting in my ass?" At this he chuckled, rubbing my ass and making me suck air through my teeth, telling him,

"That would be a no then."

"I have to say, I will enjoy knowing that you spend the day

feeling my mark upon your flesh, as it will make my cock hard knowing how well my handprint looks painted on your ass," he said, after looking over my shoulder and seeing it for himself, prompting me to say,

"Then may I suggest we just buy some red paint and save me the pain next time." He grinned at this and reminded me,

"Ah, but you forget, sweetheart, I could read your thoughts quite well, and know it was not without its *gratification*." I cringed when hearing my own thoughts reflected back at me.

"Therefore, I know you like the pain, Eden," he added, making me bury my head in his neck this time and grumble,

"Damn know it all, men!"

He laughed at this before replying,

"But praise the Gods for submissive little Sirens." I grinned against his skin before raising my head up, loving it when he pushed all my hair back from my face with both his hands. That was when I was finally brave enough to start asking the right questions, starting with,

"What is a Siren, Ward?" At this his eyes heated again, telling me he was glad I had asked this question, but instead of answering me like I hoped he would, he told me,

"I think that is our cue to leave this bed and get ready for the day... I have plans for you." Then he winked at me and kissed me for the first time that day.

Naturally, this meant we didn't leave the bed.

But instead...

We stayed in it, and I let the kiss take me to another round of...

Gratification.

CHAPTER 30
TENDER LOVING CARE

I t turned out that what Ward had planned for me was, strangely, a day of shopping. But this started when I had tried to look for my own clothes and literally the only thing that I owned.

"You don't need them," he told me casually, making me look down at the robe I was back to wearing, telling him,

"I beg to differ. Unless you plan to keep me in this hotel suite forever, then I will need clothes."

"Mmm, as tempting as that thought is, I have taken the liberty of having some clothes bought for you," he told me.

"Where are they?! Oh God, please don't tell me you threw them out!" I shouted, freaking out and throwing cushions up from the sofa, trying to search for them. But then his arms came around me from behind and he told me sternly,

"Calm, now."

"Ward, please… please tell me they are still here." My voice was pained as I closed my eyes, feeling the tears start to rise. Then he turned me in his arms, ordering me,

"Eden, look at me." I kept my eyes closed and shook my head, telling him no, before he tensed his arms around me.

"Open your eyes... *now!*" he ordered again, more firmly this time, and finally I gave into his demand, letting him see the tears there for himself.

"I had your clothes sent to be cleaned and anything I found in the pockets I still have in my possession," he told me softly, before nodding to a side table where I found my wallet sitting in a bowl. So, I squirmed out of his hold, being thankful when he let me, before running over to it. Then I riffled quickly through the wallet's pockets and as soon as I found the plastic heart with its colorful thread wrapped around the partially burned picture of me and my mother, I held it to my heart and whispered,

"Thank God."

"May I?" Ward asked behind me, and I turned to hand it to him.

"It's my mom, it's... it's all I have left of her. Gomez's goons burned the rest," I told him, making his jaw go hard before suddenly I was pulled into his hold. I wrapped my arms around his waist, fisting the material at his back, holding on as tightly I let my emotions flow. He kept my head cradled to his chest for as long as it took to calm my tears, and I felt as if for the first time in a small forever that I was finally allowed to grieve for all I had lost.

"I swear to you, Eden, with the Fates as my witness, you will be avenged for all you've had taken from you. For I will not rest until they pay tenfold for every tear they made you shed... this is my vow, my love." At this I looked up at him, and this time my tears started to fall for a different reason, as I couldn't help but ask not about his vow but instead about how it ended.

"You... *you love me?*" He granted me a tender smile in return and used his thumbs to wipe away my tears, before telling me,

"Oh sweetheart, don't you already know yet... *but I fell in*

love with you the moment you refused to give me your name."
Then, as I sucked in a quick and shuddered breath, he brought
my face up to his so he could kiss me while framing my face
with his hands. As for me, I poured all my own love for him
back into that same kiss, knowing that I too had fallen
impossibly hard in that same first meeting. Which was when I
realized I was yet to say the words by making the same claim.
However, I didn't need to as he tore his lips from mine and said
incredulously,

"You love me, Little Carino?"

"How could I not? *You've been my hero from the start,*" I
told him, whispering this last part before pulling his lips back to
mine, so I could continue to show him just how much. And in
the end, it was utter perfection as he picked me up into his arms
and carried me back to bed.

And this time, he showed me in another way.

By making love to me, proving that my dark Angel of
Vengeance could be sweet and tender but mainly…

That he could take me to Heaven on Earth.

A little time later, and once we had actually made it further
than a few feet from the bed, I found myself dressed in brand
new clothes. Clothes that I knew would have no doubt bought
me a brand-new car, for how much they cost, they were all
designer. But I had to admit they fit as if they had been made
for me. The light blue jeans no longer needed a belt like my old
ones that were too big for me. No, they were just the perfect fit,
and turned up at the bottom, as this was their style. Added to
this was a soft cotton T-shirt, and black blazer-style jacket that
had a light-gray hooded sweatshirt on the inside. A brand-new
pair of white sneakers completed the causal look that was both
stylish and comfortable.

Of course, I had tried to convince him that it was all too
much, but he wouldn't hear of it. And well, this seemed to be

the theme of the day, because I soon discovered Ward wouldn't hear of a lot of things.

Like when pulling me into shops and buying anything I spent longer than a mere second looking at. In the end, he stopped asking and simply picked things up, handing them to a shop assistant who trailed behind us at the ready. I swear it was as though they could scent the money the moment he walked in. But then again, Ward had that kind of kinetic pull about him that drew people in. Woman literally stopped dead, turning their heads in that slow, predatory way that made me feel as if I was some little gazelle trying to snuggle up to the King of the Serengeti!

But as for Ward, this lion wasn't up for grabs. He didn't even look. No, instead, I was left with no option but to bask in the attention he gave me, never letting me even an arm's length from his touch. And seeing as I spent most of my time tucked under his arm close to his side, I had thought I would get out of him spending too much money on me by being unable try anything on. However, this was not the case as he simply bought them anyway, making me pout, something he would often remind me throughout the day, was adorable.

But it was after this fifth shop, and what I knew was a carload of shopping bags, that I finally put my foot down.

"Seriously, Ward, you have to stop, or I will be bankrupt before I have even found another job!" At this he stopped walking, and therefore I was held back and forced to stop walking too.

"Eden." He said my name in that reprimanding tone and I was left looking up at him.

"What?"

"We talked about this," he informed me, and I reminded him,

"Yeah, we did, and I specifically recall telling you that I don't agree." At this he frowned and told me,

"I was there, sweetheart, and I don't remember you mentioning anything about you getting another job."

"Erm… then how do you expect me to ever pay you back?" I pointed out, causing him in turn to do the same.

"I don't, something I made very clear to you also." I released a sigh before saying his name.

"Ward."

He ignored this and took my hand in his, clearly ready for us to continue.

"Wait a second… look, I get it, you're rich and you want to take care of me…"

"I will take care of you," he reaffirmed firmly.

"Yes, but not like this," I tried to say, and again, got my name repeated back to me, as if it had the power enough to make me comply.

"Eden."

"You took care of me the only way that matters, Ward, in here," I told him, placing a hand over my heart before continuing on. "Do you know when the last time someone held me whilst I cried was? The last time someone made me feel safe? The last time anyone made me feel that kind of love? It was before my mom died when I was ten years old. That's seventeen years I have gone without that type of connection with anyone, and you gave me that today, Ward. That is the only way I need taking care of, because to me… God, Ward, *it means everything."* At this he gave me a soft, tender look before cupping my cheek, telling me gently,

"Thank you, Eden, for your words feel like a gift I do not deserve but it warms my heart to know I can give you that." I grinned up at him and hugged him to me, not caring that we were sharing this moment out in the street like this.

"Then why not take me back to your hotel room so I can show you just how grateful I am." Then I winked at him before he tugged me to him and growled,

"I've created a sex monster." At this I threw my head back and laughed, feeling my heart lighten even more, and it was starting to feel as if we were a real couple.

"I can also see now that you do not enjoy shopping," he commented with a hard jaw, making me tell him,

"Not when it's spending someone else's money, no."

"Alright, my Little Carino, I will concede…"

"Thank you, I…" I said prematurely as he was quick to interrupt me.

"Now that I know what you like, I will have someone shop for you and that way, you will have no say in how much I spend. Now, as for work, well I have the perfect job for you."

I groaned aloud, putting a hand to my forehead and silently praying to the Gods or Fates or whatever deities there were in his world that had the power to grant patience. Then I said to him,

"This job, it wouldn't happen to be in the form of a sexy maid's outfit and a sign on my back that says, Ward's sex slave… would it?" At this he grinned wolfishly and said,

"Okay, scrap my first idea, *so now* I have the perfect job for you." I laughed at this and let him lead me to the car, where Deke had been given the job of trailing us all day from shop to exasperating shop.

"Done so soon?" he asked with a smirk. He had seen my dismay every time bags and shoe boxes were brought out by the armfuls by overly helpful shopping assistants.

"I swear, she is the first woman I have ever met who acts as if shopping for clothes is akin to being punished in the fourth circle of Hell."

"Which one is that one again?" I asked on a chuckle, making him growl into my cheek,

"Greed." I giggled at this, before slipping into the car as he held the door open for me. I also heard Deke laughing, telling him,

"I would feel sorry for you but then I would be an idiot, so instead I am just going to repeat myself from yesterday... Lucky bastard." At this, Ward grinned and as he got in the car after me, he agreed with Deke while looking right at me...

"Yes... Yes I am."

CHAPTER 31
THE TASTE OF FEAR
WARD

I found myself on my feet again, as I was restlessly waiting for my girl to come out of the bathroom. I had informed her shortly after we were in the car heading back to the hotel that I wanted to take her out tonight. At which she quickly got excited, bouncing in her seat like an excitable child, making me unable to resist the urge to kiss her. Something that nearly ended as a sexual peep show for Deke, despite him quickly raising the screen between us.

I swear I couldn't keep my fucking hands off her! I knew I needed to give her some time between claiming her. But honestly, she was making it harder and harder to try and act like a fucking gentleman when she seemed just as turned on as I. Because I swear she took a great deal of pleasure from teasing me and at one point, her thoughts took me back to spanking her and I nearly dragged her into a changing room to fuck.

But then she had promised me retribution for reading her thoughts and this was her punishment, to keep me as horny as a fucking teenager! Gods, but she was almost as insatiable as I was, and therefore utterly perfect for me. In all honesty, if I wasn't spending half the day lusting after her, I was spending the other half of it marveling at how fucking lucky I was to have found her!

Although this was nothing compared to hearing her thoughts after I had spoken of my love for her. To know that she felt it in return was… well, it was nothing of the likes I had ever felt before! A moment in time I knew that I would never forget, even if my soul carried on living for another thousand years and beyond. Nothing came close, as all happiness before now paled in comparison, for I had never felt as blessed by the Gods until that point, other than first being granted my Siren.

She was my everything.

Of course, when I had seen her heart break and what it had meant to her to be held through it, well it had been like a bittersweet torture for me. As her thoughts had awarded me after getting to the point of our love being declared. Yet the journey it had taken had me wanting to commit murder all over again, when hearing of all that had been taken from her. I swear my heart ached in sight of that small burned picture of her mother, knowing it was the last thing in the world that she had left of her.

My Siren's utter panic at the idea of losing it, fuck me, but the sight had nearly brought me to my fucking knees. I had never before felt pain through that of another as they suffered. I didn't even believe such a thing was possible for one of my kind, making me wonder back once more if the King of Kings would struggle as I did now.

Would he too battle with these mortal emotions that felt a little like being reborn all over again? These experiences, like the blinding fear clawing at you at just the thought of them being taken from you or hurt beyond all healing? The irrational emotions that seemed to build and build until it was like containing a storm within your own heart?

Would he too be willing to fall to his knees like I was at just the sight of our Chosen One's tears falling? Well, if the strength of this love I felt was anything to go by, then I had no doubt that even Kings would find the floor, worshipping at the feet of their fated Queens. And honestly, I would not think any less of them... not now, not when I too had fallen under the same affliction.

Speaking of which, the moment I informed her that I had picked a dress specially for tonight, I smirked knowing she wanted to argue against it. But then, I simply whispered a soft and tender word in her ear, making her melt against me.

"Please."

After this, she found she couldn't deny me and, in turn, I filed this technique away in my mind as being successful, and to be used again when I wanted to have my way with her. Which was why I now waited for her to emerge, finding my palms itching to see her dressed in such a way. For I had a feeling she would be surprising me yet again. I'd made sure that she had everything she would need, speaking with the concierge to source everything after hearing the panicked inner dialogue of her mind, as I had no idea half the shit that women felt they needed. For I would have just been content with seeing Eden in a dress and that was it.

Of course, the moment she came out, I knew that it had all been worth the wait, for I would have waited barefoot on the hot sands of the Lut Desert in Iran, for such a sight. This was known to be one of the hottest places on Earth. However, right now, I felt myself burning as though I was actually there, for the sight of her beauty was taking my breath away.

She wore an elegant black cocktail dress that was an A-line style, with a skirt that flared around her perfect legs, in swaths of floating flock lace. A band of thick silver ribbon separated the black satin top, dipping deliciously low with its V neck, finishing with little lace cap sleeves, leaving her arms bare.

It was little wonder then that she stole my breath and kept it her prisoner until she spoke.

"I don't know if I zipped it all the way as I couldn't reach but I think if you..." I stopped her the moment I could stand it no longer, for I needed to touch her! I needed to make sure she was still real, and a fucking angel hadn't just been dropped from the sky!

"You're exquisite," I told her as I took her face in my hands and kissed her, feeling as if there wasn't a word powerful enough to express how I felt. She was beyond beautiful, and she had no fucking clue!

"Erm, wow, okay I... um... thank you, but of course you look very handsome too," she told me in a shy way that I fucking adored. Something that made me smirk down at her before giving her even more reason to blush.

Naturally, she didn't disappoint as I turned her around so I could finish zipping up her pretty dress, even though in all honestly, I was far more inclined to want to get her out of it. Especially when I was awarded the hint of silk and lace of underwear she had been bought today.

However, I gently brushed back the loose curls from her neck, that hung down in a tempting way from the rest of the curls she had pinned up in a graceful style.

"Then I am happy to be deemed worthy enough to be by your side tonight and be graced for the evening by such beauty," I told her, making her suck in a quick breath before blushing crimson. Then, after forcing the grin from my lips, doing so for fear she would think my words untrue and tainting a perfect moment, I offered her my arm.

"Shall we?" I said, motioning for the door and taking possession of the silk wrap to match her dress from the back of the chair where I had put it ready. As for myself, I was already dressed in a black three-piece suit, with black shirt and tie to match, for I felt darkness was to be the theme of the evening. Because tonight was the night that I intended to tell her all about my world.

One that would soon be hers.

"Wow Eden, you look beaut... erm okay, I will stop there before he bites my fucking head off, but you get the idea," Deke said the moment he opened the car door for my girl, making me snarl at him. Eden smacked a hand to my chest to get me to stop threatening my friend and making Deke chuckle when this didn't work. So, she grabbed the lapel of my suit jacket instead and started to drag me in the car, making him laugh harder. Naturally I followed her in and the moment she started to reprimand me, I ceased her words by taking possession of her lips and kissing all words of annoyance from her mind.

Lust was all that followed.

☙

A short drive later and we were pulling up to a restaurant that I had hired out for the evening, meaning that there were only a handful of staff in the building. But other than that, we would have the place to ourselves, just the way I wanted it. Especially for the conversation we would soon be having, as she had finally asked me the one question I had been waiting and hoping for...

She had asked about Sirens.

"Oh dear, I think we may be out of luck. The place must be closed or something," she said, looking along the street and along the wall of windows to see the place empty, prompting me in turn to wink down at her.

"Not for me, it isn't," I told her, before taking her hand in mine and walking her through the glass doors.

"But wait, we could go somewhere else if it is..." she said, obviously feeling uncomfortable at the thought of me demanding a whole restaurant be open just because I wanted it to. I grinned to myself knowing that a man like me didn't need to demand anything, I just needed ask where to sign the bill and make it so.

"Mr Za'afiel, Miss Teles, welcome to West 9, everything is ready for you, so if you would like to follow me, your table is right this way," the owner of the restaurant said, greeting us and getting paid extremely well to do so. This considering he stood to make more money tonight than ten times what he would with table covers by letting other diners inside. But like I said, I had wanted Eden all to myself and now, after seeing her in her pretty dress, I was even more thankful for it. Having the place to ourselves meant that I wouldn't have to compete with any lingering eyes, nor injure the jealous need pressing at me to gouge them out for the offence.

"Erm... why is there no one else here?" Eden asked after I had taken over the job of pulling her chair out for her and we were seated. This question made me lean closer to her over the table and whisper in a mocking way,

"Why are you whispering?" She laughed at my teasing and replied honestly.

"I don't actually know." I grinned in reply before she admitted, "I've never eaten anywhere fancy before. I mean, don't worry, I know what all the cutlery is for, I watched Pretty Woman, so no chance of me embarrassing you on that front... wait, why are you laughing?" she asked, as I couldn't help but once again find my fist held between my teeth, just so I wouldn't burst out laughing. Fuck me, but she was endearing!

"Well, apart from the part about some 'Pretty Woman', I am laughing because I find you cute as fuck, and because I wouldn't give a shit if you knew what fork to use for what course. You couldn't possibly embarrass me, even if there were other people here to witness it," I told her, making her look around and say,

"Oh yeah... well I guess that's good then, oh and FYI, Pretty Woman is a classic movie where Richard Gere plays a billionaire who asks for directions from Julia Roberts who plays a prostitute. After what I like to think of as him falling madly in love with her instantly, he takes her back to his hotel... holy shit, but other than not being a sex worker, I am pretty much living that movie right now!" she said, causing me to give in to the impulse of laughter this time and thankfully, she joined in.

"I think you're forgetting quite a few extra differences there, sweetheart, as unless this billionaire is of the supernatural variety and this Pretty Woman, I gather the movie is about, is also on the run from a soon to be dead drug lord, then perhaps we just concentrate on continuing on with our own love story, shall we?" I told her, making her lift the glass of champagne already poured and holding it out to me for me to toast.

"Then here's to us and making our own real-life movie... oh wait, that came out wrong, I don't mean like a porno or anything." At this I was once again throwing my head back, making the restaurant echo with the sound of my booming laughter. I honestly couldn't remember a time that I had laughed as much as I had since meeting her.

"I can't say I agree, as I think your idea is a perfect one," I told her, winking and making her blush again.

"Behave," she whispered, before the waiter came with our first course that I had preordered, knowing now of what she liked and disliked. But I lifted my glass up and told her unashamedly in front of our waiter,

"That is highly unlikely around you." She bit her bottom lip at that and tried to hide her smile. Again, I was left blinded by how fucking cute she looked whilst doing it and unsurprisingly, I was hard in seconds.

After this we continued on with our meal, and I had to say I had never enjoyed someone's company more. Even being around Deke had its limits for me. But as for Eden, Gods, but I swear I hung on every fucking word she said, making me bombard her with all manner of questions. Everything from her childhood memories, to how she ended up in the line of work she had. I asked if she ever considered travelling and I was elevated to discover that it had always been a dream of hers. But as of yet, she had never even been on a plane. Fuck me, but I found myself excited at the thought of being the one to show her all these new things and exotic new places the world had to offer.

As for me, I had seen the world over more times than I could remember to count, but doing so with Eden by my side would feel like seeing it all over again for the first time.

I in turn talked about my homes in Italy and other places in Europe I wished for her to see, and her eyes widened as if what she heard me speak of was only possible in her wildest dreams. As if such a thing would never happen, yet she was excited talking about it all the same. Well, she would soon discover that I would be making it all a reality, just as soon as I had dealt with that fucker Gomez!

And well now…

His death couldn't come quick enough.

"Well, I really don't think I could fit anything more into this dress," she said laughing and patting her belly, that honestly looked no different, even after five courses.

"I am just going to nip to the ladies," she informed me, and I stood instantly, as was still the habit to do so from living through more years with the decorum, than not.

"Would you like me to escort you?" I asked, making her smile up at me and tell me,

"Such a gentleman, tell me, Ward, where does he go

when... *you have me in your bed?"* she whispered seductively in my ear after her heels granted her a little more height to do so. I growled playfully and warned,

"Behave, little Siren, or I will show you, *restaurant or not."* She laughed at this and then walked away muttering,

"Promises, promises." I shook my head and chuckled to myself as I watched her leave, unable to tear my eyes from the sight, knowing exactly what I was going to be doing to that delectable ass tonight... *fucking own it, that was what!*

I sat back down and motioned for the waiter to bring the bill, knowing that I wanted it all settled by the time she came back. Mainly so she didn't see how much tonight had cost and therefore feel indebted to me or some bullshit like that. She owed me nothing, yet I felt like I owed her everything just by breathing and surviving long enough for me to claim her!

Something that had me grinning until suddenly I felt that usual pull at my dark soul, knowing that for once, it wasn't a taste I was addicted to... *it was one I fucking loathed.*

It was acid in my veins, and it was Hell's fire in my blood.

It was the taste of...

Eden's Fear.

CHAPTER 32
FIRST DATE BOMBSHELL
EDEN

I swear, I just couldn't stop smiling.

It had been the most perfect date and I knew that with a lot of the night still ahead of us, then it would only get better. But as for the evening so far, well I don't think I had talked so much or felt like anyone had truly listened before now. He had seemed so interested in what I considered quite a boring life… well, up until recent months and mob bosses aside.

Now, compared to Ward, I seemed so sheltered compared to his worldliness after he named all the places he had lived, and I knew that it was only the tip of the iceberg. But to know then that he intended to take me to these places, well it seemed like a dream, and I hung on his every word. It was as if I could see these places through his eyes for myself. Like I was being woven into his spell and even now, I couldn't help but release a loved-up sigh.

Of course, I knew that the likelihood of me ever seeing them was slim at best, but I hadn't cared, as I gladly let him entwine me into his future plans as though it would actually happen.

Which was why I was looking at myself in the mirror and

grinning like a crazy lady. Because even though this night had been perfectly romantic, I knew that I didn't need any of the fancy stuff that came with Ward for it to be so. I knew just being with him would have been what made it perfect. We could have been sitting in some diner eating greasy burgers and I would have been just as happy. But it also meant something to me to know all the effort he had gone to, despite me wincing just thinking about what such a night must have cost him. Making me wonder if I would ever get used to it. It was something I knew I would struggle with, as I had done most of the day whilst shopping.

In fact, I was trying not to think of it, or I knew it would have only freaked me out. So instead, I kept my grin in place and walked from the ladies' room, half expecting him to be standing there waiting for me, because it was clear he seemed uneasy leaving me out of his sight for too long. Hell, but even walking back into the room after getting ready, he was pacing the room like some caged, wild animal.

Of course, his reaction to seeing me had made all the effort worth it, and all the worry about trying to look nice for him. He honestly had looked dumbstruck at the sight of me, making me blush even now at the memory. Which was most likely why I didn't see where I was going, or the man I now walked into.

"Oh, I am so sorry... hey, what are you doing!?" I said, realizing it hadn't been my mistake at all. He had purposely walked into me. I knew it the moment he took my arm in his hand, making me look down to see that the other one was in a cast as if it had recently been broken.

"Oh this, yes you can thank your fucking freak for that!" He spat out the venomous words at me and the second I tried to pull away, he warned,

"I wouldn't do that if I were you. This place is rigged to blow and unless you come with me without a fuss, then I swear to you, I will let the fucker burn!" I gasped and looked back toward where I walked in, knowing that just beyond those doors was where Ward was waiting for me. But of course, I had no idea if he could survive something like that, which is why I knew I couldn't chance it!

I couldn't chance his life, not for my own. I would never forgive myself if I lost him!

"Okay… alright, I will go with you, just… just don't hurt him."

"Oh, how very fucking touching!" he snapped, before demanding me to move with his fingers biting into the top of my arm as he dragged me through what looked like the kitchen. But this was when I heard Ward roaring my name like the roar of anger first being dragged through Hell itself!

"RAWWHHH… EDEN!" I couldn't help my reaction as I screamed out my warning,

"WARD RUUUUUN!" But I was suddenly slapped across the face, before I was pushed through the door that led onto a back street, where there was a van waiting.

"You stupid bitch, get in the fucking truck!" He quickly pushed me inside before I was grabbed by others waiting in the back for me. Instinct took over, making me try and fight against them. But then just as the van started to drive from the building at speed, I threw myself against the back window and saw Ward emerge from the exit of the building!

"WARD!" I screamed, even though I knew he wouldn't hear me.

"NOW! FUCKING BLOW IT… NOW, GOD DAMN IT!" The man dressed as a waiter roared down his phone and just as I cried out, suddenly the whole building blew up in an explosion of glass and stone!

But my cries of heartache were only answered by the true cruelty of our fate. My hand shot to the window, slapping it, and

I was forced to witness as my Avenging Angel was brought to his knees, just before the building came down all around him.

His body swallowed whole as he was crushed to death before my very eyes and my love was then…

Consumed in flames.

To be continued…
Eden's Enforcer
Lost Siren's
Book 2

ACKNOWLEDGEMENTS

Well first and foremost my love goes out to all the people who deserve the most thanks which is you the FANS!

Without you wonderful people in my life, I would most likely still be serving burgers and writing in my spare time like some dirty little secret, with no chance to share my stories with the world.

You enable me to continue living out my dreams every day and for that I will be eternally grateful to each and every one of you!

Your support is never ending. Your trust in me and the story is never failing. But more than that, your love for me and all who you consider your 'Afterlife family' is to be commended, treasured and admired. Thank you just doesn't seem enough, so one day I hope to meet you all and buy you all a drink! ;)

To my family…

To my crazy mother, who had believed in me since the beginning and doesn't think that something great should be hidden from the world. I would like to thank you for all the hard work you put into my books and the endless hours spent caring about my words and making sure it is the best it can be for everyone to enjoy. You, along with the Hudson Indie Ink team make Afterlife shine.

To my crazy father who is and always has been my hero in life. Your strength astonishes me, even to this day! The love and care you hold for your family is a gift you give to the Hudson name.

To my lovely sister,

If Peter Pan had a female version, it would be you and Wendy combined. You have always been my big, little sister and another person in my life that has always believed me capable of doing great things. You were the one who gave Afterlife its first identity and I am honored to say that you continue to do so even today. We always dreamed of being able to work together and I am thrilled that we made it happened when you agreed to work as a designer at Hudson Indie Ink.

And last but not least, to the man that I consider my soul mate. The man who taught me about real love and makes me not only want to be a better person but makes me feel I am too. The amount of support you have given me since we met has been incredible and the greatest feeling was finding out you wanted to spend the rest of your life with me when you asked me to marry you.

All my love to my dear husband and my own personal Draven... Mr Blake Hudson.

To My Team...

I am so fortunate enough to rightly state the claim that I have the best team in the world!

It is a rare thing indeed to say that not a single person that works for Hudson Indie Ink doesn't feel like family, but there you have it. We Are a Family.

Sarah your editing is a stroke of genius and you, like others in my team, work incredibly hard to make the Afterlife world what it was always meant to be. But your personality is an utter joy to experience and getting to be a part of your crazy feels like a gift.

Sloane, it is an honor to call you friend and have you not only working for Hudson Indie Ink but also to have such a talented Author represented by us. Your formatting is flawless and makes my books look more polished than ever before.

Xen, your artwork is always a masterpiece that blows me away and again, I am lucky to have you not only a valued member of my team but also as another talented Author represented by Hudson Indie Ink.

Lisa, my social media butterfly and count down Queen! I was so happy when you accepted to work with us, as I knew you would fit in perfectly with our family! Please know you are a dear friend to me and are a such an asset to the team. Plus, your backward dancing is the stuff of legends!

Libby, as our newest member of the team but someone I consider one of my oldest and dearest friends, you came in like a whirlwind of ideas and totally blew me away with your level of energy! You fit in instantly and I honestly don't know what Hudson Indie Ink would do without you. What you have achieved in such a short time is utterly incredible and want you to know you are such an asset to the team!

And last but by certainly not least is the wonderful Claire, my right-hand woman! I honestly have nightmares about waking one day and finding you not working for Hudson Indie Ink. You are the backbone of the company and without you and all your dedicated, hard work, there would honestly be no Hudson Indie Ink!

You have stuck by me for years, starting as a fan and quickly becoming one of my best friends. You have supported me for years and without fail have had my back through thick and thin, the ups and the downs. I could quite honestly write a book on how much you do and how lost I would be without you in my life!

I love you honey x

Thanks to all of my team for the hard work and devotion to the saga and myself. And always going that extra mile, pushing Afterlife into the spotlight you think it deserves. Basically helping me achieve my secret goal of world domination one day...evil laugh time... Mwahaha! Joking of course ;)

Another personal thank you goes to my dear friend Caroline Fairbairn and her wonderful family that have embraced my brand of crazy into their lives and given it a hug when most needed.

For their friendship I will forever be eternally grateful.

As before, a big shout has to go to all my wonderful fans who make it their mission to spread the Afterlife word and always go the extra mile. Those that have remained my fans all these years and supported me, my Afterlife family, you also meant the world to me.

All my eternal love and gratitude,
Stephanie x

ABOUT THE AUTHOR

Stephanie Hudson has dreamed of being a writer ever since her obsession with reading books at an early age. What first became a quest to overcome the boundaries set against her in the form of dyslexia has turned into a life's dream. She first started writing in the form of poetry and soon found a taste for horror and romance. Afterlife is her first book in the series of twelve, with the story of Keira and Draven becoming ever more complicated in a world that sets them miles apart.

When not writing, Stephanie enjoys spending time with her loving family and friends, chatting for hours with her biggest fan, her sister Cathy who is utterly obsessed with one gorgeous Dominic Draven. And of course, spending as much time with her supportive partner and personal muse, Blake who is there for her no matter what.

Author's words.

My love and devotion is to all my wonderful fans that keep me going into the wee hours of the night but foremost to my wonderful daughter Ava...who yes, is named after a cool, kick-ass, Demonic bird and my sons, Jack, who is a little hero and Baby Halen, who yes, keeps me up at night but it's okay because he is named after a Guitar legend!

Keep updated with all new release news & more on my website

www.afterlifesaga.com
Never miss out, sign up to the
mailing list at the website.

Also, please feel free to join myself and other Dravenites on my
Facebook group
Afterlife Saga Official Fan
Interact with me and other fans. Can't wait to see you there!

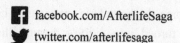

facebook.com/AfterlifeSaga

twitter.com/afterlifesaga

instagram.com/theafterlifesaga

ALSO BY STEPHANIE HUDSON

Afterlife Saga

Afterlife

The Two Kings

The Triple Goddess

The Quarter Moon

The Pentagram Child - Part 1

The Pentagram Child - Part 2

The Cult of the Hexad

Sacrifice of the Septimus - Part 1

Sacrifice of the Septimus - Part 2

Blood of the Infinity War

Happy Ever Afterlife - Part 1

Happy Ever Afterlife - Part 2

The Forbidden Chapters

*

Transfusion Saga

Transfusion

Venom of God

Blood of Kings

Rise of Ashes

Map of Sorrows

Tree of Souls

Kingdoms of Hell

Eyes of Crimson

Roots of Rage

Heart of Darkness

Wraith of Fire

Queen of Sins

*

King of Kings

Dravens Afterlife

Dravens Electus

*

Kings of Afterlife

Vincent's Immortal Curse

The Hellbeast King

The Hellbeast's Fight

The Hellbeast's Mistake

*

The Shadow Imp Series

Imp and the Beast

Beast and the Imp

*

Afterlife Academy: (Young Adult Series)

The Glass Dagger

The Hells Ring

*

Stephanie Hudson and Blake Hudson

The Devil in Me

OTHER AUTHORS AT HUDSON INDIE INK

Paranormal Romance/Urban Fantasy

Sloane Murphy

Xen Randell

C. L. Monaghan

Sorcha Dawn

Kia Carrington-Russell

Sci-fi/Fantasy

Devin Hanson

Crime/Action

Blake Hudson

Mike Gomes

Contemporary Romance

Gemma Weir

Lightning Source UK Ltd.
Milton Keynes UK
UKHW040753020922
408203UK00001B/174